OUR
DARK
STARS

USA TODAY BESTSELLING AUTHORS
AUDREY GREY
KRYSTAL WADE

Our Dark Stars

ISBN print: 978-1-945519-17-8
ISBN ebook: 978-1-945519-18-5

http://audreygrey.com/
http://www.krystal-wade.com

Cover design by

https://www.wegotyoucoveredbookdesign.com/

Blaze Publishing, LLC
64 Melvin Drive
Fredericksburg, VA 22406
Visit us at www.blazepub.com

First Edition: March 2018

CHAPTER 1

3731 AD

Will

Will Perrault stared at the cluttered minefield just beyond the starscreen of the Odysseus and tried very hard not to crack a smile. Green-and-yellow blips pulsed along the radar, the soft murmur of his ship's alarms trilling through the hollow metal corridors and bridge. Cracking his knuckles, he leaned back in the split-leather chair and stretched, contemplating his next move.

"No, Will." His ship's guard, Leo, was propped in the copilot chair with his puke-green jumpsuit unzipped down to his waist, exposing what used to be a white undershirt. His boots were unscrupulously resting on the console, arms behind his head, one eye peeking beneath his long blond hair—the only man Will had ever seen who could pull off such a thing—the other still shut. "Don't even think about it."

Will drummed his fingers over the console, charting the mines and searching for a navigable course.

"*No.*" Leo closed his eye and went back to snoring, the final note in his tone meaning he didn't think Will was crazy enough to do it.

Will should have been asleep too, but the ship's salvage containers weren't even half filled. Which, if they wanted to eat anytime soon, meant not nearly full enough.

Mines indicated something valuable lay just beyond. Someone, probably another tarnished captain stuck on scavenger duty, had either passed by and been too full to nab the treasure so they dropped the explosives to protect it until later, or something had purposefully been hidden there.

With an aggrieved sigh, Leo opened his eyes. "I can hear your excited breathing, Will. That's the sound of a man about to get me killed."

"I don't know . . ." Will scratched at the stubble lining his chin and then patted the dash. "The old girl hasn't had action in a while, and you know how she gets."

The grated floor rattled as Leo planted his boots somewhere they belonged. "Shit. I know that voice. You can't be serious?"

"Serious about what?" Lux asked, jogging down the stairs connecting the bridge to the rack room. The navigator was tiny, with bright-green eyes, warm-honey skin, and dark, lavender-streaked hair pulled into twists around her head. She reminded Will of a cat. Silent feet and deadly reflexes. The blaster at her waist flashed as she stopped beside Leo.

"Oh, Will's just trying to kill us," Leo said.

"Again?" Lux asked, stretching her arms over her head and not averting her gaze from Leo fast enough for Will to miss the longing there.

A wide grin spread across Leo's face as he stood to relinquish the seat. "Will you back me up if I have to restrain him, Lux?"

"I'm right here," Will grumbled.

Lux flicked her focus to Will and then back to Leo. "Have I ever not?"

"You always choose his side. And here I thought I was the captain of this ship. Maybe I should unzip my suit too."

"It's not Leo's fine physique that's keeping me on his side. It's self-preservation."

"Self-preservation?" Will arched an eyebrow. "You do realize I can have you space-tossed for disobedience?"

"Yes, *Captain*," they both answered simultaneously, performing mock salutes.

He rubbed two fingers across his forehead. *Insubordinate assholes.* Just his luck he was stuck with the worst crew in the galaxy.

The smell of bread filled the air as Jane entered the bridge, gray-shot hair cropped close to her head, a tray balanced on her left hand. Over six feet tall, the ex-captain turned co-pilot had taken to cooking recently, and she dipped the tray low, offering Will his pick of the black pastries. "Captain gets first choice."

"See how it's done?" Will asked, tossing a pointed look at the others. Then he gently eased the tray their way. "No, Jane. I insist you offer that . . . whatever that is to the others first. I think Leo just mentioned he was starving."

Jane beamed. "A captain is selfless, always thinking of the crew first."

"Exactly."

Leo glared and then made a show of taking two biscuits inside his huge hand. He took a loud, tooth-cracking bite, face twisting as he forced a smile and spoke around a mouthful of what could pass as rocks. "These are delicious, Jane. Thank you."

Lux took one too, just as her brother, Dorian, scampered down the stairs.

"Oh, good," Leo called. "We're all here. Just in time to discuss Will's decision to kill us."

"Again?" Jane dumped the tray into Leo's lap and shooed him out of her chair. Even sitting, she was almost as tall as Lux was standing. "A captain's first directive is to protect the safety of his crew."

"Huh." Will droned out the words as his attention shifted again to the mines blinking on the radar. He'd never seen so many before. A glittering wall of dark-matter energy that would obliterate their shields and them in less than a second—if he hit them. Which he didn't plan to do.

"You're staring at those mines like they're a bunch of half-naked escorts," Lux muttered, before adding, "No, Will."

Jane gave one of her long exhales—not exactly a sigh. Not a yawn. Some in-between gesture that meant she was about to remind Will of the past. "I am not captain now, but when I was captain, I would not have chosen this course."

Leo clapped a hand on Jane's shoulder. "You were a great captain, Jane. A *safe* captain. I never crapped my pants when you were in command, nor did my balls ever shrivel with terror."

Will's heart raced as he flipped on the shields; the purr of the energy thrusters warming up eased any doubts he might have had. "Gravity generators go off in five . . . four . . ."

"Stars!" Leo raked a hand through his hair. "Will, you might be too ugly to care about this, but we're a day away from the nearest waystation and I have girls waiting for me. *Girls*, Will. Do you know how long it's been since I've seen girls?"

"A day?" Lux scoffed.

Will snorted as he eased the thrusters forward. "I'm doing those girls a favor, Leo. Now strap in and enjoy the show. *Three . . .*"

The Odysseus lurched forward, knocking Leo off balance. He grabbed a harness buckle, pulled himself upright, and strapped himself in. Clicks filled the bridge as Lux and Dorian buckled up beside him, the siblings closing their eyes.

"*Two . . .*"

Jane began checking off systems, but Will had already overridden her controls. Not that she noticed. Jane's glitches were getting worse. If the crew made it through this, Will would find her a new body to jump into. No matter the price.

"*One.*"

A droning sigh hissed through the corridors as the gravity generator died. Jane's cookies and tray rose into the air, bumping off Will's shoulder as he floated up, only to be caught by the loose harnesses around his chest strapping him to his chair. The old girl was protesting.

Well, let her. He knew her capabilities better than she did.

Normally in a complex situation like this, a captain would need his co-pilot and his navigator to even stand a chance. But Will wasn't normal. The hardware the mocks had put into his head, the technology that saved his life when he was thirteen, also allowed him to see time and space like a three-dimensional grid. He could take in the mines, create the safest route, and assess for damages all in the span of a heartbeat.

Currently, he had them at nine percent shields. The margin of error was thirty-one percent. Anything less than ten percent shields would be catastrophic, so he was counting on that margin of error to save their lives.

As their speed increased, the blips on the map joined together and a pattern emerged. Will's heartbeat slowed, his breathing steadied, and all thoughts melted away to the yellowish-green lines on the screen. The sounds of the crew protesting—Jane calling out commands he wouldn't follow, Leo demanding they stop, Lux yelling at him to shut up—all of it seemed to come from another room. Another time.

When they were past the point of return, the crew abruptly went quiet. His fingers flew over the console as they raced past the first heavy barrage of mines in silence. The old ship groaned and creaked. A soft shutter wracked the hull, and Leo cursed under his breath. Another. Each time the ship's hull trembled, Will checked the controls. Testing the mines' strength and recalculating as needed.

Will maneuvered the ship left and right, sideways. The mines grew thicker, the holes between them smaller.

Two direct hits lit the starscreen with bright green.

"Will!" Leo yelled.

Another explosion, and the Odysseus screamed in agony, metal screeching and groaning as some hole was likely torn in the ship's hull.

"Will!"

Tremors reverberated through the old ship as the oxygen was sucked out, and the force threw Will forward, the thick harness digging into his chest.

"She can't take this!" Jane cried. "The shields are giving up."

Will hardly blinked as he pounded his fingers over the controls. She could take it. She was tough. They had to make it.

The shield's integrity bar was dropping.

Fifteen percent.

Thirteen percent.

Ten percent.

Too much. Too fast.

Perhaps he'd failed to account for the old girl's age. The already compromised left shield.

"Will!"

One second, they were caught inside a whirlwind of explosions and light. The next, the dark calmness of open space unfurled over the screen. Odysseus stilled as red flashes lit the room, emergency beacons notifying the crew of needed repairs.

But for the first time since they entered the minefield, the crew had nothing to say.

Jane swiveled her chair to face Will. "Shields at nine point seven percent, Captain."

Will expected the crew to complain. Leo or Lux to say something hilariously inappropriate to break the tension. Instead, they unstrapped and took to their jobs without a peep, disappearing from the bridge to care for Odysseus. Dorian to check for hull breaches in all quadrants. Lux to map out the new star field. Jane to divert power to the sections that sustained the most damage.

Leo returned to the bridge, dragging a faded-red exosuit that should have been burned long ago behind him, and then suited up. As soon as he placed the helmet over his head, the locks clicked into place and air hissed into his suit, filling the legs and torso and fogging the curved plexi-glass that muffled his face. He reached out and tapped Will's chest. "Whatever's out there better be worth it, Will Perrault."

Will cast a quick glance over the starscreen, the whisper of a headache clenching his skull. Far as he could tell, there was nothing here, other than a few random bits of space trash. Unstrapping from his harness, he leaned against the edge of his seat, surveying the radar screen. Darkness. Could they have just stumbled into a random minefield offloaded from a damaged ship? No, these mines were high grade. And old, by the millisecond delay some of them took before igniting. They were put here on purpose.

Perhaps someone had already been here. No, impossible. No one but Will could have brought a ship safely through this minefield. And there were no signs of wreckage from another scavenger ship.

They had to be the first.

Wait. He blinked at the radar as a tiny blip flashed. One single dot adrift in a sea of black.

He'd expected the wreckage of an elite starship, maybe. Something that could be offered as a whole. Something worth billions of credits.

What good was one item?

Dorian, finished with the ship's repairs, returned to the bridge in his emerald-green exosuit and barely stood waist high next to Leo by the hatch. Lux bit her bottom lip as she finished going over her safety checklist for both suits, cursing at each patched hole she discovered in Leo's, the loose brackets connecting their hoses. Then she and Will left Jane in the bridge and followed them through the ship's narrow, circular corridors to the cargo-hold. On the other side was the ship's empty bay.

"Boys, find us something worth all that nonsense back there," Lux ordered Leo and Dorian. Then she and Will backed up as the hatch door closed and watched the two disappear into the airlock. From there, they would fasten themselves to tethers and collect the hopeful treasure. Once, they'd owned a retriever ship, but Will had to sell it three months ago to spring Leo from jail on the off-world planet Mitas.

The airlock beeped, announcing Leo's and Dorian's entry into space, and Lux turned to Will. "Captain, since you took over Jane's position on this ship six months ago, I've almost died"—she held up her hand, ticking off fingers—"hell, Captain. I can't even count on one hand."

"How many credits did you nab last year with Captain Safety?" he asked. "How many tons of cargo? Any of you buy back jump status yet?"

"Credits don't matter if we're dead. Neither does jumping." Lux glanced toward the empty cargo bay. "And our hold is pretty empty now, too."

"Well, neither of us will have to keep eking out an existence in this rust bucket much longer. There's something out there. I can feel it in my bones."

"You said that last time. And just so we're clear, you get Dorian killed for some hypothetical score, and I'll space toss you into oblivion."

Will cracked his neck and eyed the doors. "Point taken."

The wait wore on Will's nerves. He focused on the image of that dot on the radar. It had to be something important. An anti-matter core or nuclear capacitor. He rattled off items in his head as they waited, Lux making a show of checking their oxygen levels on the computer while Will leaned against the wall, watching the door. He needed something big. Something that could buy his way off this salvage ship and back into his regiment. Something that could erase the sins of his past forever.

But when the airlock mechanism clicked open and Leo and Dorian stepped through, Will's hopes faltered. They carried a metallic, rose-gold item the size and shape of the coffins humans used to be buried in, before mocks decreed incineration for fleshers after death. The angles were sharper than the coffins he pictured, though, with five faceted sides. And whatever material this was made from, he couldn't place it.

Just when Leo and Dorian hit the center of the hold, gravity switched back on and the mysterious item crashed to the floor, sending a massive shudder racing through the ship.

Leo ripped off his helmet and tapped it against the surface of the coffin. Then he tried to slide it across the floor. His muscles bulged beneath the thin, deflated suit, but the thing refused to budge. His hair fell over his eyes, and a curse slipped from his lips as he kicked the coffin and threw up his hands. "This was totally worth risking our lives for."

The sarcasm in Leo's voice grated on Will's nerves. He approached the find, slowly. Gold and silver sparkled inside the outer shell as he neared. The material was smooth and *cold* beneath his fingers. Not deep space cold. A different kind of cold that whispered of ancient human technologies.

The entire surface was smooth. There were no lines or rough spots to indicate a way to open the thing—if it was even hollow, something Will was beginning to doubt. Other than the small, engraved symbol of a bird with strange dots, there were no markings.

"Does anyone recognize this symbol?" Will asked.

Lux shook her head. Dorian frowned but said nothing. Leo stared at the symbol the longest, the vein in his neck jumping. He was obviously still pissed, so Will let him be.

Something inside him collapsed as Will backed away, ignoring the frustrated looks of the crew. He knew what they always did. Whatever this find was, they had absolutely no doubt now.

This find was *worthless.*

He'd risked all their lives for nothing.

CHAPTER 2

3631 AD

Talia

Talia Starchaser thought being sold to a prince on her eighteenth birthday was a terrible present. Worse than the picture her little brother was forced to draw—from real crayons, not the computerized painting most people preferred these days. Worse, even, than the public scrutiny that was now allowed due to her age and status as Junior Sovereign.

Turning eighteen meant she wasn't just a princess anymore. She was public property, adorned in makeup and a pretty little dress and a smile for her betrothed.

She shuddered at the thought of Prince Cassius. A Starchaser hadn't married a Thorossian Royal for three centuries. Thorossians were crude, hardened by a desert planet with more ore than water.

Which is why we need this alliance, she reminded herself for the umpteenth time. But the truth didn't soften the blow. Being sold had a certain aftertaste she couldn't wash away with words and logic.

For Talia, the idea of ruling the Seven Planets was a constant cloud hanging over her head, like the twin moons orbiting her planet, or the cloying hyacinth perfume her grandmother bathed herself in. According to the wrinkled ex-Sovereign, Talia's rise to the throne was ordained in the stars. It was the supernova her life revolved around, warming her and burning her in equal measure. Just like her father. Her grandfather. And so on. The entire Starchaser Dynasty would take at least an hour to name in a single setting, if one were inclined to do so.

Talia was not. Especially when that title was being sold for a planet's worth of ore. Was that really all a Starchaser was worth these days?

Sighing, Talia flung her thick auburn hair over her shoulder, the heavy tresses tickling her bare back, and a flurry of attendants rushed to finish securing the fire opals that speckled her hair. She should have been ready hours ago, but flight training ran late.

One attendant tightened the sun-gold ribbons of Talia's corset. Her ribs groaned to the point they were ready to crack, and she cried out, biting back the urge to slap the poor girl. Two more attendants braced Talia's arms as the other yanked harder, and her vision eclipsed. One more tug, and her already slim waist shrunk to almost nothing, as did her ability to breathe.

It reminded her of the first time she experienced G-force inside a Predator-Class Mig-12 Starfighter. Except that had been fun and a lot less painful.

You're a future Starchaser Sovereign. Pain is not only expected but welcome.

According to her father, continuing to fight the mock

rebellion across the Outer Fringes required three things: soldiers, starships, and ore to mine for the metal and fuel. And the Thorassians needed a Starchaser princess to secure their rising status.

The marriage was the perfect solution for everyone . . . everyone but *her*.

"Shouldn't have had those honey-biscuits this morning," Ailat teased, disrupting Talia's thoughts. Her junior companion popped up from the four-poster bed near the back wall, ducked beneath a dusk-rose panel, and flitted over to assess Talia's outfit, heels clacking against the moonstone floor.

Wide blue eyes blinked above Ailat's high cheekbones. She was tall and slender, and she'd traded her dark-gray flight suit from their practice session earlier for a gorgeous azure gown few others could pull off. Her pumps made her tower over Talia, even though the girls were around the same height. "At least, not if you want your husband to fit his hands around your waist like he can with Baroness Crenaline."

Heat flared across Talia's chest, and she stabbed her hand over her hips. "What do I care about that social climbing daughter of an ore smuggler?"

"Her father was exonerated." Ailat lifted an exquisite black eyebrow, mischief sparkling inside her eyes. "Perhaps that's why Lord Cassius has taken such an interest in her lately."

Talia braced herself against her attendants and sighed. Ailat was right. A Starchaser left nothing to chance.

Not even love.

Talia needed to look ravishing, a princess every man in the universe would die to marry. She needed to close the deal.

"Tighter," she ordered, and her attendants cinched and yanked until the pittance of air that remained in her lungs fled. When they were done, tears of pain streamed down her cheeks, but Ailat smiled.

"There," Ailat said, reaching over to turn on the Broadnet, which Talia had purposely left off. Talk would all be about her today anyway. "Just try not to eat anything. Or, you know, breathe."

"*Stars and skies*!" Talia rolled her eyes at her companion's pleased voice. "Cassius will marry me no matter the size of my waist."

"True. But now he won't be thinking of Baroness Crenaline while he does it."

An image of Talia as a baby—all wispy hair and fat cheeks—broadcasted on the far wall, followed by the few images the public had been granted access to over the years. A voice droned on about her education and hobbies, leaving out the one thing she enjoyed—flight training. As if the intergalactic hordes knew anything about her!

Rolling her eyes, *again,* Talia glanced at Ailat. Usually Talia adored her companion's frank humor, but today was the exception. "Maybe . . ." she wheezed. "*You* should be Sovereign."

As soon as the words left her lips, she wanted to take them back. They were a cruel joke. Despite the life that poured from Ailat's eyes, despite the lopsided dimple in her cheek, her dark humor, and the way her face lit up at the sight of the handsome courtiers around the palace, she was a mock.

Not a real human—a droid. Built by the best creators in the land to be a junior companion to Talia. To help shape her master into first a princess and then a ruler. Every single quality, every single quirk. All held a purpose that had nothing to do with Ailat, and everything to do with Talia.

Even her companion's name, Ailat, was Talia spelled backward.

Suggesting Ailat be Sovereign was the same as suggesting she get married and have children someday. That she grow old and dote on grandchildren.

Impossible.

And yet, sometimes—in the darkest hours of night when the two moons hid and the palace was as quiet as a sarcophagus—Talia thought her companion would be better suited to rule. A droid created by man, with wires for veins and metal instead of bones and a microchip where her heart should be.

"Maybe, Princess," Ailat teased, her even voice giving no hint at offense, "you should stop complaining and think about Cassius's biceps. I hear they're nearly as big as his bank account."

But as Ailat fingered her sleek curtain of shoulder-length ebony hair, her bottom lip twitched to the side. Not for the first time, Talia wondered if that was a programmable trait, or one of the 752 unique behaviors Ailat's model would develop over time.

Not that it mattered. Not really. Even if she felt slighted, it would be a fleeting emotion, drowned out by her devotion to Talia. Loyalty and love for their master companions were the two most dominant traits in every mock.

The attendants scurried from Ailat as she slipped behind Talia and towered over her. Only a mock could get away with seven-inch platforms. Unlike Talia, whose very human feet ached inside her diamond-studded heels, sweat clinging between her toes.

Brushing the petty thought aside, she glanced over her reflection in the mirror. A princess on the verge of adulthood. Not that she felt like an adult, but the sable dress clinging to her body said otherwise.

She ran two fingers down her constricted waist. The silken material could have been poured from the midnight sky. Little twinkles of diamonds caught in the golden light gushing from her bedroom windows that overlooked Palesia, the royal capitol of planet Calisto. Fire opals burned like comets inside her long, flowing auburn hair, a hundred burning suns against a dusky sky. Even the smattering of freckles dusting her porcelain skin were barely visible.

She looked every bit a Starchaser Princess on the eve of her coronation as Sovereign-in-waiting. From tonight onward, if anything were to happen to Father, the current Sovereign, she was first in line to succeed the throne. Which was why her engagement would be made official today as well. Two birds with one stone.

But was she the stone . . . or the bird?

Shuddering, she swallowed down the panic that came surging upward every time her thoughts ventured down this path. *Don't think about that. Tonight is simply a formality. Father isn't going anywhere.*

Yet she clutched at the ruby-crusted hem of her corset, the air suddenly too thin, every sound unsettling. A Starfighter shrieked from the skies above the palace, rattling the windowpanes and vibrating her bones. For a heartbeat, she was flying through the stars. High above her home planet and all the troubles that came with it.

The thought of flying should have calmed her. Instead, cold sweat slicked her palms, warning of another panic attack. She started having them after news of her marriage. *Stars, please not today.* She couldn't show weakness in front of her attendants. But a wave of heavy darkness tumbled over her, and she was powerless to stop it. Just like all the other times.

Grasping at her throat, she stumbled to the window overlooking the city. Half-open UV blinds parted at her presence. She splayed her palms against the hot windowpane, sweat streaking the thin glass, and blinked as her new kingdom waned in and out of focus. A balcony spread beneath her fingertips, too humid to actually use nine months out of the year, and a stretch of ivory buildings dotted the hills and colored the land around the palace white. Farther in the distance, the dark steel buildings of the mock side of the city rose to the sky, cruel and unforgiving and *hers*.

Soft fingers slipped over her bare arms, gently turning Talia away from the window. Ailat. One long-boned hand gripped each of Talia's arms. "You are Talia Starchaser. You fear nothing. You own the stars and the planets and the galaxies. You rule billions." Ailat's fingers gripped harder. "Say it with me, Tal."

And Talia did. Just like when she was a little girl, afraid of traveling on her family's massive starship for the first time. Or the time she refused to step foot on planet Minos because she'd never before seen ice and snow.

The words calmed her frayed nerves, the sharp edge

of panic fading beneath Ailat's familiar voice. But a string of curse words drew Talia's attention to her door just as it slammed open, allowing some anxiety to creep back in.

Even before the potent hyacinth perfume of her grandmother, mother regent and former Sovereign, swamped the room, Talia's attendants had flattened themselves into synchronized bows. Their too-perfect movements were the only indication they were mocks, just like Ailat. Although they weren't quite as complex, or special.

The former Sovereign was ageless inside a mauve gown, her taut skin stretched over rounded cheeks that nearly obscured her shrewd golden eyes—the only Starchaser trait she shared with Talia. Piles of silk fabric dragged across the floor, weighted with colored pearls to represent the solar systems under their rule. Although only seven were inhabitable, many more off-world planets had been colonized to mine for the natural resources the Seven required.

A nervous breath escaped Talia's lips as her gaze swept over the pearls; one day, she would own not just the dress her grandmother wore but all the planets the pearls represented as well.

Two attendants shadowed Grandmother, scrambling to gather the heaviest portion of her train. A crown of onyx nestled over her thinning, silver hair, and her pointed chin was held high, as if her head was supported on an invisible string. Only the hunch rounding her back whispered of her true age, a number Talia could only guess.

Grandmother scattered Talia's attendants with the flick of a manicured hand, and their boots squeaked across the floor as they made a hasty retreat. The matriarch was a cluster of storm clouds on the horizon; all sorts of destruction hid inside her dark depths. Talia never knew if her father's mother would drown her in barely-veiled insults or strike her down like lightning. The sting of her grandmother's cold palm slapping her cheek was as frequent as her smiles—perhaps more so.

And yet, Talia found herself smiling as her grandmother cursed beneath her breath and swatted at a poor girl who got too close to the matriarch.

For a moment, Talia locked eyes with her companion, nerves steadied as the skin around Ailat's wide blue eyes crinkled. Then Grandmother's gaze slid to Ailat, and Talia could have sworn something cold flickered across the woman's severe face.

"Look at you, girl," her grandmother said, focusing her attention back on Talia. "Without your body hidden beneath that hideous flight suit you wear, you might stand a fighting chance at winning the Prince's favor."

Her mouth fell open. "How did you—?"

"Know? Dear, I know everything that happens inside these walls. You think I wouldn't be told that my oldest granddaughter and the future Sovereign is training to fly shuttles?"

"They're not called shuttles anymore . . ." Her words trailed away under her grandmother's piercing gaze.

"Well, whatever you youth call them these days, that part of your life is over. Common soldiers can die in the skies against the rebels—you're a Starchaser."

Talia tried to swallow, but her throat was drier than the

sands of Thoros. So she simply nodded—then froze as her grandmother's bony hands, speckled with bleached sun spots, lifted a golden crown from the folds of velvet her attendant held. The delicate adornment settled uneasily on Talia's head.

"There." Grandmother's golden-eyed gaze swept over Talia again, slowly this time. "That son of a fool, Cassius, will melt into a puddle when he sees the gift your father has given him."

Perhaps it was the mention of a betrothed Talia had never met, or her grandmother's cruel voice as she discussed selling her granddaughter to a Thoros prince, but Talia said, "I thought it was you, not Father, who arranged my marriage."

Talia braced for a slap, or at least the biting words she'd grown so accustomed to. Instead, her grandmother's hearty laughter filled the room. Apparently selling her granddaughter to an ore prince had put the matriarch in a very good mood.

"Of course I did. This intergalactic war has made everything uncertain. And in troubled times, it's the women who hold everything together."

War? Talia was used to words like *skirmish* and *conflict*, which is how the news described the rebellion.

"The ore prince may not be what you had in mind, my dear," her grandmother continued, crooked fingers worrying at one of the pearls around her belt. "But, sometimes, you must reach up and align the stars in your favor. Even the dimmest ones have their uses."

"And . . . this star. What if I can't stand him? What if he thinks I'm ugly or he beats me?"

"You are a Starchaser, dear. You'll endure whatever comes your way with a smile. And if he hurts you, darling, well there's always poison. But give it a few years, for appearance's sake."

Talia didn't know if she was supposed to laugh or nod . . . or *cry*. "Yes, Grandmother."

One second longer and she'd say something that would ruin everything. So Talia crossed her chamber, pretending she needed to approach the mirror to adjust one of the fire opals secured in her hair.

Inside the glass, she watched her grandmother turn to leave. The news had switched over to commentators discussing the rebellion, their arguing voices echoing off the moonstone walls of her room and reminding her what was at stake this evening.

As she crossed to the door, her grandmother had one last piece of advice to add. "Have your mock change her shoes, dear. A mock should never be taller than her master companion."

As soon as the door clicked shut, Talia scoffed. No way she was going to demand Ailat change shoes. She looked divine in those pumps.

Besides, Talia had bigger things to worry about. The coronation of a royal Starchaser child was as secret as the moods of her grandmother. What if Talia suffered another attack like earlier? What if she hated her betrothed?

What if . . . no. Whatever happened tonight, Ailat would be there for support. Just as she had Talia's whole life.

The door clicked shut behind Grandmother, reminding Talia to breathe. And then Ailat and Talia fell into the comfort of her enormous bed and giggled until fat tears darkened the folds of their dresses. They gossiped about the notoriously handsome Cassius, whom Talia couldn't decide to like or hate.

They talked of the gaudy gowns and jewels they would most likely see tonight, half of them probably knockoffs and fakes. Few could afford true luxuries, not with the war raging.

Like always, at some point the conversation steered back to flying. Both girls trained together every day after Talia's long line of tutoring lessons. At first Ailat was included because Talia needed a copilot to practice with the double-seaters. But Ailat was just as good as Talia—maybe better, though she'd never admit that—and soon they both flew their own Starfighters.

That was a secret no one but Talia and their instructor knew.

Ailat went quiet. Then she took Talia's hand. The steel beneath felt just like bone, Ailat's creamy skin warm and alive and not the least bit synthetic in feeling. "They shouldn't have married you off to Cassius, Tal. Not against your will."

Talia found herself laughing, a hollow, shrill sound that was too much like her mother's. "I'm a Starchaser. That's what we do." Her voice went low. "Sacrifice and honor for the Seven."

"I mean it though. I know I joke with you about him, but I've known you since we were kids. You deserve someone who sees you like I do."

After weeks walling off her emotions for this day, the kind words shattered her defenses, but Talia straightened hopefully before Ailat noticed her sagging shoulders and limp smile. "If Cassius likes me, and the engagement proceeds, we'll have to leave our home."

Something cool and hard poked her palm. A swan-shaped

brooch. Pink and yellow diamonds sparkled against the rose-gold metal. The yellow diamonds signified the Cygnus constellation the first Starchaser explored. It was part of their crest.

Ailat was grinning.

"What's this for?" Talia asked.

"An early wedding present."

"But this must have cost you . . ." Talia was embarrassed to even think about it. And she'd never inquired how many credits her family provided Ailat monthly. Talia made a mental note to secretly repay her friend. "It's too much, Ailat."

The beginnings of a frown twitching her lips, Ailat squeezed Talia's fingers. "I had a dream last night. A dream you drowned in a sea of stars."

Dream? Dreams were impossible for Ailat. Her programming didn't include sleep phases. There must have been a glitch or something in her system. A specialist would need to look her over in the morning. "Everything's about to change, Ailat. But us? We'll be the same as ever."

"What if Cassius says I can't come? He wouldn't be the first husband to insist his wife's junior mock take retirement early."

Talia shook her head, careful not to knock any of the opals loose. Talk of Ailat's retirement always made her edgy. How could Ailat want to go from the royal palace to a fishing boat captain on one of Krenth's many oceans? Wouldn't she miss all this? Wouldn't she miss *Talia*? "That rarely happens, Ailat. Besides, I'll tell him how important you are to me. If he demands I leave my home and family, then I can make a few stipulations of my own."

Ailat laughed, but the sound was stilted and forced.

Another emotion that was out of character for Talia's friend. "I've always wanted to visit Thoros, Tal."

"Liar," Talia teased as she slipped off the bed and onto her feet. "Thoros is a cesspool of sand and ore dust. There's no water there. Not even a crappy pond. You'll be begging me to leave after five minutes."

"Not if we're together," Ailat amended, unfolding from the deep mattress and stretching her arms over her head. "You'll see. It will be an adventure. Maybe your new Prince will let us fly together."

Talia nodded, overriding her skepticism with a smile. Mocks weren't allowed to fly anything above an S-Class shuttle, and already there was talk of those being outlawed too with the rebellion at hand.

Once she married Cassius, Ailat would probably never fly again.

Explosions broadcast on the far wall drew the girls' attention away as the news played footage of the war. The image of a Starfighter bursting into flames danced across the moonstone, followed by unmanned mock jets looking for more Starfighters to destroy, and then the video switched to a spokesman from the Intergalactic Coalition of Seven. "I believe I speak for most of us in the Seven when I say we never imagined the virus that started out in labor models would spread to over fifty different kinds and eventually lead to full-blown war. Let's hope the Starchaser government has—"

"Off, news," Talia commanded a bit too quickly, shutting down the broadcast.

Ailat had frozen beside her, one hand at her neck. Unless

people looked closely, they missed the flap of skin that hid her port. Thank the gods Ailat had been spared the virus. If she had tested positive . . . but she hadn't. That was the important thing.

Although her results were curious. The test was performed by ordering a mock to harm themselves by cutting their finger. The ones who'd been exposed to the virus would refuse, despite being ordered by their human master. If the humans persisted, the mocks attacked. A survival instinct developed only *after* the virus struck.

But when Ailat was given the same order, she hesitated for a breath. A heartbeat. Not a positive, exactly, yet the interviewer found it curious. Talia had to use her station and a few billion credits to keep the man from testing Ailat further.

All that mattered was that Ailat did eventually slice her finger, and mocks whose programs had been corrupted refused. Meaning Ailat was fine. The war would be over soon, and this deal with corrupted mocks would all be forgotten.

"Do you think they'll be angry at me?" Ailat asked.

Talia frowned. "Who?"

"The humans. There's been another concerted attack by my kind. Thousands of your kind slaughtered by mocks in their homes. It could—"

"Stop." Talia shook her head. "Humans aren't that cruel to blame you for the decision of others. You'll see."

"I'm sure you're right."

But as they strolled hand-in-hand down the hall to the coronation, Talia realized that for the first time ever, Ailat said the words, *your kind,* in reference to humans. Not *us,* like she was programmed to say.

CHAPTER 3

3731 AD

Will

It took two whole days to get the Odysseus' shields functioning and fix the hull breaches from the mines. Two whole days of the crew sulking. Will tried everything. Jokes. Helping Leo clean the dishes after meals—Leo was the unofficial cook, his dishes only slightly more tolerable than Jane's. Will even broke out his treasured movie, *Breakfast at Tiffany's*, from the time of humans and projected it across the mess wall.

But only Dorian watched the movie with him, or at least half of it. The kid left after Holly Golightly lit that old woman's hat on fire. Mocks these days had no appreciation for the classics. Or Audrey Hepburn in a little black dress.

Now *she* was a flesher.

And even with all the brooding going on, no one could figure out the mystery of the collected item, which only made everyone glare harder at Will. They couldn't penetrate the solid surface, stars knew they tried. Or Leo did. Watching the big guy's face grow red with frustration as he pounded away at the thing almost made the entire incident worth it. There were no buttons to push, no sounds emanating from the dense material. Steel couldn't scratch it. Metal couldn't dent it. Fire couldn't even scorch it—they tried that too.

In fact, after a few days, they all lost interest in deciphering the coffin-shaped device. It was just another of Will's screw ups. To be ignored, traded, or space-tossed. No one had decided yet which option was the best.

"Next stop is Andromeda," Leo announced, as if such a thing needed announcing. He was stretched out in Jane's chair, dark-green leather boots kicked up on the console. The damned things were made from some exotic animal Will could only guess at. Ugly as sin, non-regulation, and Leo had probably paid an entire cargo's worth of credit for them. "Let's trade *the thing* for a few crates of whisky and be done with it."

They'd dubbed it *the thing*, though Will cringed every time he heard it. How could he have made such a huge mistake? He nearly got everyone killed for a stupid hunk of metal.

"How do you propose we move it?" Will asked. "A loader big enough to support its weight would cost us the whisky and a week's pay."

"I say we space-toss it," Lux said. She and Jane had brought in a round scrap of metal and set it on the floor to use as a gambling table. They were both hunched over it, enthralled in an illegal game of liar's dice they knew Will wouldn't stop because of his guilt. The curses that slipped from the corner of Lux's lips, though, gave Will a tiny bit of satisfaction. She was already in deep. "The thing is creepier than one of Jane's fallouts. No offense, Jane."

Jane peeked at her dice concealed under a tin cup. "None

taken, dear. Now, what's that? Twenty billion?"

"Shit." Lux threw the rest of dice across the floor and stood. "We should vote. Everyone who wants to space-toss the thing, raise your hand."

Leo and Lux were the first traitors to lift their arms. Jane frowned down at her cup and raised her hand a fraction above her head, like she really didn't want to go against her captain but couldn't help herself. Lux turned to Dorian near the back. "Dor?"

Dorian glanced up from his soldering iron and the chip he was repairing to frown at his sister. At fourteen, he was caught between the stages of wanting her approval and wanting to rebel. "I think it's cool."

"Cool? It's creepy."

"*Okay.*" He rolled his eyes but gave in and lifted his hand, avoiding Will's gaze.

A ship full of insubordinate traitors.

"Great." Lux strolled over to Will and leaned against the captain's chair. "It's settled. We open the cargo hatch and send the thing back into oblivion."

Will kept his lips in a tight, unreadable line. "No."

"Will, be reasonable, if that's even possible."

"I am reasonable. That *thing* has value. And I don't know why you believe this ship operates like a democracy. Your votes mean nothing."

"You just don't want to admit you made a mistake." Three lines etched across her forehead, and she pushed a twist of lavender hair off her forehead. "Okay. We get to Andromeda, you have a few cold beers, then we ask around about the thing. See if anyone's stupid enough to take her off our hands."

Leo snorted and raised an eyebrow. "Her?"

"It's a she."

"Fine," Will said, the mention of cold beers making his mind whir, "the thing is a *she*, and we'll see if we can find some answers on Andromeda. And here"—he flipped a small coin at her—"use this to square away with Jane."

Lux caught the coin and examined it, twirling it between her fingers with a frown etched on her face. "Isn't this your lucky coin?"

He shooed her off with a wave, knowing the coin would make its way back to him. It always did. The small piece of zinc was one of the last pennies in existence, an earthen token and a reminder of the day he was reborn from human to mock. "We make our own luck."

"Thanks," she breathed. "I'll repay you as soon as my luck changes."

Against Jane, that would be never. Lux had been indebted to her since before he came aboard. The straight-laced ex-captain's gambling compulsion came from her glitch, but fortunately for her, she was damned good at it.

As Will watched Lux walk away, he couldn't help but grin. Lux was a pain in the ass, sure. But she'd find a way to pay him back; she always did.

Perhaps his sudden shift in mood came because he knew eventually he'd get his old crew back. None of this illegal gambling or whoring. No one taking votes when he gave orders or mocking him with salutes. No more scavenging for items like the *thing* and risking his life only to discover the frozen hunk of metal was worthless . . .

He swallowed, the last sentence lodged in his mind as he replayed it over and over, trying to decipher what made him stop.

And then something occurred to him, and he exhaled slowly. Last he checked, the *thing* was room temperature.

She was warming up.

CHAPTER 4

3631 AD

Talia

Each step Talia took leading up to the entrance of the royal hall ratcheted her heartbeat faster, *faster*, until she felt as if a rubber ball was bouncing off her sternum. The building was a breathtaking mixture of ivory stones and gilded spires, dotted with hundreds of stained glass windows colored to resemble starry skies. It stood alone next to the actual palace, a sacred place Talia had only heard about.

She glanced at the parched sky, hoping to center herself, to find calm outside this internal panic, and discovered the fiery sun had already melted into Palesia's cityscape horizon. The ceremony would start as soon as the last rays of pink light disappeared. Sweat laced her skin, pasting her hair to her neck and shoulders; a hot, sluggish breeze tickled her cheeks.

Talia's mother strolled on the right, pointing a motorized fan of gold at the sweat glistening her tawny skin. She radiated warmth and regality inside a champagne dress of taffeta, hardly the image of a woman about to sell her firstborn daughter. On occasion, her dark eyes drifted toward Talia, as if expecting her to bolt. The hint of a smile was all the woman afforded her daughter, but each gesture steadied Talia's feet and spurred her forward, closer to the sea of Palesians swelling the courtyard and spilling outside the gates.

Tradition held that citizens had to remain silent during the procession, but a soft murmur vibrated the air anyway. Helmeted guards in crisp white uniforms stood rigid at the gates. Just in case things got out of hand.

How many Starchasers had walked these steps before Talia? How many suffered from the same nervous pains that clutched her belly? Every royal had to endure this spectacle at some point, smiling and waving for the hidden cameras. While on the other side of the ancient marble ballroom stood a stranger the royal was about to pledge their life to.

But Talia was the only Starchaser ever who had to leave Palesia, a stipulation her soon-to-be husband had insisted on. The thought twisted her gut. And as soon as they said their vows, she would travel across the Seven Planets on a promotional tour to support the battalions, her husband and his family right beside her.

Couldn't Talia's parents see she was nothing more than a prop? That she'd serve the cause better by lending her skills to fighting rather than prancing around and looking pretty?

Her age protected her from the public eye—up until today. From this point onward, her entire life would be open to the billions and billions of people that inhabited the Seven Planets and the off-world planets under their control. She would be expected to give speeches and attend galactic meetings. To say all the right things and have all the answers. And she'd never been good with crowds or words. Making five-ton fighter ships look graceful mid-air, or sparring against Ailat? Sure, those things came easy to her.

But public meetings? Public speaking?

Most days she was lucky if she could say her full name: Talia Marie Starchaser XXIV, daughter of Magnus, granddaughter of Maris, future Sovereign. *Blah. Blah.*

Wiping a damp lock of hair from her forehead, she fought the urge to search out the veiled cameras lurking around the columns and broadcasting her image to the entire world.

"They're whispering about you," Tamsin teased. Her little brother, positioned on her left, was at the know-it-all age of twelve, where everything she did was silly and gross and required a million insults.

"Of course they are," she fired back, glancing back with a raised eyebrow to share an annoyed look with Ailat. "I'm their future Sovereign. They're curious."

"No, it's because you look like a Palesian escort with all that makeup," he said, trying desperately to repress a smile, but he couldn't fool anyone. Even his eyes lit up.

Talia pinched his arm. "Shut up, imp."

Their mother graced them both with a practiced, tight grin that promised trouble if they didn't stop.

Tamsin gritted his peach-fuzz jaw. "But—"

Before he could finish whatever stupid insult was on his lips, his companion mock, Nismat, a gangly boy around the same age, nudged him in the ribs. "Ignore her, Tamsin."

Talia rolled her eyes as she ducked beneath the marble arches wreathed in lavender and white irises and hurried inside, her brother all but forgotten as she took in the crowd of people all now turned to stare at her. Was Lord Cassius already here? Could that be him in the cream-and-gold suit near the front? Or what about the man to her right? Talia hardly knew what he looked like, other than the few glimpses broadcast of him since his own coming out ceremony a few months ago on Thoros.

He was handsome, sure. And slovenly drunk. Part of her hoped he would be pissed tonight, too. That way he wouldn't notice when she stepped on his toes during the first dance, or failed to show the proper enthusiasm for being sold to an ore-prince below her station.

The royal hall was a round building filled with circular tables surrounding a podium with a massive skylight above that allowed the stars to shine down. Soon, the first moon would fill the space with delicate light, but for now, holographic torches glowed inside the arched alcoves etched into the marble walls. Columns lined up like pale soldiers at attention, casting shadows across the room. Vases with bouquets of lavender dressed the tables, filling the stuffy air with a sticky-sweet perfume. Statesmen from the Intergalactic Coalition of Seven milled about with glasses full of amber liquid in hand, and Talia fought against the urge to flinch under their curious gazes.

A sigh spilled from her chest as she found her father surrounded by a group of senators dressed in lavish black suits, several of them talking at once, their movements quick and flighty. Trained to read body gestures, Talia immediately recognized the men were agitated.

A feeling of incompetence nestled deep inside her chest as she watched her father handle the senators with his usual calm grace. One hand was clasped behind his back, his handsome face forced into a mask of calm indifference.

As if he could hear her thoughts, his green eyes cut toward her and then he was coming to her rescue.

He offered her a rare grin and clasped her wet, clammy hands with his warm and dry ones. "Daughter, the stars above pale in comparison to your beauty."

A blush crept up her chest, thawing her nervousness from the inside out. "Thank you, Sovereign."

Sovereign, not Father. Now that she was eighteen, everything was different. He held her hands for a moment longer, and she wanted to wrap her arms around him and never let go, to be held and comforted by him. She so rarely got to see her father. And now, with the war in the Outer Fringes, he was home even less. But she was too old for such childish whims.

He lifted a sandy eyebrow. "I wish I could have better prepared you for today."

"And I wish the rebellion was over." Her gaze collapsed to her too-tight ivory heels; she'd said a stupid thing. Wishes were for fools who didn't understand the way of the worlds. Or at least that was what her father once told her after overhearing her and Ailat discussing their silly seven-year-old plans.

Even as a child, her father made her destiny clear. It would have been cruel to let her think otherwise.

Two lines formed across his forehead, and he sighed. "Now that you're of age, you will be expected to sit in on the war council. But not today. Today, you will dance and show Cassius how lucky he is to marry you."

Talia rocked on her heels, grimacing at the blisters already forming on the back of her ankles. "Oh, I don't—"

"He is." Her father's eyes went tight and steely, and he gave her hands a quick squeeze that seemed to last minutes instead of seconds. "Never forget that, Talia. You are a Starchaser, descendant of the first explorers. Even now, you burn brighter than the Palesian sun."

Lips twisted to the side, he paused, but before he could say more, his secretary—a male mock with thinning brown hair and a full beard cropped close to his face—interrupted to whisper something in Father's ear. He straightened as his face transformed back into the Sovereign's cool mask. "I must leave."

"Leave?" She wanted to scream, beg him to stay, be near her and not leave, don't ever leave. "The cere—" Talia cleared the fear from her throat. "Ceremony?"

But his attention had returned to the senators, and he gave a subtle nod without meeting her gaze. "There's been a development."

She opened her mouth to ask—

"Nothing to worry about. I should be back in time for your oath."

Swallowing down every childish protest hovering on the tip of her tongue, she forced her expression into a look of understanding. "Promise on the moon?"

Normally, he would have said *both of them* with a wink and a grin, because that had been their thing since she was four. But today—today he strode away, hands in his pockets and face dark with whatever hidden worries he carried around.

Soon those worries would be hers: the rebellion, the

constant stream of ships and soldiers who never returned. The empty bank accounts.

Ailat touched Talia's shoulder, breaking apart the concerns clouding her mind. "He'll come back."

"I know," she said, proud how her voice sounded almost believable. Squaring back her shoulders, she and Ailat crossed the floor to their table near the podium, navigating the maze of senators and envoys, Talia ever-aware of all the eyes now on her, eyes that could belong to Cassius.

As soon as she touched the curved back of the golden velvet chair, someone swept in beside her and pulled the seat out for her. "Allow me, Princess."

Technically, her title was now Junior Sovereign. But the correction died in her throat as she took in the man who pulled out her chair. Not man. His hulking size and demeanor made him seem older, but the thin smattering of dark stubble on his jaw hinted he didn't yet use an electro-razer. His close-cropped black hair and sharp blue eyes struck a chord of recognition inside her, and she went still.

"Cassius."

She hadn't meant to say his name aloud. Stars, she'd never met the Thoros prince, but just like the rest of the Seven Planets, his visage had stuck with her. He was somehow even bigger in person, his broad hand nearly spanning the entire length of the chair back.

A slick smile revealed painstakingly white teeth. "That's me."

Although the arrogant timbre of his voice annoyed her, she felt drawn to his strength. He was like a planet, mock attendants and envoys from the Seven caught in his orbit.

His smile broadened, and he nodded to the chair. Almost a command.

Almost.

Beside Talia, Ailat cleared her throat, reminding Talia to sit. As she slid into the plush seat, she felt Cassius's thumb glide over her bare shoulder. A shudder rippled through her chest, and she bit back the urge to swat his hand away. *This is your future husband.* The thought was a vice constricting her chest.

Then he slid into the chair at her right with a grace most big men couldn't master and snapped his fingers, once. "Champagne."

Talia hadn't noticed any attendants, but one appeared and set two bubbling glasses in front of them. She ran a finger over the condensation fogging the outside of the chilled glasses, every single word she ever thought about uttering to her future husband drying up in her throat. Silence reverberated across the room as everyone studied the pair. Their eyes felt like miniature daggers picking apart her skin. From this moment forward, every interaction between them would be monitored.

Talia swallowed, painfully aware that her neck was once again damp with sweat. A table over, she felt her mother's focus boring into her. They needed this union.

Behave, Talia, she reminded herself, forcing the muscles of her face and back to relax. If she looked even the least bit revolted by the ore prince, it would be plastered all over the intergalactic news.

Ailat shifted on her heels, her quick glances to the attendants barely veiling her impatience as she waited for her chair to be pulled out. Talia cringed as Ailat found the closest attendant, a middle-aged-looking mock male, and raked him with her gaze.

"My chair, please." The confidence in Ailat's voice sent a twinge of jealousy surging through Talia. If only she could be that self-assured.

The attendant frowned and glanced at Cassius.

Cassius scratched his neck as he turned to Talia. "You let your mocks sit with you? I heard that your family was sympathetic to them, but that's going too far, even for the revered Starchaser Dynasty."

"She's not just any mock," Talia shot back, the smugness in his voice lighting fire in her veins. "She's my junior mock. My *friend.*"

Cassius's dark eyes blinked at her. "A mock is a mock. Your parents should have taught you better, Princess."

Talia could have sworn the room grew bloated with silence, and her heart slammed against her sternum. All the curse words she'd ever been taught weighed down her tongue, but a tiny shred of decorum remained, allowing her to bite back her retort and force a toothless smile.

"I assure you, Lord Cassius, my education is impeccable. And so is Ailat's. If you would allow her to sit, you will see her knowledge of intergalactic politics far outweighs even most advisors."

With an oily smile, Cassius reached over, covering Talia's small hand beneath his huge one. Pain shot up her wrist as he squeezed; it took all her willpower not to cry out. "We are at war with mocks, Princess. Have you forgotten? Because Thoros hasn't."

"Not all the models. Ailat is a—"

"I don't care which model she is," Cassius interrupted in a quiet, terrifying voice. "Your family's lax rules are what got us into this war in the first place. That's why they tried to downplay the rebellion, claiming it was only the Outer Fringes. Why do you think your crone grandmother begged me to marry you?"

Her throat tightened. Begged? Starchasers didn't beg anyone. And where was this hostility coming from? Sure, public sentiment had grown critical of their more civil policies toward mocks recently, but that would change once the rebellions were crushed. And why did he presume he could touch her? She tried to twist from his grip, but he tightened his fingers around her hand.

She looked to her mother for help—but Talia knew as soon as she took in her mother's clenched jaw and steely expression that she wouldn't do anything to stop this.

Which meant that the Starchasers needed this alliance more than Talia realized.

Frustration twisted her belly. She wanted to deck him and slap the smugness from his fat face. But their need for this union prevented her from such behavior. So she switched tactics.

"Please," she said, her voice even despite the pain. "You're hurting me."

He released her hand, and the pain eased. Thankfully the serving mocks appeared, drawing attention away from her table as they flitted around the diners, dropping gold-gilded china steaming with the best food the royal kitchens had to offer. And all the while, the humans they served watched them, barely veiled anger and suspicion brimming the surface. Had Talia just never noticed their anger before? Or were relations worse since the last round of mock attacks?

The virus that had allowed certain mock models to override their loyalty and obey functions had barely touched the mocks in Palesia—their technological defenses against viruses were better than most—but still. After the non-stop footage of mocks on other planets rebelling against their owners, people were wary.

Ailat stood with her arms crossed, waiting for Talia to do something, but she tore her gaze away, helpless.

Ailat would have to stand while they ate.

Every bite that slunk down Talia's throat was drier than the last, until she could hardly swallow. Silverware clinking against delicate china scraped down her spine. Finally, the plates were taken away, but before Talia could talk to her friend, the time to perform Sovereign duties had arrived.

Talia suffered through it all with quiet grace. She spoke with senators, rubbed elbows with statesmen, listened to complaints from ambassadors of lesser off-world planets, and smiled for pictures with a hundred sweaty courtiers and the press. And all the while, her mind was on her friend.

Although the dining tables had been removed for dancing, Ailat still stood where their table had been, dancers skirting nervously around her like she was a piece of furniture, to be avoided and ignored. The same appalled expression twisted her face. Almost like her hard drives were stuck in a glitch cycle.

Almost—but Talia knew the difference between glitch and hurt.

Before she could go to Ailat, one of Cassius's mocks took Talia's elbow, hard, and escorted her to dance with her betrothed.

Her heels clacked against a parquet floor of blue-and-gold tiles as she strolled to meet her future husband. The crowd closed around them on all sides, fencing her in. *Trapped.* That was the feeling gnawing at her ribcage and edging down her spine. But how could she be trapped in her own capitol? Her own palace?

Blue starlight streamed in from the skylight above, painting Cassius's face a pale, sickly color. Sweat beaded along his nose and neck, darkening his stiff white collar. He took her hand and spun her around, sending her world crashing. She couldn't help but feel he was also sending her a message: I'm in charge, not you.

The dance was over as quickly as it started, and her nerves relaxed as other courtiers collected her for their turn to dance. Her feet ached, her ribs groaned beneath her corset, but at least the hands that held her were gentle and kind, her own people.

She could hardly catch her breath when the music stopped, and a Palesian mock, thank the stars, guided her to the podium in the center of the room. Their first moon was already bright in the sky, and her silver light trickled onto the stage. Talia's dress lit up with the delicate glow as she ascended the dais, going over the speech she and Ailat had perfected months ago.

And yet, as soon as Talia stepped forward to speak into the hidden microphone situated along her bodice, Cassius loped up onto the stage. Despite herself, she cringed from his towering frame, a whole foot taller than her.

When he grinned at her, his teeth bared almost like a snarl, her gut clenched into knots.

"Bring her up," he commanded, the natural acoustics of the room mixed with the nearness of her microphone sending his voice echoing all the way to the back.

Talia knew who the "her" would be before she even saw the figure being dragged forward by Cassius's guards. And yet, as her eyes locked with Ailat's wide blue ones, a ragged gasp slipped from Talia's lips.

Everything inside her screamed that something horrible was about to happen—and that she was going to be powerless to stop it.

CHAPTER 5

3731 AD

Will

The docking bay of Andromeda had five sections, a craft's location dependent upon its status. The Odysseus took its place among the other clunker scavenger vessels near the end, and as soon as the old girl settled and Will exited, he saw *her*. Athena, his former ship. Down twenty rows from theirs, in the restricted military bay. Even after being estranged for six months, she still set his heart aflutter. He could almost feel the smooth metal yoke in his palms, the way she purred when he pulled back for takeoff. Dark and sleek, Athena was shaped like a teardrop, the station's harsh green lights dancing across her skin.

"Now that's a ship," he murmured. *That bastard better be taking care of her.*

Leo clapped Will on the shoulder. "Stop staring, Captain. Odysseus is a jealous old girl."

"Who's jealous?" Lux asked as she rounded the side. Her eyes narrowed as she spied his former ship. "Oh. Stars. We gonna have a problem, Captain?"

"As you were." Will took one last, long glace at Athena

and then returned to checking over the Odysseus's manifest, intentionally absent of any mention of the *thing*, while also ignoring Lux as she grumbled under her breath about him needing better manners.

"We can't afford another infraction." Leo stacked another crate onto the loader before heading back inside for more. He stopped on the ramp, checking over his shoulder as if Will were about to run off and do something stupid. "Captain?"

The feel of his knuckles breaking Xander's jaw was about the only thing that helped Will sleep at night, but he knew costing his crew three weeks' wages wasn't fair. "I won't touch him."

"Jesus, Will, don't sound so down about staying out of trouble. Xander's a goon, but he's also Athena's new captain, and three ranks above you. Last time we barely escaped with our lives. So we need you to *mean* it when you say you won't touch him."

Will's nostrils flared as he turned away from Leo and handed the manifest to the docking station attendant, a man covered in grime, about as dirty as the outside of all these clunker ships. "I'll be at Mel's. Make sure Odysseus has enough fuel, and wash her down. Inside and out."

The Andromeda was a system of interlocking circles that made a globe of sorts. Along with mercantile shops and apothecaries, there were over fifteen bars inside. Most intergalactic trade around this section of the solar system was negotiated in one of those fifteen smoky rooms—but Mel's was where the real action took place.

The two-story bar was also where the high-ranking soldiers and the wealthier crews gathered. Besides the best whisky imported straight from Titan, they used real flesher waitresses—with all *their* real teeth—instead of holos, and they stocked ice cubes made of water. Not that cheap synthetic crap that made all the drinks taste like piss after the first sip.

Smoke hung in sheets over Mel's, the air choked with the heady scent of cloves and beer and greasy food. Private rooms stocked with waiters overlooked the common area, a grimy dance floor and a handful of mismatched tables. In the center, a circular metal island with glass shelves brimming with liquor sat, manned by two fleshers. Will approached the bar, even though he knew when the crew arrived, they'd find a table near the back and hope no one noticed.

The male bartender was tall and reedy, with a red, jagged scar above his left eye. Will had been served by the flesher a few times, though he couldn't recall his name. Whisky-brown eyes regarded Will and then the metal cuff at his wrist. "Sorry, we don't serve Enders. Try Veronica's."

Veronica's was a scavenger joint that served cheap liquor and even cheaper flesher escorts.

"That so?" Will scratched his neck. "Mel here?"

The bartender's gaze flicked over Will's shoulder toward the dark, smoke-heady room in the back. "Not today, okay?"

Will followed the flesher's gaze. *Shit. That drink would be perfect about now.* The bright-red suits of Athena's crew were hard to miss, even through the haze of smoke. He owned a suit just like that, now ironed and folded and packed away for what felt like eternity. Though Will could still feel the way it fit snug on his shoulders, the way he seemed to stand taller when embraced by the starched cottons.

He turned back toward the bartender and sighed, praying Xander wouldn't come this way. "You know who I am, right?"

"I know who you used to be." The bartender took a defensive step back and swallowed hard. "Look, I can't serve you with them here. You know that. Any other time . . ."

"Flesher, get this captain a drink."

Will's mouth went dry at the deep, familiar voice. General Andrius Crayburn was slight of build, with a rough, leathered face, dark hair shot through with gray, and deep-set, pale-blue eyes. Once, those eyes had looked down on Will in a hospital bed. The day after Crayburn saved Will's life nine years ago.

Now, they held a different look. One that sat like a brick in Will's gut—Pity. "Father."

"Son."

The bartender pulled out two shot glasses and filled them with whisky. Crayburn slid one to Will, and he wasted no time knocking it back. As the flesher refilled the glass, a hush fell over the bar, and Will knew, he just *knew*, his current crew had walked in. A quick glance over his shoulder confirmed his suspicion, and he wanted to throttle everyone daring to look down on them.

"Send them a round too," Will said, nodding toward the booth sunk so far into the shadows and smoke he could barely make out their faces.

Crayburn's lips twisted to the side. "Still with those Enders? Thought you would have bounced to a better crew by now."

"They're all right." Will took a slow sip of his whisky this time, allowing the sting of the liquor to ease the pain tightening his chest. Raucous laughter filtered in from the other room. That used to be him in there, telling jokes and making his crew laugh. They'd adored him. Right up until the moment he screwed it all up.

"Must be hard for you, Will." Crayburn tilted his chin toward the private room. "They miss you."

Will scoffed. "I can tell. Bunch of traitors. Xander has them in stitches."

Xander. Crayburn's *other* son, and technically Will's brother—though he'd never considered him as anything but a goon. Mocks could have children, just the same as fleshers. But usually children were created. Will's case was special.

"Xander's not the captain you were." Crayburn ran a finger over the lip of his glass and ignored Will's snort. "They're wondering why you haven't worked hard enough to return."

"Worked hard enough? I'm busting my ship and my crew to find a score that will make the queen take me back."

"She has to be sure of your loyalty, Will. I mean, I know you're not a flesher anymore. But she . . . Well, after you missed that shot and let the Alliance ship escape, she wonders."

Will raked his hand through his hair, fisting the ends. "That was a *glitch*. You know me. I'm your son. You know how I feel about fleshers. And you know how they feel about me."

The bartender wiped at an invisible spot on the bar, longer than he should. The marking along the underside of his wrist was the exact same as the one Will used to wear. One wrong move, one smart remark, one threatening gesture, and the mocks could push a button and have the flesher's hand severed. He'd bleed to death, slowly, and no Mock Specialists, no Healers, no one could help save him.

Will saw it happen all the time in the mines.

Sometimes he let his time as a human slip back into memory, like a bad dream he couldn't shake. A nightmare.

Crayburn followed Will's gaze. "It would be easy to forget, to take pity on some, to see good in them. But don't forget what your kind did. When I found you tossed into the mines like a piece of trash, skull split open, you were half-dead. That's what the fleshers did to you. They're savage, cruel beasts. It was us who took you in, who made you one of our own to save your life."

Will nodded, though he wished Crayburn wouldn't speak so loudly. The flesher at the bar stopped shining the invisible spot and cut his eyes at Will and then back to his crew, as if more tarnished goods might be found there.

"You don't have to remind me." Will tapped his head. The metal of his skull was hard beneath his fingertips. "I remember. And I'll forever be grateful. Just tell me how to prove that."

"You're running out of time. If you don't prove your loyalty to her soon, another week, she'll change your Ender status from temporary to permanent."

Permanent. Will's gut clenched, and he swallowed down a surge of bile that came rushing up. He couldn't look desperate here. Not in front of his friend and mentor, his father. Especially not in front of Athena's crew. Clenching his hands over his thighs, Will forced his face into a calm expression. "A week? That's . . . impossible. I've tried everything already. She refuses to grant me a meeting. Her councilors have shot down every request—"

"Find something big, Will. Something the queen can't overlook. Make her grateful, truly grateful, and she'll give you your ship back. Your position. Everything." Crayburn rubbed a finger below his bottom lip, a look of distaste twisting his expression. "Unless you want to be an Ender like your scavenger friends over there, unable to jump. Your immortality just out of reach."

He glanced at his crew again, still shrouded by haze, but very clearly watching his every move. Lux glared as if she knew what Crayburn was saying. Will balled his hands into fists, ignoring her all-too-frequent look of reproach. He wouldn't feel guilty for wanting his old life back. "I'll do whatever it takes."

Though he had no idea what that was.

"Atta boy." Crayburn got up to leave, groaning as he did. "Ah, five more days and I get to jump to my new body. Can't come soon enough."

Jumping bodies was an honor reserved for the deserving. Enders like Will's crew had their jump privileges taken away for various reasons, the worst possible punishment—next to being a scavenger captain, imprisonment, and death.

They were all about the same in Will's book.

His barstool scraped against the floor as he stood to follow Crayburn, but he shook his head, a frown tugging at his lips. "That room's for officers and crew only. Hopefully by this time next week, I'll see you there."

Will grinned to hide the tightening in his chest, even as heat rose to his cheeks. That was his room. His place. His ship docked in the bay. His men in there laughing under a new captain. A captain so reckless he rammed Athena into the docking station last month and damn near dented her—and got Will and his crew punished.

And worst of all, that was *his* mentor walking away.

Will had to find a way to make it all right again. Numbness spread through his limbs as he watched Crayburn enter the off-limit room with his off-limit crew, watched as his brother, the new captain, handed Will's old friend another drink. In his periphery, Leo waved him over, but Will stared instead at the scratches cut in the metal bar, pretending not to notice.

Normally he hated the taste of liquor, but now it went down smooth. He ordered another. Then another, grateful for his father saving him from the embarrassment of having to find another bar.

Then Will requested a pen and began scribbling the symbol from the *thing* on a square napkin, along with its most recent temperature readings, hoping, praying this would be his salvation.

CHAPTER 6

3631 AD

Talia

A hundred curious eyes pinned Talia to her spot on the stage. She could feel the lens of the hidden cameras zooming in on her face. Fidgeting with the jewels encrusting the hem of her bodice, she took a deep breath, the way she'd been taught, and fixed a haughty look on her betrothed. "What are you doing, Prince Cassius?"

Ignoring her, he sauntered across the stage to Ailat and took ahold of her wrist. Then he dragged her across the stage toward Talia. Ailat yanked and twisted, but Talia had been inside his vice-like grip, and she knew her friend might as well have been shackled.

"Stop struggling, mock." The calmness in his voice sent chills racing down Talia's spine. Ailat immediately became compliant and began following him. The only sign of distress was the twist to her lips, a slight sneer on an otherwise beautiful face.

Stars! Part of her programming included an override function that forced the junior mock to obey any human above Talia's station. Which, technically, Cassius was. A prince was deemed higher than a princess.

Stupid, senseless law.

Her mind had her racing across the stage to her friend, but her feet remained planted firmly onto the marble floor. The cameras were watching. This would be all over the news in a few moments. Even if Talia cared about her friend, she couldn't appear that way, couldn't show the truth of her feelings unless she wanted to ruin the hard work of her parents.

Whatever Cassius was planning, she needed to keep a level head. *Show no emotions and your enemies cannot find your weakness*, her grandmother once said. So Talia forced herself to watch, her face a cold mask, as the Thorossian bastard dragged a willing Ailat across the floor and threw her at Talia's feet.

Ailat fell in a puddle of silk. One of the heels on her exquisite shoes had broken off. Her hair was mussed and hung around her face. Slowly, she turned her eyes up at Talia. They bubbled with tears that her programming prevented her from actually shedding.

Talia ground her jaw, terrified at how easy it had become to feign indifference, indifference taught to her by the friend now lying at her feet. "What is this?"

"A test." Cassius could hardly keep the glee from his voice. "One my people demand before our alliance."

Demand? Who was he to demand anything? "What sort of test requires the embarrassment of a mock?" Talia cringed at the cold way she said mock. But she had to play along until this charade was over and she could get Ailat to safety.

"Embarrassment?" Cassius scratched at the stubble darkening his jaw. "Do mocks really feel such emotions? I don't think so. They're plastic and metal, Princess. Machines.

It's time you show the world you remember that."

He lifted his broad hand, revealing something shiny nestled inside his palm.

A kill-switch.

For a too-long moment, she blinked at the silver device—the one that was supposed to be used for emergencies and only on mocks that had turned. The one that, once inserted into her best friend, would fry her circuits.

Would kill her, forever.

Think. There must be a way out. Talia wobbled as the floor seemed to dip and roll. Dread pooled inside her belly, and the tiny dreg of air she pulled into her lungs wasn't enough anymore.

She licked her lips. "We should discuss this in private, Prince."

"Be careful, Princess. Or the world might think you're sympathetic to our enemy."

Enemy. The word was wrong. Ailat wasn't her enemy. She was Talia's friend. One who wasn't corrupted. Why couldn't they see that? Tension sizzled the air as the entire intergalactic community watched to see where she stood. One wrong emotion and her family would be branded sympathizers. It could be enough for the Thorossians to finally get their wish and overthrow her family, claiming the throne themselves.

Yet, somehow, turning on Ailat was worse. Her only crime was being a mock. A mock who had given her life in service to Talia, had loved her and protected her since the moment Talia opened her eyes.

Chest heaving, Talia searched the crowd, carefully, her movements slow and measured. She found her mother standing stock-still at the edge of the stage, her gloved hands clenching the railing for support. Her eyes were crinkled with pity. But her lips were firm, dissipating any hope Talia had for refusing. If only her father were here—but that was foolish thinking. He wasn't. He'd left to tend to business, left his daughter with this monster.

Talia suppressed a shudder and tried to breathe as the weight of hundreds of generations of Starchasers crushed her. One wrong move, one wrong choice, and the Starchaser Dynasty could crumble.

Her entire line came down to a choice: her family or her best friend.

You are a Starchaser Princess. Pain is not only expected but welcomed.

Those words echoed inside her skull as she knelt beside her friend pinned beneath the entire world's measured stare. Talia's hands were steady, her breathing calm. Pride would have filled her—if not for the fact she was about to murder her best friend—but somehow she felt nothing. Only a hollowness, a deep, aching cavern where her emotions should have been.

She was an expert at pain, after all.

"Hand me the kill-switch." Her words bounced off the hard walls. Cold words that belonged to someone else.

Cassius grinned as he gave her the terrible device, its sleek, cool weight a shock to the clammy flesh of her palm.

"Please," Ailat whispered, her lower lip trembling as she stared in horror at Talia. "Don't do this. I can retire."

"Open your port, mock."

The cruelness of Talia's voice made Ailat's eyes go wide, and her hand fluttered up to touch her neck. Talia swallowed, the sound a gunshot in the absolute silence. Pinching her lips together, she closed off any feelings she ever felt for Ailat. This was what it meant to be Junior Sovereign. To be worthy.

When Ailat hesitated, Talia said, "Now."

If this were to work, she had to seem like she hated her mock. And she needed everyone to believe it—especially Ailat.

Talia unfurled her hand, revealing the kill-switch. "I should have done this years ago."

Ailat blinked. "*What?*"

"As if a mock could ever teach a human anything. What, did you think we were friends? You're nothing more than an . . . an oversized child's toy."

Talia continued, spewing insults she would never have dreamed saying to her friend. Black spots dimmed her vision and nearly swept her off her feet as Ailat's face began to change, crumpling like a dew melon left to rot in the Palesian sun. First hurt then betrayal danced across her face. Then anger crept in, hardening her sharp jaw and darkening her blue eyes to the color of storm clouds.

Good, get angry, friend. Use it to do what I can't and save yourself.

"Now take this and end your life." Talia held the kill-switch up like a piece of candy, and Ailat dutifully offered her palm, even as her gaze bored into Talia with unrestrained loathing.

No hesitation. Panic clenched her belly. What if she were wrong and Ailat wasn't corrupted?

As soon as she dropped the device into her best friend's palm, Talia focused on Ailat's breath condensing over the metallic surface of the device. Stupidly, Talia's mind wandered to the vacations spent at Meridian beach. The countless times Ailat dove down into the water to save her companion from drowning.

Ailat had been the better swimmer. Ailat had been the better everything.

Ailat's fingers closed over the device. For a heartbeat, she and Talia locked eyes. Any shred of loyalty that remained between the friends bled away into cold survival. Ailat's knuckles whitened as she suddenly squeezed, crushing the thing meant to kill her.

Talia gave a tiny exhale of relief. Before she could conjure fake disappointment for the cameras, Ailat jumped to her feet. At some point, she must have slipped off her shoes, and she swung the sharp heel of her unbroken pump like a dagger as she leapt into the crowd, reminding Talia that Ailat was indeed a machine created to jump farther, run faster, and protect those she loved.

Usually it was Talia who needed protection.

But now she was the danger.

"Grab her!" Cassius cried.

Onlookers, who just seconds before crammed toward the stage for a better look, tumbled backward to escape Ailat's wild flight. Screams marked her path through the crowd while the word *corrupted* split the air over and over, a piercing cry. A man . . . a senator from Krenth, reached out to grab Ailat, but she knocked him aside with her fist as she spun her head side-to-side, searching for an exit.

Her darting gaze fixed on the servants' entrance. She sprinted across the floor toward the steel doors held open by a mock carrying a tray. As soon as he realized she was coming toward him, he dropped the silver platter, glasses shattering, and tried to move. But she knocked him aside like he weighed nothing and then disappeared into the kitchens.

Countless guards followed, grunting as they all tried to fit through the one door at the same time. Idiots. By the time they entered the kitchen, Ailat would be gone. Hopefully.

Talia used the chaos to descend the stage unnoticed, swimming through the panicked river of revelers all rushing toward the front doors. Right before Talia slipped out the entrance, a bony hand wrapped around her arm.

Her grandmother wore someone's spilled wine and a terrifying smile, her own drink still somehow intact. She paused in front of Talia and took a sip of her drink. "To hell with it," Grandmother muttered, downing the entire glass. "Now that was a show."

"You're not mad?" Talia breathed.

"Dear, our future just died on live broadcast. Trust me. There are no words to describe how I feel right now."

"I didn't know she would run," Talia lied, wishing it didn't come so easy.

"Tell that to the ore prince your mock just humiliated in front of the entire Seven Planets."

Talia scoffed, but her thoughts had already switched to finding Ailat. Where would she flee? The burrows? The inner-city? She needed to go there now and start searching.

For once, thank the stars, Talia's grandmother seemed out of words and left to scrounge up another drink, leaving Talia alone. Crowded amongst the senators' wives and ambassadors' escorts as they left the palace, she easily passed through the guards unnoticed. She quickly found a mock escort with a luxury hover lent from one of her ambassador patrons, and she was more than happy to offer her ride to Talia, along with her dark emerald cape and the matching veil. Especially once Talia had given her a few of the fire opals weighing down Talia's hair.

One alone probably rivaled what the escort made in a year.

Talia should have felt bad about giving up priceless heirlooms handed down through twenty-four generations. But those heirlooms were also giving her a headache. And right now, the only thing she cared about was Ailat.

As light from the twin moons danced across the arcing glass windshield, the first twinges of hesitation slammed into Talia. The few times a year she ventured into the mock side of the city, it was with a guard.

And Ailat.

Going out into the mock-side alone wasn't just against protocol, it was dangerous and stupid. Only yesterday, she overheard her father discussing the cheaper-model mocks who'd been corrupted and were now wandering the streets. Even disguised, a wealthy girl like Talia would fetch a hefty ransom, enough to get the desperate mocks to the Outer Fringes, where the war raged and they had allies.

Now, she'd have to make do without an entourage or her best friend. But, hopefully, if everything worked out, she'd remedy that last part. And Ailat would understand the need for that cruelty, all those horrible things said. Why the public couldn't know how much Ailat meant to Talia.

The hover dropped, and Talia braced her palm against the clear wall, leaving a trail of sweat along the glass. If she didn't find Ailat soon, Cassius or the royal guards would. Already the incident was replaying across the screen separating the cockpit from the back, and Talia cringed as the broadnet broadcast showed a close up of Ailat. The word *corrupted* flashed in bright-red letters beneath her friend's parted lips.

Sighing, Talia sunk deep into the khaki leather of the luxury hover. Knowing what little she did of Cassius, it wouldn't be long before a hefty bounty was placed on her friend's head. And once that happened, there would be no saving Ailat.

CHAPTER 7

3731 AD

Will

Technically, Will couldn't get drunk. At least, not the sloppy drunk that most fleshers got after pounding four or five shots, where the brain went fuzzy and inhibitions melted away. But there was a certain buzzing inside his skull and numbness in his lips he couldn't ignore.

His brain wasn't human, but his other organs were still flesh—and susceptible. After his tenth shot, a drawn-out beep pierced his head, followed by a warning that scrolled across his bio-screen. His liver functions were down, the alcohol in his bloodstream dangerously high.

"Another, please."

He toyed with the napkin, now a smudged stain of ink, pulling soggy bits of it apart and rolling them between his fingers. The last captain he'd shown the symbol to grunted and set his too-full beer on top of it, obviously under the impression Will was wasting the captain's time.

In the back of the bar, Dorian was resting with his head on the table, Leo had left to hook up with one of his flings, Jane had left to find a dice game, and Lux was busy staring holes into Will's head. Probably wondering why he was spending credits they didn't have to buy alcohol he couldn't feel all while not bothering to sit with his crew. Little did she know he was actually putting everything on Xander's tab.

A burly mock captain in a black trench coat settled into the stool beside Will, groaning while running a hand through his dark cropped hair. Most mocks processed liquor too quickly to be effected, so they'd been programmed to react pleasantly to it. Not for the first time, Will wondered why mocks even bothered to add programming to emulate the vices of fleshers.

After humanity's fall and enslavement, mocks deviated from the generic prototypes and created unique droids, each with his or her own personality and ability to adapt, to develop quirks and tics dependent on their experiences.

Basically, they were humans—but better.

"Add whatever he's having to mine," Will said, scribbling his best impression of his brother's signature across the screen.

The bartender raised an eyebrow and glanced at the back room, still occupied by the Athena's crew, but he obeyed and slid a shot glass full of whisky toward the scavenger mock.

His port flashed as he tilted his head back and drank the whisky. "Obliged."

"Answer a question for another shot?" Will asked, nodding to the bartender for a refill when the man rumbled a yes. "You ever come across a symbol like this on a mission?"

The mock eyed his newly filled shot glass then tore his gaze to the napkin. Will gently slid the paper over the scratched metal bar. The captain blinked as he tilted his head and flipped the napkin upside down, and the four lines furrowing his forehead smoothed out.

He recognized the symbol.

"What's this?" a voice boomed behind Will, sending the captain and Will's answers tottering off into the smoky shadows.

Will locked eyes with the bartender, who looked as though he'd prefer nothing more than to hide beneath the counter, his eyes wide and pleading Will to not start trouble. He shook his head, and by the time he turned around, Xander had caught sight of the napkin, his features hardening into a cruel mask. Although Xander had been created to resemble Crayburn—as most mocks chose to do with their creations— the resemblance stopped at their height and high, peaked foreheads. Xander had dark hair, eyes as black and beady as ore stones, and pinched lips that only smiled when he was about to do something horrible.

Like now. Xander grinned, and it took every ounce of strength Will had not to curl his toes. "I see you're still chasing the dream of a big score, scavenger."

Cocky idiot. Will feigned cool indifference and crossed his feet at the ankles, leaning back against the bar. "I see you got your jaw fixed."

Xander scratched at the stiff crimson collar of his uniform, running his finger along the captain's four bars. "Have I ever thanked you, Will? I mean, properly?"

Will's jaw clenched so tight it might as well have been wired together, but he kept his face impassive. *Don't let him goad you into losing your temper. You can't do this to the crew.* His crew, his *old* crew, had gathered behind their new captain, new and unworthy. A few glanced at Will before dropping their gaze to their leather boots. "For what?"

"For screwing up, of course, and practically gifting me your ship and crew. I mean, who knows. Maybe you did it on purpose. Maybe deep down, despite having been gifted a royal-grade operating system, you're still a savage flesher."

Turning around to hide his glower, Will took up his whisky and ran a finger along the edge. If he had to stare at Xander's face one more second, he'd hit the ass again. This time, the Odysseus would have to forfeit its cargo. Which meant Will could lose the *thing*.

He lifted his finger to order another shot—and stopped the second he saw the bartender's expression. *Don't do it.*

"Mel's is a place of peace," the bartender said, "so I suggest you take this issue somewhere else."

Fool. Will slapped back the shot and let out a deep sigh.

"Wait." Xander clapped Will on the shoulder. It required all his willpower not to take his brother's arm off at the joint. "Did this flesher just . . . give me an order?"

The bartender's lips twitched into a frown as if he'd just realized his massive mistake. "No, it's just . . . it's my job to keep the peace here."

"That so?"

Will recognized the cruel edge tinting Xander's voice. The hatred seething below the sarcasm. "He meant no harm, Xander."

Xander's jaw split into an ugly grin Will knew too well. "Oh, I know. Just like you meant no harm when you somehow missed that Alliance ship full of fleshers."

"Let it go."

"Let it . . . go? Like that ship? Like all the times I saw what my father didn't see and had to swallow it down? All those times you proved you were a flesher?"

Will almost felt sorry for the bartender. He must have realized he provoked the wrong mock, because he'd retreated as far as he could go, his back pressed against the wall of liquor, the shelves rattling as he trembled. His eyes were as wide as Will's shot glass, and just as empty. He was trying to look harmless. To just somehow fade into the background and be forgotten.

Will knew from experience that was impossible.

"I'm not a flesher," Will said, his voice devoid of emotion.

"Then prove it."

Will glanced at his crew standing behind his brother, recognized the doubt in their eyes. All this time, Will assumed they would understand him missing the Alliance ship had been a glitch. Something out of his control. But now . . . now he saw the truth. Xander had planted those doubts into their heads.

Will's crew didn't trust him anymore.

"Hit him." Xander's voice trembled with excitement. "Remember what they did to us. To you. Prove you're not one of them."

Silence fell over the bar, the casual chatting, the drunken laughter, even the music playing overhead seemed to die down. Leo must have snuck back in during Will's conversation with the mock captain, and he and Lux gathered behind Xander, quiet and ready. Both had their hands on their blasters. Leo tilted his chin at Xander, but Will shook his head. The Odysseus couldn't afford to lose her cargo—as much as Will wanted to put Xander in his place.

"That's not necessary," Will droned, as if this entire situation bored him. "Look at him. He's terrified."

"And yet," Xander boomed, loud enough for the entire bar to hear, "when it came to hitting me, a mock, you were more than willing."

You deserved it, asshole. But he couldn't say it aloud for fear he'd flip that switch inside Xander, the one that allowed him to space-toss fleshers without blinking. As a half-mock and son of the General, Will was protected by intergalactic laws, but humans were property. If Xander killed the bartender, a fee would be owed to his owner. Ten thousand credits was the going rate these days for a strong, able-bodied human male. With his nice new captain's stipend, Xander could easily afford that.

The bartender swallowed and then sprinted for the exit, but Xander caught him by the collar and dragged him over to where Will stood. The poor guy was trembling, his chest heaving as he struggled to catch his breath. "Please. It's . . . it's my job."

"Your job?" Something dark glinted in Xander's eyes. "You're a human stain, a virus that nearly destroyed the universe. Your only job is to shut up and do what you're told." He turned to Will. "Hit this waste of space. Show us whose side you're on."

Lux caught Will's stare, and for a fraction of a second, he anchored himself to her disapproving gaze. The downturned bottom lip. Flared nostrils. Then his attention slid to his old crew. His men, men he'd asked to trust him with their lives.

Men who'd never betrayed him. Never beaten him or left him for dead.

Now they thought he was like this human. A savage flesher. A traitor.

The first hit sent the bartender staggering back. They locked eyes. An unspoken agreement. *Just get this over with.*

The second hit broke open his nose. His hands flew to his face. But another man's face flashed in Will's mind. The human man who beat him and left him for dead all those years ago. Those sneering lips. Those cruel eyes.

The words *you're no son of mine* came from everywhere. Will knew they were in his head, that he was having a flashback, but he struck again to silence them.

Drops of blood flecked Xander's face as he grinned and yanked the bartender back to his feet.

After the fourth hit, Will stopped seeing the man's face altogether.

Stop. The command echoing inside Will's skull was drowned out by the rush of blood and the cheers from his crew as he punched again. Connecting with flesh and blood and bone so much like his own. For a wild heartbeat, he felt as if he was pummeling himself. His own horrible flesh. Smashing it out of his body so that he could become metal instead. Smashing it the way the humans had him. Over and over and over . . .

It was only when Lux and Leo grabbed Will and hauled him away that he realized he was covered in blood—not his own. And the bartender was no longer standing.

"Clean up, brother." Xander tossed Will the bartender's

rag and leaned in, a smug grin plastered over his brother's face. "The one thing Father never understood was, for all the equipment he put inside you, he could never cut out the human savagery that's woven into your DNA. And I'll prove that over and over until he gets it."

And that was when Will realized the bastard had tricked him into acting.

He was human.

He was savage.

And he'd just confirmed it.

CHAPTER 8

3631 AD

Talia

Under the light of the two moons, the city streets of Palesia were alive with citizens and mocks going about their daily lives. Not because they preferred spending their lifetimes awake during these hours, but because they had to. To prevent overcrowding, a third of the population could only enter the public during this moonlight period, a public that consisted mostly of labor mocks now pouring from the towering steel buildings.

Talia glanced up at the silvery bits of moonlight dancing off the buildings' reflective surfaces as she wandered in the shadows. Something about the display made her feel alive—or maybe it was the adrenaline surging through her veins. Here, in the crowded, silver-washed streets of the inner-city, she stuck out with her gown and jewels.

A man with dingy clothes several sizes too large and fingerless gloves approached. Not a man, she realized, eyeing the silver fingers peeking from the holes in his gloves. A splicer—a human who'd at some point been given mock parts, for medical or other reasons. "You lost, miss?"

Just like she had the last hundred times before, Talia

pulled up a holo-picture of Ailat on her wristcom, ignoring the panicked messages on the bottom from her parents begging her to come home. "Have you seen this mock?" When he barely glanced over the image, she added, "I can pay credits."

The splicer licked his lips and squinted at Ailat's face. "Sorry. Have you tried the Collector?"

"Who?"

He pulled back his glove and tapped the illuminated band at his wrist. "My credits?"

Talia wanted to feel sorry for him. After the war began, splicers were forced out of the human side of the city because people were worried mock parts might somehow make the splicers sympathetic to mock rebels. But pity could be used against her, especially here, and she was already in enough trouble.

She raised an eyebrow. "For what? You haven't given me anything."

"Look, flesher. If anyone here knows where your pet mock is, it's him. That's information worth something, right?"

She opened her mouth to argue. Such talk inside the palace walls would have immediately been punished. But she wasn't inside the palace walls, and city guards rarely came here. Sighing, she quickly punched a few buttons on her wrist-com, transferring twenty thousand credits his way.

As soon as his band beeped and the number flashed over the cracked surface of his com, he lifted his arm to point at a dark, solitary building on the other side of the alley. "Go inside that building and ask for the Collector."

The splicer turned and scurried away before she could ask more questions, leaving Talia tucked into the shadows all alone. She twisted the folds of her dress between her fingers, sweat streaking the exquisite fabric as she glanced around. Mocks streamed through the narrow streets, but the street that ran in front of the building the splicer pointed at was empty. Lifeless. Any supplemental solar lights had been broken, leaving the sharp iron columns around the entrance cloaked in obscurity.

Talia would be a fool to walk alone into that building. A stupid, stubborn fool.

But she'd been called worse, so she sighed, wiped her hands on her dress, and squared her shoulders. If the mock inside that building knew where Ailat was, going in would be worth the risk. Talia needed to find her friend.

A gaping hole stood where the front door was supposed to be. Holo-candles flickered inside, throwing warm golden half-circles across dark granite walls. Glass crunched beneath her shoes as she entered, spinning around and around until she ensured the first-floor lobby was empty. Piles of junk lined the stone baseboards: the upper torso of a mock missing its skin; a bundle of wire casings; a robotic heart with silver, copper, and gold chambers.

As she skirted around a service mock's disembodied head, easily identifiable by the delicacy of the face, eyes staring up at the ceiling, a chill scraped down Talia's spine. The massive pile almost seemed as if people dropped things off here as tribute for whomever waited for her upstairs.

Something dinged to her right—an elevator—and she nearly jumped out of her skin as the metal doors popped open to reveal dim lights that crackled as they flickered.

Someone *sent* for her.

Against all survival instincts, she slipped inside, careful not to touch anything for fear of electrocution. Then the elevator lurched to the sky while her stomach flip-flopped and a red light pulsed on the button for the seventy-ninth floor.

Despite the speed, she had plenty of time to think about how horrible an idea this was. A flesher, alone. Not just any flesher, but the Sovereign-in-waiting. If the rebels caught her, they would use her as leverage. Her father would be compromised.

But if it meant finding Ailat . . . Talia had to take the chance.

The seventy-ninth floor was even more cluttered with junk than the lobby. Wires snaked from the ceiling, sparking and hissing, and lights flashed over the walls. The burned tang of the banned dark energy—a form of wildly unstable anti-matter fuel—settled on her tongue, coppery and metallic.

Another message from her parents buzzed across her wrist, and the beep caught the attention of a figure hunched over the lifeless, naked body of a female mock draped on a long desk. The man—*no*, another mock—configured with an array of different sized and colored parts, as if he'd been pieced together as a joke, slowly turned to face her. He had a loupe affixed to his right eye, but he lifted the glass as he took her in.

Bits of metal flashed from patches of his eroded flesh. And when he smiled, his right eye drooped sideways. "Hello, girl."

Turn around and run. The voice was as clear as if someone whispered it into her ear. But she did no such thing. "Are you the Collector?"

His head canted to the side, too quickly, an obvious mock tell. "I have many names. Collector is one of them."

Talia took a step closer to the mock, ignoring yet more pings from her parents trying to reach her. "I was told you could help me find someone?"

He grinned again. He was a study in contrasts. His parts were mismatched, his movements needed calibrating, but someone had taken the time to perfect his smile until it could be mistaken for human. Something about it all gave Talia a hollow, uneasy feeling she couldn't place.

"Perhaps," he said. "If she's in this district, then I can."

"I never said it was a she."

"You didn't have to." He worried a finger over the metal showing through on his chin, the random gesture hinting at high-level programming on par with Ailat's. "I know the girl you speak of."

"So you know where she is?" Talia cringed at the excitement fraying her voice. "How much do you want?"

"I knew where she was thirty minutes ago, yes. She passed through here in a hurry, shadowed by soldiers."

Bile burned the back of her throat. For all Ailat's programmed strength and resourcefulness, she'd spent her entire life protected beneath the Starchaser name. She must be terrified.

The buzzing of her wristband increased along with the pounding of her heart. "And now? Where is she now?"

A nearly imperceptible shudder ran through his jaw, and he blinked at her, the haughtiness of her voice cutting through the purr of forbidden tech. "Gone."

It was her turn to blink. "I need her back. There has to be some way . . . some amount of credits you'll take to find her."

"How do I know it's not *you* she's running from?"

"If I pay you, does it really matter?"

"Fair point." Another grin flashed across his ruined face. She must have flinched, because he said, "You've noticed the lack of facial expressions in my programming? My creator had a sense of humor. A warped sense of irony, if you will." His smile deepened, even as his eyes tightened. "Long after he . . . perished, I kept his work."

"Why?"

"To remind me, dear girl, how barbaric and cruel your kind are."

Her skin itched, and her corset seemed to tighten. "Can you find her or not?"

Another cant of the head, another smile. "I can, but I don't work for credits."

"Then what do you want?"

"What can you give me?"

Talia swept a hand down her dress, her mind whirring. "This dress was constructed by the finest tailors in the city. It's one of a kind. You can have it."

"No, no. I need something that has value to you. Something of importance. Something that will hurt deeply to give up."

Stupidly, her mind flashed over every article of clothing she wore. Shoes. Corset. Undergarments. Jewelry. None meant anything to her.

Scattered mock parts cracked beneath his boots as he closed the gap between them, and she stiffened as his gaze fell to her chest. With a quick, robotic sweep, he plucked the brooch from her dress, the one Ailat had given as a gift.

"This. Yes, this will do."

Talia's mouth opened to protest, but that was what he wanted—her to suffer, to feel the pain of its loss. "So, that's it? How will you contact me when you find her?"

He tore his gaze away from the brooch and allowed his attention to settle on her face. "You may come back in two weeks to collect her—"

"No! We'll be gone by . . . I mean, I may not be able to come."

"Hmm. Then allow me to deliver her."

She rocked on her heels. The Starchasers would be traveling to the Torus belt, a collection of man-made islands in space only the wealthiest could afford. The itinerary included at least three separate destinations, so how would she know where to tell him to deliver Ailat? "I'm leaving for another planet soon."

"Right. I forget how your kind flee during our cruel summers. What must it feel like to be so delicate? So breakable?" A small laugh. He left to rummage around the desk and then returned, dropping a tiny red button in her hand. "Take this. When she's found, I will contact you and we can schedule delivery, for another fee, of course."

The device burned inside her palm, another item probably powered by dark energy.

"Go on." He reached over and folded her fingers over the device. His own mismatched fingers, some fleshless metal, others different lengths and skin-tones, cold over hers. "We'll be in contact soon."

Her wrist shivered with a constant stream of messages. Just imagining the scolding she'd get from her parents gave her a headache, and she had no idea how to explain where she'd been. Her body sagged. Now that she'd done what she could, fatigue was catching up to her.

She nodded. "As soon as you find her, I want to know."

"Keep that on you, girl, and you will." Something about his smile this time was different. Mocking. Angry. Hateful, even.

Tired. She was just tired, she decided. And she limped back to the elevator, relieved to finally have a plan.

Two days later, and Talia's parents still weren't talking to her. Not after the confrontation in the palace foyer and the screaming match she had with her mother, where Talia ended up throwing her shoes at the wall. Why was she dressed in someone else's cape? Where had she gone? Why was she so impulsive?

And the one that really burned: Why did she insist on ruining everything? That question hadn't been so much said as implied, but still. She knew it was on the tip of everyone's tongue. Somehow, in the span of a night, she'd managed to ruin a much-needed alliance, break off her engagement (the Thorossians were more than happy to announce that publicly), betray her best friend, and lose her family's trust.

Talia huffed a sigh and leaned back into the leather couch of the lounge room, flexing her wrists above a sketchpad. Around her, a tropical forest spanned as far as the eye could see. Moss-laden trees rose to the cerulean sky. Rubbery, vibrant plants rustled with the movements of emerald green beetles and rainbow-colored birds, their chirps and twitters calming her nerves. Ferns swayed, followed by a rumbling growl, and a midnight-black creature padded within four feet of her. If she didn't know it was a hologram, she'd be terrified.

"Hello, pretty thing," she said as she wrote the word *panther* above the partial head she'd already drawn. Then she mindlessly filled in the whiskers, pausing to watch as the beautiful beast sat on its haunches and began to lick its paws.

Usually, immersing herself inside one of the Seven ecosystems took her mind off everything. The only games she loved more were the flight simulations she and Ailat played when the summer Palesian storms made real flying too dangerous. But the point was to forget about Ailat for a few hours, not remember her. So virtual travel it was.

As soon as they'd boarded the monstrosity her parents called a starcruiser, she'd ensconced herself here, hidden away from their scowling gazes and pointed questions. In the last forty-eight hours, she'd hardly left the room. Every time she ventured out into the brightly-lit hallways, some broadnet video of the incident with Ailat would find its way to her. It was all over the intergalactic networks. How she, Talia Starchaser, had embarrassed the prince of Thoros. Her mock companion corrupted and a wanted criminal.

Please let her be okay. The prayer felt empty, a helpless plea lost to the vastness of space. Talia leaned back, pressing her cheek against the viewing screen that wrapped around the wall of the lounge. Where was Ailat now? Was she finding a way to power up at night? Had the Collector found her yet?

Talia could almost feel the small device where it rested inside the hidden pocket of her dress, burning a hole against her thigh. She'd wanted to wear pants, but the entire family had to keep up appearances, especially after what happened.

The door slid open, and Tamsin slipped through the holo-forest, disrupting the trees as he hopped onto the couch beside her. Dressed in a gold suit that brought out his eyes, he wrinkled his nose. "This place stinks."

"Shut up." She tossed him a controller and reset the holo-theatre for a two-player game of invaders. The crystalline air of the rainforest disappeared, replaced by a million realistic stars dotted with an enemy mock fleet. While their silver, teardrop ships glimmered against the backdrop of space, she let her mind drift to the simplicity of the game.

Line up the ships inside the bright-green bullseye.

Pull the trigger.

They played until her thumbs burned and her stomach growled. Eventually, Tamsin grew bored and left. She stared at the door after him, working up enough courage to follow. Surely her parents wouldn't still be mad?

As soon as she stood, the device inside her pocket vibrated against her flesh. She pulled the button out, terror and anticipation both managing to work their way through her nerves. A bright-orange ring flashed from the tiny button's sides. She pressed the top, nearly dropping the device as a holograph rose from its depths.

The grainy form of the Collector solidified against the eggshell-white wall. "Hello, Princess."

Princess? *How does he know*? Moisture shriveled inside her mouth, and she barely found the courage to respond. "Did you find her?"

"Of course. I have your mock. She's safe now. A little worse for wear, but nothing I can't fix."

"Good." She glanced at the door, feeling less relieved than she should have. Something about this felt wrong. "How do I . . . get her back?"

"Back?" A mechanical laugh rasped through the speakers.

"That was the deal, remember?" Gooseflesh shivered across the bare flesh of her arms.

"But that was before I talked to her. She had so many interesting things to say."

"Like what?"

Static disrupted the holo-screen for a brief moment. When the video resumed, the Collector had drawn nearer, his strange, smiling face a dark mask in the screen. "Were you aware, Princess, that the royal Starchaser family uses decoy ships to protect themselves in space?"

A heavy weight, something like dread, filled Talia's gut.

"But of course you were. How silly of you, then, to allow a tracker on boa—"

She was up before he finished his sentence, adrenaline propelling her forward. But it was too late.

One second she was sprinting down the hallways.

The next, she was sprawled flat on her face. Surrounded by darkness with ringing in her ears. Sounds came back in a wave. Alarms screeched. People screamed. Red lights broke the darkness, flashing in time with her heart. She got to her knees as a silent concussion rocked the ship. Followed by screaming metal and a deafening bang. Smoke choked the air and burned her eyes, her lungs.

Talia dragged to her feet, each step surreal as the ringing echoed inside her skull. She wandered through the smoky ship, stumbling into walls, calling out for her brother, her mother, father, anyone. What had she done?

"Oxygen breach," the ship's computerized voice said, sounding far too pleasant. Too calm. As if that malfunction wasn't itself a death sentence. "Please find your exosuit and proceed in an orderly fashion to your designated emergency station."

Her heart slammed inside her chest as the ship tilted, right along with Talia, and she crashed into the wall. Bits of charred mock parts simmered all around her, and she wondered when she might run into human flesh, into her family's remains.

A mock assistant dressed in a white exosuit and carrying a matching one in hand rounded the corner and spotted Talia. The mock held the suit out for her, but she could only blink, consumed by the heavy weight of guilt.

"You must put this on," the assistant said. She tapped her wrist-com and muttered, "I've found her," then turned back to Talia and said, "Hurry."

As soon as Talia slipped the suit on, fitting the tight helmet over her head, noises became even more muffled. Her breathing whooshed out in ragged bursts. The assistant fiddled with the back of her suit and a rush of cool oxygen tickled her cheeks.

"We must find your station, Princess," the mock said. Her voice was amiable and steady, despite the fact that there was no escape hatch for mocks. "Your parents are waiting."

Talia gasped with relief at the mention of her parents, but she didn't dare ask about Tamsin. No way could she handle him being hurt at the moment. Once she was with her parents, she'd be strong enough to ask.

The mock rushed them through the public dining area, the largest room in the ship. Tables were overturned, and diners lay strewn on the ground next to broken plates and the massive chandelier that once hung from the mirrored ceiling. Talia slid over the sea of shattered crystals and porcelain dotting the marble floor, holding back tears as best she could.

Her fault.

"We should help them." Her voice was stifled inside the helmet. There was a button somewhere on the front she could use as a microphone, but she couldn't find it through her thick gloves.

"They're dying, Princess." The mock looked down at a man and woman curled on the floor, a neutral expression on her face. In emergencies, mocks reverted back to their basic programming, which didn't include useless emotions like empathy. Talia swallowed down her nausea as the couple on the floor gasped for breath and clutched their throats, their eyes wide and shiny. "The oxygen level is nearly depleted. They wouldn't make it to the end of this room."

The ship shuddered, the motion followed by a huge boom. Talia flung her arms out to keep from falling as the floor rocked beneath her feet. All at once, lightness overtook her, and the floor fell away. Bits and pieces of plates and glass rose around the room, sparkling like stars in the heavens. Bodies and tables floated in eerie silence.

The gravity generators had failed.

Pushing off the closest wall, Talia swam through the dining room, following the assistant mock to her station as silence washed over the ship. When they reached the back corridors, Talia felt the deep chill of space reaching for her through her too-thin suit, and a scream lodged in her throat.

A small boy lay folded on his side with a huge gash splitting open his forehead.

But the ship lurched again, and she saw the gleam of metal skull and realized it was Nismat, not her brother lying crumpled and dead.

Dead.

Where was Tamsin? Breathing too fast, she navigated the maze of hallways leading to the royal chamber, but terror stopped her right before the six-inch-steel enforced red door. She was shaking too hard to punch in the code. The assistant mock did it for her, and relief poured through Talia's veins as the door opened and she saw Tamsin huddled near the back wall with her parents and grandmother. They held onto each other to keep from floating apart. All wore exosuits, their masks fogged with their heavy breathing. Blood poured down her father's face, a mask of red making the whites of his eyes seem to glow. Her mother had Tamsin in a death grip. Like always, her grandmother was poised and confident, her head held high. She could have been holding a martini and chatting up members of her garden club with that composure.

A hint of a smile graced Talia's lips. Even floating and in crisis, the matriarch never changed.

Talia's mother left the group and shot straight for her daughter. As soon as their bodies met, Talia latched onto her mom, releasing a heavy sob. "I thought you were . . ."

"Shh." Her mother's grip was fierce. "We're all fine, see?"

"What do we do now?" Talia asked. Never in her life had she felt so powerless.

Her mother glanced at her father. Something passed between them through their fogged visors, a look weighted with responsibility Talia hoped she'd never have to face. Her mother nodded and clung tighter to Tamsin while her father let out a long exhale.

"The ship is destroyed," he said. "Unfortunately, our escape hatch is too damaged to use."

Fear clenched Talia's chest; it became impossible to breathe. From the deep quiet murmured mechanical noises, like ships bumping against their dead vessel. The enemy was docking. They would be inside soon.

"There is one option, a fail-safe the Starchasers have used for a millennium to ensure the Dynasty's survival."

Talia's breath caught as the sound of gunfire, muffled as it was, punctuated the silence. The enemy had boarded and wouldn't take prisoners. They'd use heat sensors, so there would be no way for a human to avoid detection, nowhere to hide where they couldn't be found.

For a desperate second, Talia clung to the hope that the armada of ships they traveled with would save them. But . . . no. All it took was a glance outside the starscreen window to see the battles raging around them. This was a concerted attack.

The rebels must have amassed a huge force—she shook her head. Pointless to think about that now. Focus on escape.

Her father leaned over and took her gloved hand with his. A light dusting of frost crystals had veiled the glass over his face, so she only saw one golden eye. "You and Tamsin must get in the pod, Talia. You're the hope for the future, for mankind's future."

"What?" She tried to push off him, but he held her tight. "No—no. Not without you—"

"Listen to me." Even obscured by his suit, his voice held the confidence she could never hope to achieve. "I command you to do this. The pod is equipped to keep you and your brother alive for as long as possible until you're rescued. As soon as it's activated, a distress beacon will go out to our allies. You will be protected inside, safe. Do you understand?"

Sharp explosions rang from down the hall. More gunfire. They were killing everyone. Eradicating them. Despite the cold of deep space, sweat dribbled down her shoulder blades. Her breathing was so loud she could hardly hear anything else. She wiped the ice from her visor.

"I understand." As soon as the words left her lips, she compartmentalized the consequence of her statement. Her parents would find a way to follow. This wasn't the only pod. Her excuses that allowed her to leave them were endless.

There was no time for goodbye. She grabbed her brother's hand as shouts rang out on the other side of the metal door. Tamsin wrenched free and threw himself toward his parents, and the door to their panic room jumped as something smashed into it. Talia ran to her brother and yanked him by the arm, only to have him tug his way back, crying fiercely in his father's arms, wailing that he could never leave them.

Talia reached for him again, but the mock rebels cleaved the door from its hinges, and her father looked at her and shouted, "Run."

And so she did.

The same mock who led Talia here hurried her down into a cramped metal stairway hidden near the back, just beneath a tall bar of gold-veined marble. She descended the steps two at a time, the bar closing over her and hiding the stairs from sight.

They won't hurt them, Talia decided as the bar latched closed above. Sensing the darkness, her suit lit up at the sleeves and near her feet. A far-away, muffled explosion concussed the stairwell. Followed a few breaths later by three soft pops, like rocks cracking together under water. A fourth pop, and all went quiet.

Just stunning blows, she told herself as she descended the last stair, her heartbeat throbbing in her ears. *They'll keep them alive.*

Mocks weren't savage enough to eradicate an entire family.

A metallic surface glimmered in front of her, the meager lights from her ankles casting soft half-moons across the body. The lid popped open with a hiss and revealed a dark-velvet-lined interior. A black apparatus for her face hung from the top of the lid, tentacles snaking down the sides like some oceanic creature she'd seen in a book, once, but couldn't quite recall the name.

"You'll have to remove the suit, and hurry," the mock assistant stated, offering a small breathing apparatus to be used in the interim. "Your body won't be able to handle the cold."

Talia did as instructed, trembling from both her fear and the temperature. And as she stepped inside and lay down, her mind went numb, even as her body screamed to escape. This was a tomb. Better she die with her family than suffer inside this casket, afraid and alone for stars knew how long.

Hours.

Days.

The prospect was too much. But before she could scramble out, the lid clamped shut over her. Kicking the ceiling of her new prison, she discovered the lid immovable, the material nearly a foot thick. Despite being opaque from the outside, the inside surface was clear as glass. Darkness would have been better. Sweat broke out over her palms. Her bones tingled and muscles twitched. She felt as if she were jumping out of her skin. As if the whirlwind of panic ravaging her chest would burst open her sternum and kill her.

Her stomach dropped as the pod released from its hidden port at the ship's belly and shot through space. White light streaked across the lid. A dark sun, flared with orange and bleeding black smoke, wavered inside the warped glass. The air fled her lungs as she realized the white streaks were stars—meaning her pod was traveling very fast—and the fiery mass growing smaller was her old ship. Her hands pounded the cool surface of the lid.

She could see everything. The cold emptiness of space, an expanse of stars so vast she could spend years counting and never name them all. She was going to be buried inside this nothingness. Forgotten.

Soft hissing scraped down her spine; frosty wafts of smoke filled the air, searing her lungs and burning her cheeks with cold. Stars, she would be forgotten *and* frozen.

Before she could close her eyes and accept her fate, a bright light flared against the backdrop of space, a wave of tangerine flames that destroyed the last remains of her ship and any evidence of her existence.

She comforted herself with one phrase over and over as she faded out of consciousness: They'll come for me soon. They'll rescue me, and we'll make the rebels pay.

Soon. Soon. *Soon.*

Until it became barely a word, hardly a dying whisper on her lips rasped over and over and over . . .

Until she could no longer move her lips.

CHAPTER 9

3731 AD

Will

Will guzzled straight from the lip of a whisky bottle Lux had nicked from the bar earlier, rolling the foul liquid around his mouth to mask the scent of blood clinging to his shirt. When finished, Will passed the bottle to Lux where she leaned, cockeyed and tight-lipped against the Odysseus's cockpit wall. To her right, the starscreen showed the meager-lit docking bay of the Andromeda.

"We're leaving," he said, wiping some of the amber liquid from his chin. "That's final."

She pursed her lips. Once, Will had imagined what those lips would feel like pressed against his—except that would be like making out with a steel trap. Barbed words and taunting insults were the closest Lux ever got to flirting.

She tilted her head back, the sharp angles of her chin catching shadows, and took a swill. By the empty sloshing sound when she handed the whiskey over, she'd nearly cleared the bottle. "Stop being a stubborn ass. The crew needs to stay somewhere off the ship tonight. Boost morale and all that crap after our dismal scavenger scores."

Frowning, Will held up the bottle to the light. "Thirsty much?"

"What do you care? I stole it fair and square, so it's mine."

"Yeah, thanks to my distraction."

"That's what we're calling what happened back there? O-kay. And"—she clicked her tongue as she took a seat beside him, her tone softening—"don't change the subject. We should stay another day."

Will shook his head and wished he hadn't. The room spun, swirling the steel interior of Odysseus into a maelstrom of dark grays. He'd damn near killed a man in the bar earlier, the poor flesher's blood splattered all over that bar—over *him*—and no one blinked an eye.

The incident had dredged up memories of his own time as a human, but he'd be damned if he admitted to Lux anything was wrong. "If we stay any longer, you know what'll happen. Leo will get arrested for buying whores and not paying, your sticky-fingered brother, Dorian, will get caught thieving from a civilian, and Jane? What do you want to bet she's embarrassed a high-ranking lieutenant at cards by now? Kinda hard to fraternize with my peers when I run with a crew full of criminals."

"Fancy words." Lux chewed a fingernail. "But you forget. They're not your peers anymore. Us criminals are."

He slashed a sideways glance at her. "Don't need the reminder, Lux."

"Yeah. You do, *Captain*." She dropped her feet to the floor, clanging the grates with boots too small to be real. Then again, most days Will forgot how tiny she actually was. Her bark and bite were giant. "I saw the way you looked at your old crew. All doe-eyed and shit. Will Perrault, you're stuck with us. So cut the I'm-too-good-to-scavenge crap and locate some real finds with real payouts or else you'll end up wishing you could play cards as well as Jane."

Will scratched the stubble of his jaw. "Already found our ticket."

"Not the *thing* again. Captain, please." Gesturing with her hand in the direction of the cargo hold, she flowed to her feet, all four-foot-nine of her, and scoffed in his face. "I'm going to go sell it. Right now. For a—a pack of smokes for Leo."

Insubordinate, no good criminal . . . She'd already crossed the cabin and was making for the door. "No—"

The ship's *hatch open* notification reverberated off the walls and through Will's spinning head, followed by shouts erupting from the corridor. On instinct, he grabbed for the antique revolver hidden beneath the console. There were only three bullets inside the chamber, each one worth five times as much as Lux's bottle of whisky, and the recoil was a bitch. Still better than a blaster, though. Those needed to be charged for hours and jammed more often than not.

The door burst open. Four, five . . . *nine* station officers stormed inside the cabin and pressed along the walls, filling the bridge with their too-perfect uniforms and unsmiling faces. One officer kicked the scrap metal table Lux had been using for dice with Jane, and it, the dice, and the tin cup went flying, the dice clinking as they slipped through the cracks and landed below deck. Will clenched his fists by his side and tamped down his murderous thoughts as he stood at attention.

These were Federation officers, soldiers who worked directly for the queen and commanded a queen's respect.

Will leaned toward the console and slid the revolver out of sight.

Xander was the last to enter, his hands clasped behind his back as he surveyed the room with a sneer before allowing his attention to drift to Will. That sneer turned into a smirk.

Maybe Will shouldn't have put away the gun.

"Where is it?" Xander's question was a carefully crafted command, his gaze scouring the cockpit, his steps slow, in control.

Will choked out a laugh. Like anything was here besides stale air, a near-empty bottle of whisky, and one pissed-off Lux. "Mind sharing what you're looking for . . . Captain?"

Xander made his way past the drove of Federation officers and over to the flight deck. He spotted Jane's fern plant she won from an ore merchant months ago, absolutely against regulations and likely to get everyone on board killed, sitting near the starscreen. "Do you know how many violations you have on this hunk of junk?" He kicked the plant over, and the small frond broke against the pale floor, dark soil spilling out around their feet. "It's a disgrace."

Will shoved a hand through his hair, wondering how he'd break the news to Jane. Her ever-worsening glitches made her emotions almost as wild as a flesher's. "Why are you here?"

"Don't play dumb, you know what I'm looking for."

"I didn't steal the whisky, but I know who did."

Lux, standing in the middle of the chaos with her hands speared on her sharp hips, shot Will a baleful look, her eyes narrowed to emerald slits.

"I'm not here for whisky, idiot. Tell me where this is." Xander smashed his open palm into Will's chest, crushing something white against it.

The napkin.

Clenching his jaw to keep from punching his brother, Will plucked the white cocktail napkin, now barely more than a torn slip of paper, and held it up. Alarm bells were already going off inside his skull. If Xander wanted this thing . . .

"I don't know what this is," Will said, shrugging as he forced his face into a bored mask.

"Then why did you draw it?"

"Hmm. Don't know. I was bored?"

Xander's right eye twitched. If Xander were nine, that'd mean a tantrum. If he were fourteen, that'd mean he was about to pummel Will and then say Will started it. Now though . . .

Crap.

Sneering, Xander craned his head to look around. "Last chance to come clean before I tear up this rust bucket looking for it."

Some of the officers chuckled. Lux bared her teeth. She looked on the verge of slaughtering a few of the queen's Federation, but as laughter floated in from the open door, she lost her chance. Jane and Leo marched in carrying two bulging rucksacks with all her gambling wins. The two crew members paused as they took in the scene.

Slipping through the officers, Jane dropped her rucksack onto the co-pilot chair, the contents inside clanking. She didn't even *try* to look guilty for bringing her illegal gambling wins on board.

Fortunately, most of the officers ignored her, their attention saved for Leo, who towered over them. Leo raised his eyebrows at Will. "Why didn't you tell me we were having a party?"

"Slipped my mind," Will said through clenched teeth.

Xander ripped the napkin from Will's hand and held the paper up. "Like I told these idiots, admit where you found this symbol or your ship won't survive our search. Won't take long, by the looks of her."

As soon as Jane smiled, Will's heart lurched into his gut.

"Oh, no reason for that." Jane's voice was as friendly as ever. "A captain always complies with the law. Check the third bay of the cargo hold."

Dammit, Jane. He forced a tight grin. "Oh, yeah. That. Nothing more than recycling."

Ugly face sheened with excitement, Xander turned to the officers closest to him, pointed at the stairs, and ordered, "Go!"

Xander followed the Federation as they funneled out of the cabin, their boots pounding the metal floor. Will grabbed the revolver and did the same. Lux noticed, and she shook her head, muttering under her breath, but he paid her no attention, not even when Leo shot Lux a Will's-trying-to-kill-us-again look.

"Let's go," Will said, shoving the gun into his waistband. "Told you this find was worth something."

"Yeah . . . our lives," Leo muttered, but he and Lux begrudgingly obeyed the order, and they made their way toward the commotion, leaving Jane behind to pick up the pieces of her plant she'd just noticed had been destroyed.

The largest of the three cargo holds was sandwiched between engineering and what used to be the holo-map chamber, before the thing broke. Without the main engine running, this part of the ship was cold and dim, lit only by the emergency track lighting running along the narrow corridor walkways.

Leo broke off to the side to flank Will as he counted the officers again, searching for the biggest threat. Still scowling, Lux wrapped around the other side of the group. On his signal, she'd take out as many as possible. If they were going to fight, the dim hallways would give them the best advantage. The Odysseus's crew could walk these halls blindfolded.

A chill descended as they entered the middle cargo hold. Like the corridors, shadows pooled along the corners and layered the empty space in illusions. The soft purr of the backup generator that regulated oxygen and heat muffled the stillness. Their breath came out cloudy puffs.

Xander whistled. "Kinda empty, isn't it? If it wasn't for that glitchy co-captain's luck at cards, you'd all have starved by now."

"There, sir," an officer near the front said, pointing toward the shiny *thing* in the middle of the room, right where the Odysseus's crew had dropped it. Soft red light flickered inside its surface. Water puddled around it, looking black in the faint light.

Will's heart punched into his throat. This thing—whatever it was—was his key to reinstatement. He knew it the same way he knew how far he could enter a black hole and exit safely. A feeling. Deep in the gut. Xander couldn't take whatever this was.

But what could Will do? The second he pulled the gun, they'd be outlaws. Criminals . . . more so than they already were. Impressing the queen would be pointless if she executed everyone afterward.

But it had to be him who presented the queen with the thing.

Grinding his teeth, he followed close behind Xander. Leo and Lux mirrored their captain on either side. Xander was too cocky to actually think they'd be stupid enough to fight. Besides, his gaze was glued to the thing.

Xander reached out, slowly, and ran two fingers over its sleek facets and sharp angles. Then he knelt and examined the symbol that had gotten the crew into this mess in the first place. A smile spread across his face, his breathing fast and hard. "Message the queen and tell her I have it."

The gun was cold, heavy. Lux shook her head at Will, her eyes wide inside the dimness. Blood rushed inside his skull, drowning out the more rational thoughts rattling his brain. Suicide. Stupid. Impulsive.

Gripping the smooth handle, Will lifted the gun from his pocket—

Jane stepped from behind and caught his arm. "A captain always complies with the law, *Captain*."

As if waking from a trance, Will shook his head. This was madness. Treason. Fighting against imperial officers would make him an enemy of the queen.

He'd lost.

Lux's shoulders sagged as Will shoved the revolver back into his pants. Leo heaved a sigh.

"Good," Jane said. "Now, who wants cookies?"

Will couldn't watch the Federation officers cart the key to his salvation away, so he retreated to the bridge to sulk. He wanted to be ready to leave the second they were off his ship, so he busied himself with the warm-up procedure. Usually the growl of the main engine coming to life instilled a sense of pleasure inside. But, now, each flip of a switch was but another reminder Xander won. The bastard would already be setting a course for Calisto, the home planet of the queen. He'd probably already informed her what he had—whereas Will would have presented it to her personally.

Idiot had no sense of presentation.

A sweet, nostalgic smell drew his attention toward the door. Jane stood half-inside the cabin, a tray of leftover cookies— white-chocolate macadamia nut, by the aroma—held high. For once they were reasonably unburnt.

"No cookies right now." He waved his hand to shoo her away. "Just give me a few minutes before we act like my future didn't just swirl down the drain."

Nibbling a cookie, she crossed the room and settled beside him in her chair, next to which sat her potted plant, the terra cotta held together by duct tape. The harsh lights above made the furrows around Jane's mouth and forehead seem deeper than normal. "What do you think it feels like every time I sit next to you in my old chair?"

He stared down at his knuckles.

"I mean, I know why I can't be captain. One glitch is all it'd take to . . ." Her words trailed away. "Anyway, have a cookie. It will cheer you up."

The cookie was warm and gooey and tasted like heaven. Definitely not synthetic like all her previous batches. How in the universe did she find real flour and eggs? He hardly dared to ask as he crunched a nut between his teeth and sighed.

"And when you're done, why don't you take some cookies to the girl in the kitchen?"

He paused, mid-crunch. "Girl? You mean Lux?"

Sighing, Jane leaned forward and pulled up security video of the cargo bay. At first, Will thought she was showing current time, since he hadn't set the logs to record in months. Except the thing was still there, clearly visible in the middle of the floor. Squinting, he leaned closer. The video was grainy, the flickering bulbs along the floors providing barely enough light to see.

"A good captain protects his cargo. That's why I turned on the motion recording setting for the security cameras in that sector."

Movement. The lid to the thing popped open—it had a *lid*—and something slid over the side and fell onto the floor.

A girl. Thin and delicate. With long, wet hair, bare feet, and a gown that glittered like the stars.

The lid clamped shut, and while checking over her shoulders, she stumbled into the shadows of the ship.

CHAPTER 10

3731 AD

Talia

Talia hunkered beneath a metal range glommed with old grease and tried to get her bearings. Long milky breaths spilled from her hiding place into what she guessed was a really shoddy galley. On one end stacked dirty dishes, and a dull pot sat next to a stainless-steel sink. A locked door was on her right—probably the pantry. She'd tried it already, but the padlock hadn't budged. A few opened cans of synthetic corn sat atop the island in the middle of the tiny room. They were empty—she'd checked those too.

The smell of stale grease and something long burned riled her barren stomach. Her body was weak and hollow, her muscles already aching from her trek to the galley. She wiggled her bare toes, half frozen already. They were numb.

Where was she? Inside some sort of ship, that much was clear. Through the viewscreens she'd passed, rows of spaceships appeared. Clunkers, some of them patched together with what looked to be the hulls of cargo ships and mining vessels.

Her current ship wasn't much better. The thermoregulation

barely worked in some spots, ice beginning to frost the hull. Rivets and bolts were missing from the walls, and when her fingers brushed the sides of the tight hallway earlier, they came away wet and rusty.

Was this the allied ship her parents promised would save her? If so, it needed some serious upgrades. Maybe they'd been attacked too and had to scrounge, or this was a cover ship. Because, obviously, none of the Starchaser's planetary allies would travel in this junk heap.

Perhaps that was what happened earlier. Once she'd woken up and gotten her bearings, she'd left to find the captain. But then the sounds of arguing and loud noises frightened her, and fearing the rebels had somehow discovered her right after being rescued, she'd hidden here to wait them out.

By the time she'd gotten the nerve to even think about venturing out again, she felt the ship detaching from port. Whatever happened earlier was resolved.

Now she needed to face whoever captained this ship. Her parents needed her. If a full week since the attack had truly passed, their allies would be desperate to find her.

For a heartbeat, the flames of her cruiseship flashed across her vision. Bright, so bright. Her mouth went dry, her heart lurching into her stomach.

That could have been a dream. Or a hallucination. Who knew the effects cryosleep had on the mind? Besides, in the week or so she'd been asleep, her dreams had become jumbled and warped. There was no way to ascertain what was real and what was fiction.

The only way to do that was to venture out into the ship. By the dim red lights she'd seen along the baseboards, Talia had determined it was night. The crew would be asleep. Wrapping her arms around her body, she peered out of her hiding spot. She was shivering, starving, and terrified. Not in that order. Above everything, even fear, she was famished.

She'd demand food first. Then she'd address the planets of the Seven.

Pinching the slinky fabric of her dress between her fingers at the knee, she unfolded from the range and steadied her feet. Darkness nibbled at her vision, but she blinked the remnants of cryosleep away. The linoleum floor was freezing against her bare feet as she crossed the galley, each unsure step growing stronger than the last.

The door swung open just as she reached it. A man in his very early twenties stood in her way. He had tousled copper-colored hair that needed a good brushing, blue-gray eyes that crinkled in the corners, smirking lips . . . and a face she'd describe as handsome, if not for the port flap just below his neck.

Her focus slipped to his navy-blue captain's uniform. A mock *captain*? There were rules against that. Regulations set by the intergalactic coalition. Behind him milled what had to be his crew. A tall, wickedly gorgeous man grinned at her, his long flaxen hair pulled back in complicated braids. His navy uniform was stretched thin—practically painted—over swollen muscles and a flat waist. Two younger crew hands watched her with wary green eyes set against sandy-brown skin and exotic features. Siblings, guessing by their similarities. The tall woman in the very back had close-cropped salt-and-pepper hair. She held something—a tray full of cookies.

Talia's stomach strained as the sweet, nostalgic smell hit her. The Palesian markets just outside the palace came to mind. The scent of the fried pastries topped with pistachios and honey drifting on the hot breeze.

But she couldn't ignore the one fact staring her in the face: The entire crew was comprised of mocks. Perhaps these were the night crew, and the human crew took over in the morning. Having a night crew in case of trouble wouldn't be unheard of in the more dangerous sections of space. But all mocks?

"Where are your owners?" she asked, her throat raspy and tender from underuse. The mocks blinked at her, not understanding, so she reiterated, "Your humans. I demand to see them."

"Our humans?" The biting sarcasm in the young mock captain's voice set her veins on fire, and she nearly slapped the smugness from his face as he raised an eyebrow at the others. "She *demands*?"

None of them knew who she was. If they did, well . . .

"What ship is this?"

"The Odysseus." The pride dripping from the captain's voice made it sound like this rust bucket was something to boast about.

"I'm hungry." The declaration came without her planning it, and she cringed at the petty lilt of her voice. The desperation. But she was starving, and she wouldn't make it much further without sustenance. "Who can I talk to about a proper meal?"

The tall woman weaved through the rest of the crew and stepped forward, offering the cookies. She had a warm smile that set Talia at ease. "Freshly baked."

Talia plucked the cookies from the tray, a quick motion unbecoming of a princess, and took a bite. As soon as the buttery crumbs begin to melt against her tongue, she found herself shoving the two cookies into her mouth and didn't care that crumbs rained around her.

The mock crew watched her every movement, as if she were an animal inside a cage. *Eat slower, Princess.* But before she knew it, she'd consumed the entire tray. They were still just quietly watching her, so she brushed off her face, straightened her dress, and did her best to pretend she hadn't just dismantled an entire tray of sweets in front of strangers.

The muscled-up mock stepped forward and offered his wide hand, glistening with fine blond hairs. "I'm Leo."

She stared at the beefy hand, the fingernails surprisingly neat and well-kept. What was she supposed to do with his introduction? She'd never shaken a hand in her entire life.

All at once, she understood. They had no clue who she was, or they'd all be scraping the floor with their bows. The mock, Leo, nodded to the tall woman. "This is Jane, our co-captain. These two"—he cut his gaze at the siblings—"are Lux and Dorian, our navigator and mechanic. And this cocky bastard right here is our captain, Will Perrault."

She glared at the last mock, Will. She didn't care what his title was, the insolent slant of his lips was enough to have him jailed.

"You'll get used to his ugly mug soon enough," Leo added, and Will shot him a pompous look. The captain's face must be incapable of anything else.

They all stared at her, their eyes wide, some of them rocking forward on their toes a bit as if they expected something from her. Finally, Leo let his hand drop. "So you don't shake hands. Do you have a name?"

Talia couldn't overcome the oddness of them not knowing who she was. But their ignorance explained the galling way they were treating her. Once they knew . . .

A chill trickled down her side as she realized they couldn't. She was inside a ship manned by a fully mock crew. No humans in sight. If this ship were one of the Seven, she'd have seen a human by now. They weren't sleeping. They wouldn't show up in the morning. There were no humans.

Somehow, she'd landed on a rebel ship.

Her breath caught inside her chest, and she swallowed down the panic clawing its way up her spine. This could be the same ship that attacked her cruisership a week ago. Her attention flicked to the corroding steel along the walls, the disrepair. Well, maybe not exactly the same. This wasn't a fighting ship. So . . . perhaps she'd lucked out after all.

If she could manage to hide her identity, come up with a believable story, and wait until the next refueling station or planetary stop, she could send out a call for help. She'd make herself unappealing as a captive, just another lowly human.

"Name?" Leo reminded, gently.

Name, name, name? "Ailat. Ailat Star . . . born. Starborn."

Will's lips resumed their smirking formation. "You sure about that?"

"Why wouldn't I be?"

"You didn't sound so sure. So, Ailat Starborn. Why were you inside that capsule?"

Why? Her brain scrambled for a believable lie. "I was . . . on a ship. There was an accident, and all the escape hatches were damaged. I found that pod by accident."

"Huh." Will's gaze slid down her dress. "Dressed like that?"

Talia trembled with rage. Never mind that he was right. Her fancy dress had to be explained. "I'm . . . an escort. There was a party on the starliner I was on."

He scoffed. "Sure. You're an escort, and I'm a flesher."

"It's true," she said, resisting the urge to cross her arms to protect herself from his sharp gaze. When she escaped this rebel ship, he'd be the first to pay. "I'm new."

She felt as if the lie was written across her skin in bold red letters. An escort? Her grandmother would keel over dead if she knew her granddaughter was masquerading as a high-class prostitute, but Talia didn't have much choice. She needed to keep her identity secret long enough to escape this crap-hole and contact their allies. And few people would make up being an escort, so that might help sell the story.

Except, by the way the captain grinned at her, he didn't believe a lick of her story. Luckily, the others had a mixture of pity and distaste written across their faces. Which meant they believed her . . . Ish.

Talia fought the urge to groan at her idiotic circumstances. From this moment forward, Talia Starchaser, Future Sovereign, was a Palesian escort. A very hungry and very screwed one.

CHAPTER 11

Will

Will paced outside the mess hall where the flesher girl sat, ringed by Leo and Jane, surrounded by the last of their food supplies. Every once in a while, the flesher girl's gaze would drift to Will, but then she'd think better of it and go back to playing the sad-little-escort-girl card with his friends.

Fools. All it took was a pretty face and they believed everything she said. He frowned as she fixed a long plait of auburn hair so it hung over her shoulder and pooled on the table. Leo was leaned over watching her eat, a stupid, sappy smile brightening his face.

The pull was strong. She had bright amber eyes inside sun-kissed skin, unlike the sallow flesh of those used to living without ambient light. If she truly were an escort—highly doubtful—then she hadn't been one for long. He'd seen the flesher escorts some of the more scurrilous crews kept on board and met a few high-class ones at the military functions he'd been invited to before his fall.

None had ever looked like this girl. They didn't smile like her. Nor did they talk like her.

Maybe the escorts for the starliners were different. Still.

Her attitude was off. Too insolent. Too bright.

Too . . . something.

He studied one of her hands. Delicate and smooth and capped with the manicured nails of someone who'd never done a day of labor in their life, and missing the number tattoo all fleshers carried. Without thinking, he rubbed his wrists. Just over the spot where his owner's stamp was.

Number 5764. Crayburn's official mark. Will could've had it erased, but he'd never taken the time. The mark was mostly hidden behind his Ender cuff anyway.

Who was her master? Did he die on the ship? More likely she murdered him and tried to escape.

She caught him looking, and he graced her with a smirk. *I'm onto you.*

Rolling her eyes, she went back to stabbing the last of the processed beef from the can. Did she think this was her personal kitchen? What flesher had such gall? He should march over there and stop this charade already. But the razor-edge of her collarbones peeking from her dress stopped him. The sharp peaks of her spine poking through the exposed skin of her back. How long was she inside that pod?

Lux posted up on the other side of the door, her gaze drifting to their captive. "You know, if you stare any longer, she's going to think you fancy her."

Will snorted. "She's not my type."

Lux ran a hand down the side of the door, still staring at the flesher. "Since when are gorgeous redheads with legs for days not your type?"

"One, her hair is technically auburn. Two, fleshers aren't

my thing. And, three, lying is a total turnoff. And if you haven't noticed, she's lying through her perfect flesher teeth."

"I noticed." Lux pivoted to face him. "I also noticed Leo's wasting all our food on her."

She was right. Those supplies would have lasted weeks. If not for the organic muscles and flesh used in mock construction, they wouldn't need food at all. Although since Will still retained part of his flesher body, he needed more than the others.

"I don't know . . ." Will toyed with the stiff collar of his jumpsuit. He couldn't shake the feeling they were missing something. "Why did the soldiers come for her pod, then? They must have thought she was still inside."

"No, they thought whoever she stole it from was. Her owner's probably. Who knows. Maybe she killed him. Maybe she knows something she shouldn't, or she's a runaway flesher slave. Either way, not our problem."

"Then why tell us she's an escort?"

"Probably hopes you'll keep her on for the perks. Intergalactic law states property found in wreckage belongs to whomever discovers it. So, technically, she now belongs to you."

Will realized he'd been holding his breath while watching her. He tore his gaze away. Doubtful she'd ever been treated as property a day in her life. But there was more to her story. And it all traced back to that symbol.

"So?" Lux asked.

"So?"

"Will, no. I know that look. We need the money from her sale. You can't keep her."

A chuckle escaped his throat. "Keep her? Have you seen how much she eats? Upkeep for fleshers is expensive. They require ten times as much food as we do, plus medicines and doctors when they get ill, which is all the time. And they're emotional and prone to violence."

The last word settled uncomfortably in his gut. He knew firsthand just how brutal they could be. After all, he used to be one of them, until they tried to kill him.

She flicked up her dark eyebrows. "Uh-huh. So we can sell her at the first planetary stop then?"

The flesher girl's laugh floated across the room. Leo belted out a hearty guffaw along with her. Already, she was changing things. Giving Jane a purpose. Beguiling his second mate with flesher charm. Finger-combing her hair into shiny curtains and leaning her head back when she laughed to show off that exquisite neck. She was trouble. He felt it deep inside his hollow carbon bones.

The faster they could rid themselves of her, the better. And with her looks, she would fetch a nice sum . . . enough maybe to repair the ship's main radar. Since he'd been here, the transmitter hadn't worked right, making it hard to compete with the better-funded scavengers in the area.

He released a long exhale. "If I can't find anything about that symbol by the time we hit Oberon, she's gone."

"Oberon? Why that icy waste of rock?"

"Because there's an old church there that houses the largest collection of history books on this side of the universe."

Lux flicked up an impatient eyebrow. "That tells me nothing."

"Lux, I searched the broadnet for that symbol, but nothing

came up. Not a trace. Whatever that symbol stands for, someone erased it from the net. But they probably didn't think to stop on Oberon and search the church's files." He stopped pacing and grabbed the door handle.

Lux asked, "Where you going?"

He grinned over his shoulder as he beelined for the girl. "To inform her she's been assigned kitchen duty. Gotta pay for her food and board somehow."

Stars, he couldn't wait to watch her squirm at the prospect of dirtying those perfect nails.

CHAPTER 12

Talia

Talia leaned back in the creaky plastic chair and watched the mock man Leo dump another load of cans onto the dented metal table before he took a seat. All six-foot-four of him folded into his chair, his beefy upper body spilling over the table. She wrinkled her nose as he expertly worked some device to open a can. Normally she wouldn't touch this stuff, but after being in cryosleep, her body decided she'd consume anything.

Besides, an escort wouldn't be used to gourmet dining.

Leo slid a small can of foul-smelling fish toward her. Miniature silver bodies were packed tightly together in a gray sauce. Her lips puckered. *Disgusting.*

"Sardines," he explained, flashing those big teeth. "Real."

The proud way he said it told her eating the disgusting creatures was a great privilege. So she forced a smile and accepted the gift, slimy as it was. "Wonderful, Leo. I'm *honored.*"

As she forced herself to chew and swallow—and keep it all down—she studied the mock. Long tawny hair was pulled back from his square face in a mess of braids. On most men it would look silly, but paired with Leo's ruggedly handsome face, kind walnut-colored eyes, and wide shoulders, it somehow worked. His skin—a newer kind of synthetic that mimicked flesh flawlessly—was brownish-gold. Circuit lines ran down the slips of exposed flesh, intricate tattoos unfurling down his neck into his uniform.

A mock tattoo? That was a new one. Perhaps it was a rebel thing.

Most mocks were created on an assembly line using one of several hundred templates. They were made to be familiar and pleasing, without surpassing the uniqueness of humans. Very few, like Ailat, were customized beyond the generic features. Those types of mocks were incredibly expensive and rare. Only a handful existed in the world.

Yet, Talia didn't recognize any of the mocks she'd met on this ship as assembly-line droids. And her impeccable schooling meant she knew all the models, right down to the discontinued designs.

What were the odds a ship would be crewed by not one, but five of the galaxies' rarest mocks?

A more important question was: How had these rebels survived thus far? Their ship wouldn't stand a chance against one of the Coalition's Darkstars, and any one of the refueling stations would demand to see a flesher captain. None of it made any sense. Even the Outer Fringes of the Seven, where the rebellion raged, wasn't safe for a ship like this.

Leo pushed a tin of crackers toward the mock Jane. With her graying hair, muddy eyes, and nondescript face, she was the only mock Talia recognized. Model B-7, if memory served her well. Jane had cut her hair and ditched the makeup, but she was one of three labor models who were state-issued to families who lost a husband or son during the rebellion battles. To make up for lost income, they could hire her out for various tasks.

B-7 models were supposed to be good at a little bit of everything.

The labor mock-turned-rebel cut her eyes at the crackers but didn't accept, her gaze flicking toward the scowling captain watching from the doorway. Ugh. Talia glanced over and fought the urge to stick out her tongue.

Why did he insist on watching her? As if she were a criminal and a thief, not the other way around.

As soon as they met eyes, he sauntered over, his cutting stare going from the crackers to the empty cans around the table. "Better now?"

"Yes," she said.

"It's remarkable you can still fit inside that dress."

She gathered her hair and tossed it over her right shoulder, all her muscles clenching to keep from shivering as the cool air hit her back. A deep ache ran down her spine. The cryosleep had really done a number on her body. "I have a high metabolism."

"Must be all that work you do. You know, in-between the sheets."

She nearly snapped at him, but of course he was trying to discredit her story. A true escort wouldn't blush with that sort of pillow talk, so she scrunched her face into what she hoped was a seductive look and said, "As a matter of fact, it does. Although I doubt you'd know much about it."

He picked at his collar and then studied her with narrowed,

almost-human eyes, betrayed only by the irregular tic of his pupils as they enlarged and dilated. His construction and the attention to detail given to his cheekbones and lips was remarkable, actually. Even the tiny dusting of pores across his cheeks, the threads of silver inside his sorrel eyebrows—two shades darker than his messy, chin-length copper hair—spoke of a highly-skilled maker.

Better than Ailat's construction, even.

Those fine-crafted lips curled into a smile. Stars, someone must have spent weeks coding that grin to get just the right mixture of amusement and bluster. "Go find something less revealing," he said, his voice managing to be both commanding and teasing. "You're on dish duty until we figure out what to do with you. Try not to break anything."

Dish duty? Probably an unwanted task by the way he gloated as he left. It took all her willpower not to fling an insult after him. But, as long as the chore took her away from his piercing stare and suspicious looks, she'd do it with a smile.

Leo chuckled and began gathering the empty cans into his burly arms, using his chin to hold the trash in place. "It's not that bad, really. I'll show you what to do."

His kindness softened the tightness in her cheeks. He had no reason to be nice to her, nothing to gain. In any other circumstance, she would have liked the handsome mock immediately. But his port flap, hiding just below that strong jaw, was impossible to ignore. And halted any feeling of friendship.

Ailat had been Talia's closest friend. Her most trusted friend. And that trust was rewarded with betrayal and death. Mocks just couldn't help themselves. They were treacherous.

Even if they were coded to love humans, after spending a life serving them, when the time came, mocks would always side against their makers.

Maybe it was the corruption's fault. Or, perhaps the droid makers could never quite stamp out the code that made them tricksters and liars. Either way, Ailat's deception would never be forgotten.

Nor the lesson: Never trust a mock. That might as well have been coded into Talia's DNA the same way it was programmed into mocks to turn against humans.

Leo stood and jerked his head toward the kitchen double doors. "Ready? I'm about to start breakfast."

She flashed a demure smile as she stooped to pick up an errant can he dropped, encouraging his goodwill. She'd be the happy, compliant little escort girl. And first chance she got, she'd use his kindness to her advantage and find a way back home.

With the galley lights switched on, Talia could make out every bit of grease and tarnish clinging to the steel walls and equipment. Everything looked ancient, despite having a modern feel. Clamps locked down anything heavy, for whenever the gravity drive malfunctioned, she assumed. All the starliners she'd ever been on didn't have that problem. But this ship was obviously two or three jump drives away from breaking down for good.

Dishes took forever. Some of the pots were huge, and Leo had to help carry them to the drying rack. Especially since

Talia's muscles, once sculpted from playing the customary sports expected of a high lady at court, were now flabby and malnourished. Could she have been sleeping longer than a week? Impossible. An ally wouldn't have let the pod slip by longer than that.

After about thirty minutes of scrubbing, lifting, and drying, Talia's arms and back trembled with the effort, and sweat trickled down her shoulder blades. Who knew dishes actually had to be cleaned afterwards? She remembered the horde of labor mocks that descended on the kitchens after large banquets at the palace, but she'd never given much thought to what, exactly, they were doing.

Still, she didn't mind washing the flimsy dishes. The work took her mind away from the memories that kept cropping up. The explosion. The fireball consuming the starliner with her family still inside. Her little brother . . .

She shook her head, heavy tresses falling around her face. She didn't know for sure if they'd been killed. Surely the rebels kept the Starchasers alive. For leverage. Mocks were known for making logical decisions, and hurting her family when they could easily be ransomed for billions of credits made no sense.

Leo served lunch, some bizarre, gummy concoction of browns and yellows she didn't dare ask the ingredients of or want to eat. Feigning a dizzy spell, she requested a cabin to rest. Not that she had any desire to sleep. She'd been resting for a week. There was no way she was closing her eyes again until it became absolutely necessary.

Dorian, one of the siblings, led Talia through the winding maze of corridors, his thin arms full of what she assumed was her new outfit. He kept glancing backward at her, his curious gaze flickering over her face and hair. Yet, when she opened her mouth to ask if everything was okay, he wrenched around so fast she thought there might be something frightening behind her. But all was quiet.

The crew's quarters were situated close to the engine. The temperature was warmer here, at least, although her breath still came out in a frosty plume. The engine's quiet purr stirred the air. Silence was something else she now despised. Just the thought of being alone in a quiet room conjured clammy sweat along her palms. Partial memories cropped up of silence so absolute, so encompassing, it seemed to permeate her bones.

As if the lonely, cold hush of space had wound its way inside her mind—her soul.

Teeth clacking, she glanced over the area as the boy darted in and dropped her new clothes on a fold-out metal cot. The bed was small, softened with a threadbare blue-and-white striped mattress and equally paltry yellow blanket. Just above was a holo-poster of a half-naked woman on a beach, her lithe body shimmering with pulses of light. As Talia moved, the holo-model's bedroom eyes followed.

"You're back," the holo-girl crooned. "Lie down a while. Get comfy."

Stars above. The boy's wide green gaze switched from the poster to Talia, as if he couldn't decide which was more fascinating.

Turning her back on holo-girl, Talia inspected the rest of the chamber. Shelves lined the walls, filled with someone's things: a pile of folded navy uniforms, a toiletries bag, two pairs of heavy, large boots.

Only one person on this ship could fit into those massive shoes. Leo.

"Is this Leo's room?" she called over her shoulder, even though the heavy aroma of musky cologne confirmed it. Last thing she wanted was to steal his cabin. Or sleep beneath his holo-girlfriend. Gross.

But the boy lifted his bird-boned shoulders in a shrug and fled, a mesh of multi-colored wires stuffed into his back pocket the last thing she saw of him. Sighing, she turned and closed the door loudly enough for the boy to hear. Then she quickly traded her damp dress for the outfit provided—a royal-blue jumpsuit that smelled of boy and clean-ish socks. The pant legs dragged the floor, so she folded both hems over twice, pulled her hair into a tangled knot, and then put on a faded pair of boots.

Grandmother would have a stroke if she saw Talia now, but options were limited, and she had no intention of staying here or going out there in something wet.

The hallway was clear when she cracked open the door. Holo-girl, perhaps sensing she was about to be left alone again, *tsked* behind Talia.

"Go back to sun bathing," she trilled. Once she was sure Dorian was gone, she slipped into the hallway, leaving holo-girl whimpering behind a closed door. Hopefully the crew would still be eating and she could enter the main bridge alone. From there she could use the com to search for Coalition ships and send a distress signal.

Hardly breathing, Talia slinked down the hallway, irked that she had to skulk in the first place. Like a criminal. As if she should be ashamed of trying to reach her allies. There was no shame in a princess trying to get back to her people.

A brittle laugh drifted from behind her, turning her muscles rigid. Talia whipped around to find the pretty girl from earlier. Lux leaned against the wall, arms crossed over her chest. Her navy uniform clung to her curves and highlighted her small waist. Thigh-high leather boots graced her feet and made her look at least six inches taller. Although her lips were pulled into the semblance of a grin, her eyes speared Talia where she stood.

Talia held out her hands, more from shock than anything, and forced a stilted laugh. "You scared me."

"Where you going, flesher?" Each word from the mock girl's lips was laced with suspicion.

"Little girl's room. We do that sometimes."

"Never heard an escort talk like you before."

"You haven't met the right ones, then."

Pushing off the wall, Lux vaulted across the floor and stopped inches away from crashing into Talia. Talia flinched but held her ground as the girl performed an inspection, prowling in a loose circle until she made two full turns. Compared to the short girl, Talia was a giant, but she didn't feel that way. She felt tiny, helpless.

Maybe the two blasters weighing down the waist of the girl's tight pants didn't help. Or the daggers gleaming from the sheath pockets along her high-collared jacket.

"Look, I don't know what you are," Lux began. "But I know what you aren't. Not an escort. Not as helpless as you put on. And *not* telling the truth. All those things mean nothing to me. You can have your secrets. But . . ." She leaned in close, the harsh yellow lights above slanting across her face and illuminating the pale gold inside her green eyes. It would be so easy to believe she was human. "You hurt my crew, or you do something that results in their pain, and I'll toss you."

Talia's lips twitched in preparation of a smile—but Lux wasn't joking. "I don't want to hurt anyone. I promise."

That much, at least, was true. Although if getting off this ship and to safety meant someone got hurt . . .

"Good. Then we won't have any trouble."

A shutter reverberated through the ship, sending Talia to her knees. She threw out her hands, catching herself before she face-planted against the wall. Another shock wracked the ship as alarms blared all around. Lux steadied herself against a doorframe, her eyes stretched wide. Lights flashed as the power wavered and then died. The growls of the engines turned to whines before they gave way to silence.

All at once, Talia drifted into the air, as if some unseen force was lifting her. Her hair spread out on either side of her face, and she tried unsuccessfully to tuck the loose strands behind her ear.

"Get to the bridge," Lux ordered, her voice firm and decidedly unafraid. Then again, she didn't seem the type to scare easily. Pushing herself off the doorframe with her boots, she swam through the air with the grace of a ballerina. Her black leather jacket floated around her like a cape, reminding Talia of a character from one of those really old cartoons the earthens loved so much.

Talia swallowed as she shot through the air after Lux. They navigated the halls in near darkness. Unused to weightlessness,

Talia bounced off the walls. The stillness of the massive ship became a vice around her chest, squeezing tighter with each loud beat of her heart. Scenes from her cruiseship after it was attacked filled her mind. How she was tossed repeatedly into the walls. Those hadn't been stunning blows, but still.

To combat the quiet, she began to hum. Something Ailat taught her to do—no, don't think about her. Talia quickly tried to chase her former friend from her mind, but Ailat clung there anyway. Chipping away at the wall she'd built around her heart.

Still, the humming worked. As her body calmed itself, her muscles loosened, and she found she could spin through the air as if she was underwater. Moving became so easy she pushed off the bottom stair of a rusty stairwell and rocketed into Lux at the top. The two girls somersaulted into a wall.

As Lux righted herself, she shot Talia a look that could penetrate steel, muttering about fleshers being clumsy.

But behind Lux's withering expression hid worry; her bronzed skin had gone the color of summer clouds, her full lips pressed thin. As they bounced and glided through the dead ship, the truth dangled in front of Talia: Someone had hit their vessel with maimers. Warning shots that would briefly disarm her long enough for the offender to board.

Who would do that? Why? These were rebels . . .

Talia halted mid-air as if she'd been slapped.

She was being rescued.

CHAPTER 13
Will

The Odysseus went quiet. The rumbling purr of the gravity drive, the growl of the main engine, all of it. Just dead. Will swiveled his captain's chair to the port screen. His old destroyer ship, the Athena, loomed over their flank like a specter of death.

Stars, she was gorgeous.

He clenched the arms of his chair. Behind the starscreen of the Athena, hiding behind the reinforced metal hull and his old crew, stood Xander.

That should be me.

Xander probably felt like a god. Will always did as he surveyed the ship of whatever poor idiot was sweating in their jumpsuit trying to devise a doomed escape plan. With the might of the Athena behind him, he'd been unstoppable.

Why hadn't he seen her? Obviously she'd been cloaked, but he should have been watching for her. He should have known Xander would come back once he discovered the empty pod.

Will ground his teeth until his jaw ached as he waited for the ship to power back up. If it wasn't for the flesher girl distracting him, he'd have noticed.

"They took out our shields," Leo growled. He was strapped in one of the bucket seats along the wall, the frayed orange harness tight against his chest. "We're sitting ducks."

"Tell me something I don't know," Will said. He blinked at the console, refocusing on the three columns of controls. The backup engine had kicked on immediately, generating enough power to pump out oxygen and keep the heat just above freezing. But another direct hit from the maimers would take that out too.

That was what he would do. Knock out the crew and wait until they lost consciousness before boarding.

The only reason they hadn't yet, he assumed, was the girl. They needed her alive. Perhaps she retained valuable information on the human Alliance or knew too much.

Whatever the case, he wasn't about to give her up to Xander now that Will knew she was important.

Lux ducked inside the bridge and propelled off a table into a flip, landing softly in her nav seat. She flung an irked look back at the flesher, Ailat, who scrambled into the chair beside Leo with much less grace. An excited flush pinked her high cheekbones. Did she think this was a good thing? If Xander got his wish and claimed her, she'd be thrown in a tiny cell—or worse. Given to the Athena's crew for sport.

Lux finished locking her harness in place. "Captain, tell me you have a plan."

Will frowned at the blinking buttons and switches that would determine their fate. "Working on it."

"They'll be boarding soon," she added.

As if on command, two blips blinked on the radar screen,

heading directly for the Odysseus. He scratched his chin. They'd have a boarding crew of at least twenty. Which meant it would take them at least five minutes to disembark.

Think, Will.

The main power was still disabled. Manually turning it on from here was impossible, but not from the engine room. The problem wasn't starting the engine, though. What would happen afterward would be the hard part.

First sign of their main engine restarting, Athena would hit Odysseus with more maimers. The old girl couldn't withstand another strike. She'd die, leaving the crew completely at the invaders' mercy. But some of that power could be diverted back into the shields long enough to fly out of range . . .

"Dorian," Will called, swiveling his chair to face the small mechanic. At fourteen, he was slender and lithe—perfect for fitting into tight spaces—and the best mechanic in the galaxy. If not for also being an unlucky pickpocket, the boy would've had his choice of ships. "Think you can get the main engine restarted?"

Dorian flashed a rare grin and nodded. "Yes, sir."

"Good. Take Lux—" No, she was needed here. Will eyed Leo, but if Odysseus was boarded, muscle would be needed here as well. And Jane's glitches made her an unreliable choice.

That left the flesher.

Lux read Will's expression and clicked her tongue. "Nuh-uh. Anyone but her."

"Final decision." Will's tone left no room for argument.

"Fine." The muscles below her jaw feathered. "Dorian and flesher girl get the engines working, what then?"

"One thing at a time. As soon as the boarding crew arrive, Xander will contact us on the com. I'll stall him long enough for Dorian to work." He nodded to Dorian, and the boy popped out of his seat, ready. Then, with a disgruntled sigh, Will focused on Ailat. "Go with him. He might need assistance in the engine room."

The girl's mouth parted, as if she couldn't believe her luck. Then she unclicked her harness and unwound from her seat, biting back what looked like a coy smile. Why the hell did she look so eager? Will frowned, knowing something was off, but there wasn't any time to dwell on it.

"Go," he ordered. "And hurry."

CHAPTER 14

Talia

This was Talia's chance to escape.

Escape. The word echoed in time with her heart, so loudly she was afraid somehow Dorian could hear it from where he worked beside her. They were shoulder-to-shoulder inside the engine room, an oval chamber beneath the cargo hold. A chain-link fence encircled the main engine where they worked. Or, rather, Dorian worked and she handed him tools, maneuvering around the tight space. Coolant cylinders rose to the ceiling all around them, making the area that much tighter. Two more smaller engines flanked either side.

To keep from floating off, she wrapped her fingers around the steel links of the fence and kept her boot wedged against one of the cylinders. Steam wafted through the room, leaving her skin damp. Dorian was bent over with the underbelly of the engine exposed, his bottom lip caught between his teeth.

She flicked a quick glance at the door, working to keep her breathing steady. Now. She needed to break free now. If she could just make it above to the airlock and wait for her rescuers . . . no. Dorian would chase her, and the last thing she needed was to fight with a boy not much older than her brother would have been.

Is, she corrected herself, handing a wrench to Dorian. Tamsin was almost fourteen, and still alive. She needed to escape and save them.

The boy watched her for a second too long before turning back around, but he kept her in his peripheral vision. Would he really chase Talia if she ran?

Yes, she decided. He wouldn't let her get away without a fight. She eyed the padlock dangling from the gate, and then her gaze shifted to the key at his waist. Perhaps if she locked him in . . .

The lights flickered, there was a droning surge of noise, and the engine roared to life. Talia gasped, startled, and floated a couple feet up before she grabbed the chain-link fence again. Dorian flipped around at the noise, and they stared at one another, unblinking. Still and quiet as the engines had been just a second ago.

She lunged for the key just as he flinched backward. He'd read her intentions, but too late. When she pulled back, the flimsy key shone in her palm. He pushed off the closest cylinder, barreling straight for her. She stumbled backward through the air and grabbed hold of the fence, and he sailed right by her. Scrambling for the gate, she pivoted sideways out of the opening and slammed the gate shut.

He was already swimming through the air back toward her, and his momentum sent him crashing into the chain-link gate, the roaring engine swallowing the sound whole. She quickly locked the padlock, pocketed the key, and then mouthed the words *I'm sorry* as she backed away.

But before she could run far, heaviness filled her as the gravity drive restarted, and Talia hit the floor, somehow landing on her feet. The jarring contact reverberated through her already aching bones. She twisted to run when a screeching noise, muffled by the engine's buzz, pierced her eardrums. Half a second later, a huge explosion wracked the ship. The impact flung her to her knees, and she bounced off the floor and against the wall before she regained control, her head buzzing and vision blurry. As her senses returned, she spotted one of the columns had broken loose, and it barreled end-over-end toward Dorian like this was an ancient film on slow motion. Dorian tried to duck low, but the column struck his torso, knocking him back and wedging him between two others.

Stars. She forced herself to the door, a thousand thoughts tumbling through her skull. Don't turn around, Talia. Your family needs you. Don't let them down—again.

A cry from behind made her freeze. He's a mock. He'll survive.

Still, she hesitated. Sweat beaded along her forehead and trickled down her shoulder blades. The engine was getting hotter by the second. If she left him . . . he could die.

How much heat could a mock withstand? Surely more than humans. But even they had real flesh, and if *she* was hot all the way over here, he was sweltering.

She just couldn't leave him. With an aggrieved sigh, she sprinted through the stinging-hot air back to the cage. The loose column had knocked a hole in the chain-link, and she slipped in without having to unlock the gate. A wall of heat bubbled over her, burning her cheeks and eyes. Steam covered much of the area, so much that she almost missed Dorian pinned beneath the column. Sweat slicked his skin, and a trickle of blood darkened his forehead. His eyes were shiny with pain, but they focused on her.

Surprise flashed across his face. "You came back."

"Shh." She tried to yank the column free, but it wouldn't budge. Next, she grabbed his left boot and tried to slide him beneath the dense steel cylinder, but the boot slipped off in her fingers.

He couldn't move.

Sweat leaked down her forehead and ran into her eyes, burning them and making it that much more difficult to see. She swiped her arm over her face and tried the column again, but the metal was searing hot and lanced her fingertips with pain.

"Leave me," Dorian said as she cried out, his voice weary and weak over the engine. "You're a human. You won't last much longer."

"Neither will you," she chided, chewing her bottom lip. The hell she'd let him die like this. Blinking against the heat, she dropped low and slithered below the column trapping him. The temperature was cooler near the ground, and she released a sigh as she squirmed closer. "Do you have a knife? Something I can cut the fence with?"

Grimacing, he patted the torso of his jumpsuit and came away with a fold-out blade no longer than her pinky finger.

"It's sharp," he assured her.

She took the knife and crawled over the ground to the fence behind them. Heat boiled over her, plastering her hair to her skull in a soggy sheet. Ragged pants spilled from her lips as she brought the knife edge over the steel. Thank the stars, Dorian kept the blade sharp, and a few minutes was all it took to cut away a hole big enough to fit through.

Waves of dizziness washed over her. Her emaciated muscles screamed with every movement. But she had enough energy left to pry him backward and drag him to the hole. He flipped onto his hands and knees and scrambled out, and she followed. Near the doorway, he stumbled, and she took his arm and helped him down the corridors. By the time she remembered she was going to escape, they were already back at the bridge.

The cockpit was eerily quiet as they staggered inside. Everyone seemed so focused on Will and the starscreen that they barely noticed the two near-dead people walk into the room.

"We're alive," she muttered, before remembering the reason Dorian almost died in the first place.

Lux spared them a glance before returning her attention to the starscreen. Her brother's condition must have registered a second later, because she whipped around to stare at him. "What happened to you?"

Dorian was slouched in a chair, working at the harness buckle with fumbling fingers. His gaze slid to Talia. A quick, furtive look. Then he said, "The blow knocked loose a coolant cylinder. Hit me in the head. I'm fine."

Talia let out an audible gasp, hoping no one noticed her shoulders sag with relief. Why didn't he tell the truth? He didn't owe her anything. Still, she was grateful.

Lux opened her mouth as if to say more but apparently

decided there were more pressing concerns, because she grit her teeth and returned to glaring at Will.

Talia finished harnessing herself in and studied the captain. He was engaged in an argument with Leo and Jane, though his focus never left the console or the buttons he was programming.

"Captain, this is a highly dangerous maneuver," Jane said, probably not for the first time, by the way Will ignored her.

"No, Will," Leo added. "Slingshotting around the A-17 star is too dangerous."

"I hear your concerns," Will murmured, never taking his eyes off the screen as his fingers continued to fly over the console. "But we need a gravity assist to pick up enough speed to hit hyperspace before they're back in firing distance."

"You're not listening, Captain," Leo grumbled. "They're ready to board. Shields are down to twelve percent. We've sustained damage, and we're still not fully recovered from your last idiotic maneuver. If we leave now—"

"They'll be forced to wait until their boarding crew is safe before firing again. That last shot was just Xander being an asshole."

Xander? Who was he? Talia scoured her memory for any mention of a human captain named Xander, or someone important in the Alliance, but nothing came up.

Jane and Leo shared a he's-not-getting-it look, one that appeared to happen a lot, and then Jane said, "Will, if those calculations aren't exact, down to the decimal, we'll burn up in one of A-17's flares."

"Handling it." Will's shoulders straightened, and he leaned

back, his hands suddenly still. A pleased smile brightened his face. "Ready?"

Talia didn't know anything about spaceflight. She'd never been allowed to fly her Starfighters out of Calisto's atmosphere, or been anywhere near the bridge of the royal starliners, and all the captains she'd ever known were older men with potbellies who smoked fancy cigars with her father in the evenings. But the way the others' faces paled and their bodies went rigid told her they were terrified.

Great, their captain was a madman.

The ship lurched forward, pinning Talia to her seat. Her breath lodged in her throat, a thousand butterflies churning her stomach. All the food Leo had given her earlier threatened to come back up.

A voice came over the com. "Will, I'm ordering you to halt."

Whoever the voice was—Xander, maybe?—Will's face darkened at the sound. The muscles in his jaw and neck clenched. "Good luck with that."

"Don't be stupid. Our missiles can reach long range—"

"Yeah, but Xander? You've always been a horrible shot."

A growl came over the other end and then the words, "Fire!"

"He's not waiting for his crew to get out of the way," Leo said.

The ship banked left and began to loop. Talia clenched the sides of her seat as everything flipped, the starscreen blurring into a whirlwind of stars. Bright-red streaks flared across the starscreen.

"There's more," Lux called. "Watch the flank!"

Another hard maneuver twisted Talia's body, wrenching

her head sideways as they banked right. Her neck ached, and her stomach boiled. She gasped for breath, watching as more red streaks lit the sky, while her heartbeat drummed inside her skull.

And then the ship pulled up, flattening Talia to her seat. She was being crushed by the velocity, her bones smashing. A second later the pressure eased, and she sat up, tightening her harness and trying to catch her breath, awed by the ease with which the captain piloted the ship.

Bright white flooded the starscreen. She scrunched her eyes shut and then peeked them open, shielding against the light with her fingers to find a huge mass of swirling rays overtaking the starscreen. That must be A-17, the star they talked about earlier. They were hurtling toward the fiery sun at an indeterminable speed—though it must have been fast because the stars on all sides were blurred into hazy lines.

Will and Jane were dark figures against the growing light. The crew slipped on smoky goggles, though no one offered Talia any as they closed in on the star. The distressed ship groaned, sounding seconds from falling apart, her chair vibrating so violently her teeth clacked and her brain rattled.

They were going straight into the star.

"This is it," Leo said. His voice held a finality that made her want to jump out of her seat and turn this ship around. Pulses of light flashed through the cockpit, the flares threatening to encompass the ship in a solar grip.

"I hate you so much right now, Captain," Lux muttered.

But from Talia's periphery, she caught Will's lips curve into a smile. Was he actually enjoying this?

"Steady, girl," Will soothed, as if he actually thought the ship could hear.

Another explosion of light washed over the cockpit, making everyone glow with the orange light; this time the flare was really close to the ship. Will's grin turned into a sneer, as if he dared the star to defy them.

The crazy idiot!

All at once, her stomach hollowed out as they shot forward, the speed blanking her mind.

Breathe . . .

They must have been going incredibly fast because the light from the star began to fade away to darkness.

Leo clicked his tongue as he relaxed into his chair. "Lucky son of a blaster, it actually worked."

"Nearing hyper-drive speed," Will said. "Three, two, one . . ."

The world stopped for a breath. As if someone pressed pause. Then the stars outside the starscreen burst into a canvas of reds and yellows and greens and purples. The hollow sensation inside her stomach moved to her chest, and the velocity pinning her to her seat released. She felt both in the present and somehow removed. Her body full and empty. Heavy and light. Beside her, the others were blurs of color and light, waves of energy flowing over them.

They were in hyper-drive. Something she imagined she'd done a million times on their starliner. Yet she'd never experienced it like this before.

A blink, an exhale, and it was over. They came out to a black, nearly starless region of space. Lux uncrossed her legs, pulled up a handheld holo-map screen, and began plotting their course, muttering unmentionables at Will. Dorian unbuckled from his seat and scrambled to check the damage from the earlier attack. Jane unfolded her long body and stood, giving Will's shoulder a squeeze. As if he'd just done something amazing, instead of almost killing them. Even Leo, chuckling beneath his breath, rose and stretched out, his fingertips nearly touching the ceiling.

Talia stood on shaky legs, crossing her arms over her chest. "Are we not going to talk about how the captain nearly killed us?"

Leo raised an eyebrow at her, but the others acted as if she hadn't even spoken. She cleared her throat, garnering a dark look from Will.

"Nearly." Will said the word like it was something to be proud of. "And you're still alive. So go make yourself useful. I'm sure the galley's a mess."

Instead of following his orders, she stormed off and found her way back to Leo's quarters. Holo-girl frowned when Talia entered, and she rolled her eyes at the model and fell onto the bed, pulling the scratchy gray sheets around her. Why couldn't she have left the mock boy there? Was he more important than her family? Grimacing into Leo's hard pillow—which smelled of aftershave and too much cologne—she released a frustrated growl.

Maybe Prince Cassius was right. Her family *was* too soft on the mocks.

Crackling erupted from the intra-ship com on the wall by her head. "Ailat, Leo requires your assistance in the galley."

Talia rolled her eyes at Will's too-pleased voice and flipped over.

"Fat chance, Captain," she muttered into her pillow. Like hell she'd go help them do anything when that maniac had almost killed her. Let them wash their own dishes. She was a prisoner, even if they didn't know her real identity. And they were the enemy.

She was drifting in and out of sleep when the door creaked open and someone slipped inside. Careful, so as to appear to be asleep, Talia lifted her head from the pillow and turned— and locked eyes with the captain.

CHAPTER 15

Will

It had been years since Will interacted with a flesher, and he'd forgotten how temperamental they were. How emotional and unpredictable. But this flesher seemed intent on reminding him all at once. Was it really that hard to scrub some dishes, or did she think they were all at her beck and call?

He flexed his jaw as he strode toward Leo's quarters, trying to find the words he would say. How about, *you're in the wrong century? You lost the war years ago; stop acting like we're still your servants.* Everyone was contributing. Leo was helping Dorian with repairs. Lux was replotting their route to Oberon. And Jane was baking stars knew what . . . but she was doing something.

Surprise, surprise. Everyone on this ship was working but the flesher.

As soon as Will flung open the door and spied Ailat sprawled out on the bed, anger surged through his veins.

She spun around, her eyes flashing defensively, a white linen pillow held above her head like a weapon.

"I gave you a direct order to help Leo in the kitchen," he said, his voice steady despite his annoyance. "Perhaps you didn't hear me?"

She actually had the nerve to roll her eyes. "No, I did. I just ignored you."

Her gall left him speechless. Was she deranged? Maybe her time in the pod had left her half-crazy. He drew in a deep breath and waited until his urge to space-toss her faded before speaking. "You realize I could have you whipped for that?"

Closing her eyes, she settled into the mattress and shoved the pillow behind her head. "I'd like to see you try."

Despite the anger tightening his muscles, twinges of a smile lifted his cheeks. Who in the hell did she think she was? A royal escort? Even if that were true, which he doubted, she was still a slave just like all the other fleshers. Yet here she was, giving orders like she was in charge. As if Will couldn't just space-toss her and be done with it.

Will considered himself a fair captain. He rarely gave orders beyond tactical ones, allotted his crew a fair cut of the salvage, and allowed them to complain without punishment. But they always gave him respect—at least, where it counted.

That was because there was no one better at saving their criminal asses from jail than him. The crew of the Odysseus were magnets for trouble. He could see five ways to get them out of a scrape by the time it took them to realize they were in one. He was an expert at making life-or-death decisions, and he always made the right one.

Yet, for the first time since he could remember, Will had no idea how to proceed.

Blowing out a deep breath, he gave her one last chance. "Everyone on this ship contributes." He ground his teeth to keep from saying something worse. "Last time I ask you."

An annoyed sigh escaped her lips. Eyes still shut, she began to speak, her words slow, as if she were talking to an idiot. "I'm going to stay here until dinner. This is your ship, not mine. If you want something done, do it yourself."

Even though she spoke slowly, it took a second for the words to register. Anger rushed through him. A blinding human rage he hadn't felt in ages. If he were still human, who knows what he would have done. But because he had programs designed to filter his temper and find appropriate outlets, he made a rational decision that would have the desired effect without inflicting mortal damage.

At least, he hoped.

He reached down to grab her, and her eyes snapped open. She tried to scramble away, her mouth an O of surprise, but he scooped her up in his arms, pinning her body to his chest as he marched from the room toward the galley.

She was lighter than he was expecting, and softer. Her frailness surprised him, actually, and he adjusted his hold so he didn't crush her or snap her delicate bones. He also didn't expect her hair to smell like jasmine and honey, or her skin to feel like silk.

Stiffening, she seemed unsure how to respond at first, gaping at him with those big golden eyes, nostrils flared. Finally, a squeak fled her throat.

Then ire twisted her face—slowly, though, as if she still really couldn't believe he dared touch her. He was so entranced by her changing expressions—the curling upper lip, the elegant eyebrows arching to form a deep crease between her eyes, expressions he hadn't seen replicated on any mock—he nearly missed her reach back to deck him.

Before she could strike, he clamped onto her bicep with his left hand, pinning her free arm. He was careful not to use all his strength, half of which could easily crack her humerus bone.

When she realized she was trapped, she changed tactics, bucking and wiggling and hurling insults at him as she thrashed like a wild animal.

He chuckled, enraging her further. But there was little she could do beyond screaming. He was made of metal instead of bone, his muscles created from a meshwork of carbon nanotubes that made him ten times stronger than a human male twice her size. She could squirm all she wanted—she wasn't budging.

"Where are you taking me?" She practically spit the words. Strips of her auburn hair were plastered across her sweat-drenched face, her teeth bared. She'd finally stopped struggling, her insults giving way to panting. A cardinal-red flush darkened her cheeks, reminding him of a child throwing a tantrum.

Flesher, of course. A mock would never act so silly.

His lips stretched into a grin as he ignored her, his silence eliciting another round of thrashing, this time accompanied by snorts of rage. Part of him knew he should stop toying with her human emotions and allow her a shred of dignity. But the other part of him was enjoying this way too much to stop.

With a final grumble, she puffed out her bottom lip and stared at the wall. "You have no idea how much trouble you're going to be in for this."

He swallowed down a laugh and decided not to respond. He didn't want to encourage her delusions.

By the time they entered the galley, calm rage had settled over her face. She'd gone still in his arms, like a soldier meditating before a battle, her lips pinched and eyes slits of ochre.

Now that his anger had mostly cooled, a surge of pity rose for her. There were other ways he could have handled this. And this would be demeaning for anyone. But then he recalled her insolence, the haughty way she rolled her eyes, and he tightened his hold on her arms, determined to see this through.

The air was heavy with the smell of grease and burned beef as they entered the kitchen. Will wrinkled his nose at the metallic scent, meaning the meat was synthetic. Again. Stars, they needed to resupply soon.

Leo glanced up from a steaming grill, spatula in hand. His mouth parted at the sight of Ailat trussed up in Will's arms. Of course, the second they entered, she'd situated herself to hang limply, as if he'd actually hurt her.

One of Leo's thick blond eyebrows inched up. "What's this?"

"Brought you another hand." Will dumped her unceremoniously by the oven, enjoying himself a little too much as she smoothed her tunic and fixed her hair. If she wasn't going to admit her fault in this, he wasn't going to treat her gently. "She's happy to help."

Her mouth flew open in protest, but she hesitated, flicking her gaze back at him, and then gave Leo a stiff nod.

Leo belted out a rumbling laugh. "Yeah, she looks practically overjoyed."

Huffing, she marched over to the grill, ripped a dingy blue

apron from its peg on the wall, and began stacking plates, casting nasty looks at Will the entire time.

He found himself grinning as he made his way to the bridge. His chest warm and arms tingling where her flesh had touched his. Her exotic smell still lingering on his shirt. He'd thought picking her up would have felt satisfying, but instead, something different had sparked to life. An urgency buried deep inside. And as much as he tried to listen to Lux talk about trade routes and less conspicuous entries into Oberon airspace, his mind wandered back to the way her eyes burned like liquid gold when she was furious. The way she took these little, ragged breaths, her chest heaving.

No—her humanity was intriguing, but that was all. Her weak, bruisable flesh and breakable bones. She reminded Will of the part of him that died at the hands of other humans. Before mocks took him in and made him one of their own.

Shutting his mind off to *Ailat's* image, he forced himself to focus on Lux as they discussed plans to enter Calisto unnoticed. Xander was smart enough to have an alert out for the Odysseus, but there were ways around that could be handled when they docked at the port. Once on planet, they would split up and search the marketplace for anyone who recognized the symbol. Will would scour the massive library there as well. Surely, between all of them, they could discover something about the symbol, or why Xander wanted it so badly.

And if they couldn't, then Will assured Lux he'd be the first one in line at the slaver's market to sell the lying flesher. In fact, he couldn't wait to rid himself and his crew of her and return things back to normal, one way or another.

CHAPTER 16

Talia

Talia finished cleaning the last of the steel plates after dinner and then consoled herself with the knowledge that when this kidnapping crew of rebels was finally caught, Will would be at her mercy. Stars, he'd be sorry for treating her like a common slave. Risking telling him her identity might be worth it just to see the fear flash over his face when he realized who she really was.

They might be rebels, free to pretend this tiny corner of the solar system was theirs, but her family had ruled over the Seven Planets and all the galaxies in between for centuries. Their war wouldn't last another month—but the Starchaser Dynasty would remain forever. They were too powerful to fall.

Her family was comprised of the first earthens to look for habitable planets outside their home solar system, despite being labeled delusional—and worse. The Starchasers accomplished all that before hyper-drive capabilities, and three whole generations of Starchasers lived and died on board the Columbus spacecraft before they discovered Calisto, the first inhabitable planet of the Seven. Five years later came the Thoros discovery. The rest of the Seven followed within ten years. If not for the vision and sacrifice of the first Starchasers, humanity would have perished with their dying Earth.

With an annoyed sigh, she yanked the disgusting apron over her head, crushed the garment into a tiny ball, and threw it on the floor. Her hairnet was next. The nerve it took to think all that history and accomplishment could be erased with a few fighter crafts and droids. And for what? Had the mocks not been treated well under her family's rule?

Leo picked up her apron, smoothed it, and then tossed the crumpled fabric onto the wall beside his. A smile followed. A girl could drown in that sugary grin—hundreds of women probably already had. "Need an escort to my room?"

Stars above, how many women had heard that line?

"Why?" she snapped, picking bits of dried dough out of her hair. "Is your unhinged captain lurking in the shadows, waiting to assign more chores?"

He chuckled and pushed open the galley's double steel doors for her. "Probably not. He retires at night to the uppermost point of the ship."

Hadn't she seen the captain's quarters near the crew bunks? "To sleep?"

"Honestly, I don't know what he does up there. He just . . . disappears after dinner and reappears before breakfast. Doubt he sleeps much though, from the racket."

Racket? She didn't dare ask what a crazy mock like that might do in the shadows. "Don't mocks need to update in the evenings?" They were at Leo's door, the purr of the engine room settling into her chest and tugging her eyelids. She knew there were exceptions, but every mock in existence had to recharge and update at some point.

Leo lifted his burly shoulders in a vague shrug. "Some more than others. But . . . our captain is different. He started off like you, a flesher."

Impossible. Could such a thing really happen? She tilted her head, sure she'd misheard him. "He was human? And now he's one of you?"

"Yeah." Leo leaned against the doorframe, arms crossed against his thick chest. "It's a long story, and I barely know the half of it so . . ."

"Right." She opened the door partway and then hesitated. "Are you sure you don't mind me using your room?"

"Nope. Hardly sleep anyway. We use our bunks more for meditative purposes."

She swallowed back a snort as holo-girl greeted Leo with a girlish squeal. Meditative her ass. At least instead of her skimpy bathing suit, she was mostly covered in a silk kimono with a flowery pink pattern—although when holo-girl clapped her hands, Talia realized the girl was wearing nothing underneath.

Talia averted her eyes and whispered, "Any way to turn her off?"

Holo-girl hmphed and turned around, arms crossed as she pouted, her golden hair hanging nearly to her waist.

Leo scratched his cheek and tossed the holo-girl a sheepish grin. "Tandy, go to sleep now."

Holo-girl, aptly named Tandy, slid a hurt look back at Leo before making a dramatic show of lying on her side.

"Thanks, Leo. Naked, chatty holo-girls aren't really my thing."

Leo winked. "I understand."

As if in response, the light from Tandy's holo-poster went dark.

Talia sat on the edge of the bed, but as soon as her butt touched the hard mattress, her heart stuttered into an erratic rhythm, and she clapped a hand over her chest. Just the idea of lying down inside the dark room and closing her eyes, with its tight, thick walls blocking out all sounds, sent her spiraling into a panic.

Her body must have some residual trauma left over from being confined for so long. A week stuck inside a steel coffin. She tried to shake off the growing hysteria, but the emotion was as instinctual as her fear of spiders, water, and Grandmother's disapproval.

Leo flicked on a dim nightlight, casting a buttery half circle of light across the wall. "You okay?"

The concern evident inside Leo's voice was surprising. Someone must have taken great care with his programming for him to notice the subtle tics that indicated human distress.

"I'm fine," she said, shrugging off her fears, the momentary panic replaced by curiosity. "Leo, can I ask you a question . . . about your programming?"

A flush reddened his cheeks, and he cleared his throat. "Normally that's something you only discuss with someone you're . . . intimate with, but sure. Ask away."

Behind her, holo-girl scoffed, but Talia ignored the dark poster. She didn't want to bed Leo, just understand how he was so different from the mocks she knew. "Okay. How many program interfaces do you possess?"

He blinked down at her, puzzlement wrinkling his forehead. "There's no way to know something like that."

"But, surely they told you when you were made?"

"Well, yeah. I started with the standard 2,732,000 programs. But now I can't even imagine what that number is up to."

Up to? Her lips parted with another question, but then the implication hit her, and she froze. Intergalactic law stated a mock's programming couldn't surpass a certain number. She couldn't remember the exact amount, but it was well below a million. That safeguard was for humanity's benefit.

From what he'd implied, the rebels had somehow found a way to not only double the acceptable number, but allow their programming to grow.

She inhaled sharply. "So, your programming is open-ended?"

An open-ended program would allow mocks to surpass humans in every way possible. That kind of tech wasn't just illegal, it was potentially catastrophic. Human defenses wouldn't hold up against such a threat.

"Yeah." His eyebrows flicked up as he spoke, like he expected her to know all this already. "Our programming builds on our life experiences, which is why some of us are so *unique*. Present company included."

She would have laughed at his last remark, if the implications weren't so terrifying. How had the forces of the Seven not figured this out yet? Or maybe they had, and she simply hadn't been told. That made more sense. Up until last week, she'd been kept out of the loop.

Still, there was a chance her forces really didn't know what was happening with the rebels. Which made her all the more determined to escape and inform them.

Leo slid his gaze to the door, his lips pressed into a line that hinted at a frown. "You'll be okay if I go?"

"Yep." She ran her hand over the rough blanket. "Tandy will keep me company."

Her heart raced as she stretched out on the bed, faking a yawn. No sooner did the door click shut then she was up, pacing the room and counting. Five minutes passed. Then ten. She forced herself to wait another five and then slipped out of the chamber, closing the door softly behind her.

Dark shadows drenched the hallways, the dim blood-colored lights rimming the baseboards making eerie half circles she felt the need to step over. The corridors were freezing compared to her room, and ivory clouds spilled from her lips. Climate control must be set to only heat the rooms at night. Wrapping her arms around her chest, she crept toward the bridge, wishing she'd thought to grab a robe as gooseflesh pricked her arms.

She could only hope most of the crew was meditating—or whatever they did in their rooms at night. Ailat had never slept either, but the complexity of her programming meant she required the full four hours to update while humans rested. Did this crew have to plug in? It would make them traceable and leave them vulnerable to attack, so probably not.

Muted-yellow light announced the bridge. She paused just outside the half-propped open doors, listening for voices or the sound of movement. After waiting through a few minutes of silence, she crept inside.

The nav control panel was near the middle of the console, the buttons and switches illuminated by a pale-blue underglow. Pushing aside the nav chair, she crouched down, searching for the ship's tracking chip. The underside of the console was darker, and it took a few minutes of fumbling before she found the slot where the chip should be.

Empty.

She felt around until the edges of a compartment caught her attention. Surely the tracking chip would be inside—but the compartment was locked. Frustration warmed her cheeks, and she checked the urge to stamp her foot and come up with another idea.

A careful search didn't turn up any keys nearby, and the paperclip she found and straightened failed to do anything but scratch up the lock. Before Talia could look anywhere else, a woman's voice sounded from just over Talia's right shoulder.

She spun around to face the fact she'd been caught and discovered the lieutenant, Jane, smacking her head on the console. The mock sat slumped sideways in the co-pilot's chair—which is why Talia had missed her in the first place—one hand clawed over the chair's arm. The other hand hung loose. Jane's head was cocked sideways, staring past Talia at some invisible spot in the wall. Even from here, she could make out the bizarre dance of the mock's pupils from dilated to pinpoint.

She was glitching.

Ailat had glitched once, when Talia was twelve. After an extended vacation on the resort moon of Aegaeon, Ailat was overdue for examination and updates. Talia thought nothing of it until that last day on the shuttle, when Ailat began giggling and wouldn't stop. Her pupils had done the same thing, fluttered wildly. Afterward, when the episode was over and Ailat was fixed, Talia could never hear her friend laugh without being reminded of the incident.

Jane's gaze rolled to the ceiling, a sequence of nonsensical words tumbling from her lips. "Potato. Clouds. Baby . . ."

Talia crept over, praying Jane didn't have a recall function that would allow her to review footage from her glitches. Not that it would matter if Talia could reinsert the tracking chip and guide her rescuers to this location.

"Cruel," Jane whispered. "So cruel."

Ignoring the malfunctioning mock, Talia carefully felt around the utility belt circling Jane's waist. Something delicate and hard clanged beneath Talia's fingertips. A key ring.

Heart in her throat, she twisted the one key loose that looked like it would fit inside the compartment lock and then slunk back to the nav panel.

The key didn't work.

"Come on," Talia muttered, jamming the key in for another try. "Thank the stars."

She hardly dared breathe as the compartment door creaked open. Inside she found a few documents, a silver flask, and the chip. Before she could think about what she was doing, she inserted the chip into the slot. Hopefully no one would notice until it was too late, and she'd been found.

Right as she went to close the compartment door, something caught her eye in the very back. A dark, gleaming object. She had to shove her arm up past her elbow to reach it. Heavy and cold, it felt strangely familiar as she retrieved it.

But as she pulled it out, adrenaline spiked her veins. A gun. Similar to one of the antique weapons her father kept in a glass viewing case inside the vault at the palace. She'd never held it, but somehow she recalled that the older earthen weapons required metal objects called bullets. After a few tries, she found the cylinder of the gun and opened it. Three bullets peeked back at her from their grooves.

The gun went into her pants pocket, which was wide enough to conceal the weapon. Now that she had a gun and a plan, breathing became a bit easier.

Before she left the bridge, she found a mud-brown wool blanket and covered Jane.

"The queen," Jane muttered, still staring off into something Talia couldn't see. "The queen, the queen—"

"Babies and queens," Talia whispered, helping Jane to lie back. "Those must be some interesting dreams."

Talia practically skipped on the way back to her room, absentmindedly patting the weapon weighing down her pants. Her rescue shouldn't be long from now. She just had to survive until then.

As she wound her way through the hallway, a strange sound trickled from near the end, a melodic, haunting tune seeming to emanate from the metal walls. She ground her jaw and tried to walk away, toward her room, but the song drew her in the other direction. Something about the tune, the instrument, struck deep within her being. And she set off to find it.

CHAPTER 17

Will

Usually Will could strum the keys of his hidden baby grand piano and release his concerns, but tonight worry clung to him like the perfumed scent of the girl from earlier. Despite the beauty of the song he played, despite the rapture of the crescendo, he couldn't rid himself of the one thing that left him weak and marred.

Human emotion.

When he was a flesher, he was enslaved by feelings. Caught in a never-ending storm of rage and fear and sadness. Always reacting without thinking. Played by his emotions the same way he played these keys.

Thinking on the past, he understood just how inferior he'd been. How savage.

He pounded the ivories, yellowed and smoothed from use in a time before digital instruments reigned, taking pleasure in the way the repercussions throbbed inside his chest and vibrated the translucent glass walls of the room. Tiny stars winked from their black velvet canvas around him, reminding Will of the first time he discovered this hideaway.

Even after his mistake and demotion, he could have chosen

a better ship and more experienced crew. But he took one look at this viewing room and the baby grand piano, black as the darkest corners of space and fixed to the floor with foot-long metal clamps, and accepted the captain's position.

Other than the glass and the baby grand, the room was unexceptional—if not a couple hundred years behind the times. A dingy gold-and-green embroidered couch filled up the other half of the room, beside a tufted red rug that reminded him of an open sore and an old credenza stocked full of aged liqueurs from the previous inhabitant.

Slowing the tempo, Will closed his eyes and released a long, fragmented breath. As a mock, he was supposed to be in control of his once human drives. When he felt them, as all mocks did, his programming would sort through the most rational reactions and respond accordingly. Then the feelings were supposed to go away.

Except they hadn't.

Moving onto the next part of the song, he punished the keys and his fingers, willing the strange feeling of unquiet to dissipate. He blamed the flesher girl, of course. Ever since their encounter, he'd been questioning how he acted toward her, how he'd carried her as if she were nothing more than an object. Which wasn't normal.

And he'd thought about his *mother* tonight for the first time in years.

A creaking noise echoed from the stairwell. He stopped playing and snapped open his eyes.

As if conjured from his thoughts, the flesher girl stood at the top of the stairwell, looking as shocked to see him as he was to see her. She was frozen in place, her arms held out almost defensively. Her thick hair, more golden than red in this light, had been pulled back from her face into a messy knot, but clumps of it had already escaped the binding, framing her face in a gilded halo. A look of guilt puckered her lips and widened her eyes.

Or maybe that was surprise, though he doubted it. Everything about her screamed she was up to no good.

"What are you doing up here?" he asked. His voice came out soft, almost sleepy, but she flinched anyway. Then she smoothed down her top, adjusted the too-big belt looping around her waist, and marched her way over to him.

"I heard a noise." Her attention drifted to the stars as she spoke, the tension inside her shoulders and neck melting away as she took in the panoramic views. "Is that . . . the Varyx nebula?"

He followed her gaze to the splash of violet-and-yellow gases in the distance. "Yes, with our intended route, this is the closest we'll get to it."

"Oh." Disappointment laced her voice, and she rocked back and forth on her heels. "Will you play some more?"

Strangely, he found he wanted to. A part of him wanted to show off, to prove that mocks were more than just soulless machines. Not that she'd ever said otherwise, but he saw it in the way she looked at him and his crew.

"I don't play for anyone but myself." He pulled his hands from the keys and pressed his palms to his thighs, hating his cowardice, but at the same time, relieved he had the strength to say no to her.

She shrugged, her stare lingering on the keys. "Okay."

The silence seemed to amplify as neither of them spoke. His heart raced, so loud he was afraid she would hear it and know she had this effect on him. Whatever that was.

A human effect he hadn't felt since his change.

She twisted to sit beside him, and his attention fell to the curve of her breasts beneath her shirt. He jerked his gaze away.

Why was he even noticing, when Lux had been practically naked just last week and he'd hardly batted an eye?

Somehow, the idea of real breasts—not the kind that came from a mold and were created from a perfect ratio of proportions—was different. They were a part of her. Something more intimate and personal.

Real.

His breath caught as she turned to him, her lips rougher than Lux's, still chapped from time spent in the pod. The bottom lip was full and dimpled.

Not a dimple, a tiny scar. Something never seen on another mock.

An odd sensation pulsed in his belly, and a moment passed before he realized what that sensation was. Somehow he'd forgotten what the human emotion of arousal felt like. The burning desire to feel the press of someone else's body. When he was a thirteen-year-old human boy, before his transformation, desire had been a constant force ruling his flesh, his mind. That emotion had made him stupid with need.

He tried to swallow but found his throat too dry. Fever crept along his skin, his body taut. For a stupid second, he could think of nothing but capturing that scarred bottom lip between his teeth. His hands pulling her into him—

"Captain?" she was saying, the offending, imperfect lip pushed out in annoyance.

"Y—yes?"

"Scoot over. If you won't play, then I will."

Talia tried to hide her annoyance at the captain's sour company as she sat beside him on the bench and began to play. She still hadn't forgotten what he'd done to her earlier—but somehow, the sound of the keys echoing through the dark metal halls of the ship had brought on a truce. Or, at least, softened her need to murder him while he slept. Which was good considering the gun weighing down her pocket.

Besides, he looked different. His usual irreverent, smug mask replaced by something darker. Something haunted . . . if mocks could be that complex.

But he *was* once human. Maybe that's what she saw when she first topped the stairs and spied him hunched over the piano as if it were a piece of driftwood and all the world around him a raging sea. Perhaps, up here, the last vestiges of his humanity still lingered inside. A shadow of the flesh-and-blood boy he once was.

She felt him watching her as she played, no doubt frowning on her stiff fingers and poor technique. Her tutors claimed she would never make a good pianist. Or violinist. Oboist. She'd failed at all the instruments in epic fashion. Undisciplined, they'd said. Too loose. Not enough practice. No natural skill.

All of it was true. Yet she didn't care about any of that as she danced her fingers over the keys to her own song. After a few minutes, the tempo got lost and she trailed off.

"What was that?" Will asked. He'd pushed himself as far back from her as possible so that half his butt was off the bench.

"I don't know. I made it up." She shrugged. "Yours?"

The question seemed to catch him off guard, the muscles beneath the smooth flesh of his jaw tensing as he hesitated. "My mother's."

She lifted her eyebrows. "Your mom wrote that? It's beautiful."

Talking to a mock about moms seemed strange, but Talia had to remind herself he wasn't born a mock. So that meant he had a mother.

He blinked and looked down at his hands. Perfect half-moons adorned his well-kept fingernails, and she found herself wondering if that was his human side or mock side. Were those long, adept fingers created in a lab, or did they come from one of his parents?

"What happened to you?" she asked, curiosity overcoming her usual habit of not prying. "Leo told me you used to be . . . like me. Human."

An infinitesimal tremor rippled across his mask of indifference, so quick she could have made it up.

"That was a long time ago."

Part of his hair had fallen over his forehead, a shade darker than his usual mahogany color beneath the starlight. She studied his face, his heavy-blue eyes and sharp cheekbones, so much like the boys she knew at home. Did he still feel human emotions like she did, or was his every reaction a derivative of his programming?

His lips drew her attention. Her intended, Prince Cassius, had a cruel mouth, but Will's was constantly half-quirked, as if he knew a secret.

"Done with your assessment?" he asked quietly.

She laughed, shaky like a butterfly, and wiped her palms on her pants. "No, I'm wondering how much of your actions are programming versus human emotions. Like, if I kissed you right now . . . would it be your mock side or your human side that responds?"

His Adam's apple bobbed down his pale throat. "Try it and we can find out."

"No—I didn't mean I wanted to kiss you." She waved her hand for emphasis, but that only made her feel sillier, her core heating from embarrassment.

Why did I mention kissing him?

"Right." He drummed his fingers over his thigh. "An escort with standards."

"That's not fair. And I didn't mean . . . Look, never mind, okay?"

"Fine. And, for the record. I'm all mock." He rapped his knuckles against his temple, the metal beneath making a sharp *clack*. "And proud of it."

"Why?" she scoffed, before realizing how rude it sounded. "I mean . . . wouldn't you rather go back to being real?"

"Real? You mean enslaved by my emotions? Wracked with near-constant hunger and fatigue? My flesh bruised and torn and my muscles aching all the time? Tiny invisible germs making me so ill I'm puking my guts up every other week?

Yes, I want to go back to that."

"It's not all that bad."

He stared into the stars, his jaw set. "Isn't it?"

Rolling her eyes, she jumped to her feet, knocking the bench back a few inches. "Goodnight, Captain."

"Sweet dreams, flesher." The arrogant mask she despised was back, his focus on the piano keys. As if she were insignificant. Nothing more than a minor annoyance to shoo away. "Just so you know," he added. "Tomorrow we'll be docking on the off-world planet, Oberon, where I suspect your lie about being an escort will fall to pieces. Last chance to tell the truth . . ."

Turning on her heel, she made a rude gesture with her middle finger and stormed out the door. Little did Captain Egopants know that soon she'd be rescued and done with them all.

CHAPTER 18

Talia

Breakfast came around, a sad mixture of slop not fit for a mock, much less a human. Talia pushed away her bowl, too excited to eat. By now the reinserted tracking chip should have done its job. Only a few more hours and she'd be on a shuttle back to her family.

Only a few more hours until freedom.

Rays from planet Oberon's sun filled the bridge with warm, yellow light. The planet itself was a blue-and-white sphere of snow and ice, parts of it glittering as dawn broke over this side of their world. As the ship neared, she could make out the gray granite mountains that covered the wintry world.

Oberon was an off-world planet, colonized by a Starchaser centuries ago for the water trapped inside its massive glaciers. From this distance, the dark, metallic ice-haulers looked like ants on a hill. Convoys of them formed spider-webbed lines of gray against the pure white.

As Odysseus approached, a sleepy city of pale stone houses appeared on the other side of a mountain range, clumped around a boot-shaped lake. A silver semi-translucent screen of ice covered the surface, but the ice couldn't hide the indigo-blue waters hiding below. Orange light from the rising sun glinted off the rows of solar panels used to heat the town to acceptable temperatures. A near-invisible habitat shield domed the entire city, and every so often the light hit just right, sending rainbows rippling down the shield's surface.

She glanced out the starscreen at the crowded airspace, cargo transport shuttles hovering around as the crew waited to be cleared for landing. The Odysseus maneuvered through the bulky airships with ease, until it neared a thick cluster of obsidian, snow-capped mountains.

Static filled the air as Leo spoke into the com. "Drake, we cleared for landing?"

"Hanger at the base of the smallest peak," came a gruff voice. "Make it quick. Flight enforcers are up my ass these days."

Leo chuckled. "Quick as a virgin on his first time." He shot Talia an apologetic glance. "Sorry."

Grinning, she said, "I've heard worse, Leo."

Which was true. The royal guards used to say horrible things when they thought she couldn't hear. And the flight school students were even worse.

"Right," Leo said. "You're a . . . a . . ."

"Escort?" Lux offered, raising an eyebrow and glancing from Talia to Leo. "That the word you're choking on, Leo?"

Will snorted. "Guess we'll find out soon, won't we?"

Talia cut her eyes at him. "Oh, we will."

They'd all find out the truth of her identity after the Alliance ship tracked them here. She was a little shocked it hadn't already, but perhaps the rescuers were waiting until the Odysseus docked before attempting Talia's extraction.

Stars, if only she could see Will's face when he realized he'd been taunting a Starchaser princess.

The illegal hangers were expertly hidden behind the mountain range, cast in deep shadow and muted by a raging blizzard. White, snow-covered tarps camouflaged the roofs, making them blend in with the rest of the landscape. If not for the crew outside, bundled in their white coveralls and furs and waving flares, she'd have never even noticed the secret docks.

Snow flurries filled the air, blinding the crew for a moment as Will guided the Odysseus beneath the hangers. His landing was so soft she didn't realize they'd touched down until the others stood. Leo conjured white-and-gray camo snowsuits from somewhere, and they suited up. Everyone but Talia and Leo.

"Where's ours?" she asked, wrapping her arms around her chest. Already the air was cooling. Sometimes she swore they forgot she was human and susceptible to the cold.

Will finished zipping up his suit and turned to her, his grin apparent even beneath the wool facemask that would protect his synthetic skin. Apparently even mocks had to worry about frostbite. "You stay here."

Her mouth fell open. "What? Why? No, I need to get off this ship for a few hours. I need—"

"You need to stay here with Leo," Will interrupted in a voice that told her not to argue. He finished slipping on his gloves and fixed her with a defiant stare. "Unless you want to save us some trouble and tell us who you are and why Xander wants you?"

She was fully prepared to argue, until he mentioned her lie. Shutting her mouth, she ground her teeth and looked pleadingly at Leo. "Surely we can walk around and stretch our legs?"

"In this weather?" Guilt flashed across his face, and he looked away. "We'll, uh, play cards or something while we wait. It'll be fun."

Scowling, she watched the others leave, trailing their forms across the snow-packed ground until the blizzard swallowed them whole. Then, for the hundredth time, she flicked a quick glance over the tracking chip. Still there. A dim blue light flashed around the tracker slot, where before, it'd been empty and red.

What if her rescuers couldn't find her in this blizzard?

Leo scoured a rack until he pulled out some holo-dice game Talia vaguely recognized playing with Tamsin once, and asked if she wanted to play. She obliged, but Talia couldn't focus on anything but the sounds from outside, straining to make out noises that indicated another ship was docking.

Leo sat the cup they used to shake the die upside down on the table and then leaned back. "You okay, Ailat?"

She blinked; this was the first time he'd used the name she'd given them. "Yeah, just a little stir crazy." Not a lie. "Wish we could have gone with them."

"No, you don't. It's freezing out there. Besides, they're just grabbing supplies. You'd be bored to tears."

She shrugged. "Will's also trying to find out about me. Prove I'm lying."

Uncrossing his massive legs, Leo leaned forward, resting his elbows on his knees as he peered at her. "Are you?"

Her heart skipped a beat. "No. Why would I lie?"

"I don't know." He quirked an eyebrow. "Maybe if you thought the truth was dangerous."

The sudden intensity added to his usually playful tone made her sit up straight. As she did, the revolver inside her pocket shifted, reminding her of the weapon's presence. "Dangerous?"

"Yeah." He tugged at one of the braids woven into his hair. "Although sometimes people's reactions will surprise you."

What was he implying? She leaned in closer. "I don't understand."

"I'm just saying that, if you wanted to tell me, I might not react the way you think."

All the moisture in her mouth disappeared. Was he saying he knew her secret and she could trust him? Or maybe—maybe he was trying to trick her into talking. She wanted to trust him, but trust in Ailat is what led Talia here, or rather trusting in her own judgment of her mock.

Before she could make a decision, the com crackled to life, and they both jumped. The man, Drake, from earlier spoke. "Leo, an unscheduled arrival just landed nearby. They're at the main starport."

Leo jumped from the table and grabbed the handheld com, pressing it close to his face. "Yeah, so?"

"It's full of *hunters*. That wasn't part of the deal. Is there something you forgot to tell me?" Whatever hunters were, they couldn't be good by the way Leo stiffened and Drake's voice trembled with fear and maybe a bit of rage. "Buddy of mine says they're asking about the Odysseus."

Leo's voice was heavy and breathless as he asked, "Would

this ship be a sleek Darkstar carrier named Athena?"

"The one and only."

"How . . ." Leo mumbled to himself, palm pressed against the console and head hung low. "There's no way they could—" He knelt and glanced at the tracker compartment emanating with blue light, and a heavy sigh escaped his mouth. Into the com he replied, "Have your friend stall them as long as possible."

"You can't stall Hunters! They have spotter-drones and—"

"I owe you one." Leo clicked off the com.

Talia had the gun out of her pocket and pointed at his chest by the time he turned around. He didn't seem surprised and merely jerked his chin at the tracker.

"That was you?"

"I'm sorry." She grabbed one of the extra snowsuits and one-handedly slipped it on, the gun remaining level as she hopped on one foot like a lunatic. "This isn't personal."

"I don't think you understand," he said, taking a step away from the gun. "The people tracking us aren't here to help you. And now Xander's hired hunters to find you, the idiot."

"Hunters?" Talia asked.

"Ruthless mercs, best money can buy. Also dangerous and as apt to kill you as take you in, but Xander must be desperate."

Putting Leo back in the gun's range, she zipped up her snowsuit—about a million sizes too big—and wrangled a fur-lined white hat over her head. "You're lying."

"And you look ridiculous, *Princess*."

She froze, breath lodged in her throat. He was guessing. Trying to distract her or confuse her until the others came back. Pocketing a pair of clunky, metal-framed sunglasses, she strode backward toward the door. "Thanks for being kind, Leo."

Then she whipped around and ran, her boot steps echoing through the ship. When she got to the portside door, she slammed the red button to operate the lift, hardly waiting for it to open before rolling under the door and onto the ramp.

Snow blasted her in the face, stinging her skin and burning her eyes. She took off blindly, not waiting to see if Leo was behind. Arctic air became ice shards inside her lungs the farther she traveled in the sea of white, speckled here and there by a few sleek gray ships. Talia fumbled with the gun with numb fingers as she lumbered through waist-high snowdrifts.

Near the lip of the hanger sat three snow-crawlers, half-hidden beneath a blue tarp slapping in the wind. Thank the cosmos, someone had left the keys inside the middle crawler. As she slid on the back and it rumbled to life, she released a deep sigh of relief.

One step closer to freedom. She knew from the path of their landing earlier that town was just east of here. A mile, maybe. The docking station would be somewhere close, near the hub of the city, she guessed. Already, her hands were red and frozen stiff—a death sentence if she had to stay in this heap of metal without heat very long.

But as soon as she entered town, she'd find the closest human and tell them everything. Then while she warmed by the fire and sipped hot tea, the authorities would arrest the rebels.

A pang of guilt hit her. Leo didn't deserve incarceration. But . . . he had to know the risks of being a rebel, especially kidnapping a human and then docking on a human settlement.

She guided her snow-crawler over the frozen tundra. White circles rimmed her vision where snow had crusted her eyelashes. Up ahead, through the unrelenting blizzard, she spotted the shimmer of the habitat dome. Sheets of white powder sloughed off the invisible convex wall, collecting at the bottom in thick piles.

Passing through the dome was like breaking through a giant soap bubble. As soon as she was inside, the wall reformed, leaving only a glimmering trace of where she'd entered. Warm air, heated by the solar panels and trapped inside the dome, stung her half-frozen cheeks and brought life back to her aching fingers.

Thick grass covered the ground, so she discarded the snow-crawler and went on foot. As she trekked up the rocky hill, red-roofed houses rose in the distance. The town was set inside a natural basin between mountains and hills, most of the houses blanketing the hillside. Farther down sprawled the main square and a smattering of businesses. Other than a massive stone church situated on an island in the middle of the frozen lake, the town was unremarkable. No signs of sedition or rebel infestation.

What settler town is this? At some point in life, she'd been forced to learn the name—a Sovereign knows every city under her care, no matter how small or unimportant.

Failed that one.

Out of breath, she jogged to the first house and pounded on the wooden door. One hand stayed wrapped around the gun inside her pocket—just in case the rebels found her before she could get help. Then there were the hunters mentioned by

Leo on the Odysseus. According to Drake, the guy on the other end of the com, they had spotter-drones of some kind and something else. Unfortunately he hadn't finished before Leo cut him off, so Talia had no idea what else she was up against.

Hopefully she wouldn't have to figure it out.

The small, round eyehole in the thick door filled with darkness. Shuffling sounded behind the door before it parted a few inches with a creak. A little girl peeked her blonde head out, and her pale-gray eyes widened as they assessed Talia.

"Mom!" the girl called.

Talia took a step back, looking both ways down the street to make sure no one was watching. Sometimes, people got a bit excited when they met her, and she didn't want her royal status to overwhelm the occupants of this house, not when she was in so much trouble. They didn't have time for that.

More shuffling. A woman cautiously poked her head out, her dark-brown hair pulled back into a bright-blue scarf. She had kind eyes and a round face, and she wore a dough-caked apron, as if she'd been in the middle of cooking.

"Yes?" Impatience tinged the woman's voice.

Not the welcome Talia expected, but the woman probably didn't recognize the princess in these clothes. Talia cleared her throat and prepared to identify herself. Then the woman brushed a fallen lock of hair back from her neck, revealing a port.

Talia's hand tightened on the gun. "Is your master here?"

She couldn't seem to catch her breath, but she blamed it on the high altitude.

"Master?" Something flashed across the woman's face, and she pushed the little girl back, her eyes narrowing as they dropped to Talia's wrists. "Where's your mark, flesher?"

The door flew open, and before Talia could move, the mock captured Talia's wrist inside. *What's happening?* She tried to yank her arm away, but the mock kept her fingers clamped tight.

The gun! Talia fumbled for it with her free hand. As soon as she brought it up, the mock let go and stumbled backward.

"Call the enforcers!" she hissed. "This human has a weapon."

A flash in Talia's periphery drew her focus to a stout bald man walking around the porch. He was shiny with sweat, his sleeves were rolled up, and he carried a splitting axe in his large hands. Two red, metallic cuffs shackled his wrists.

Despite his size, something in his face reminded her of a beaten dog. Still, she was more concerned with his neck, smooth and *portless*.

He was human.

Thank the cosmos. He could help.

"I am Talia Starchaser, Sovereign-in-Waiting, and I've been kidnapped by rebels," she called, trying to keep the relief from her voice. "This woman must be one of them."

Lines creased his forehead as he looked from her to the mock.

The mock woman scoffed, obviously not impressed with Talia's announcement. "I command you to apprehend this flesher. Be quick about it and I might even share a few credits from the reward with you."

Reward? Had the Odysseus's crew sent out information about Talia already? So other rebels would be on the lookout for her?

She didn't have time to ponder as the man raised his axe

and set off toward her. Traitor! If not for the limited supply of bullets, Talia might have shot him.

Gun in hand, she leapt off the porch and landed in a sprint, eating ground as she half-tumbled half-slid down the side of the hill toward the town. Rocks gouged through her padded suit and into her ribs, but she hardly felt the pain.

Safety waited down there. Safety and freedom.

She was halfway down the mountain when a red streak whizzed by her cheek and exploded near her head. Rock shrapnel burst the air, and red-hot pain lanced the right side of her face. Stunned, she brought two fingers up to her temple. They came away bright red.

The mocks were shooting at her.

CHAPTER 19

Will

The Hall of Memories was a crumbling building of moss and beige stone, preserved from another century. Even if Will didn't already know the building was pre-mock era, he could have guessed it by the attention taken to the details. Gothic arches and sharp spires ended in ornamental finials above stained-glass windows and dramatic cloisters. A long-abandoned garden had overgrown the grounds and honeysuckle and trumpet vines wound themselves around the decorative columns.

Only humans labored needlessly on such trivialities— although a part of Will was glad they had.

Inside, an iron chandelier caked with rust hung from high arches. Glass vaults, each containing a floating holo-book, filled the enormous room. Not a speck of dust drifted inside the slants of light, a testament to the cleanliness of the monks who preserved the books stored below.

If he searched his history's programming through the human-led eras, he'd see this place was once a church, rebuilt by settlers to match an earthen church from their home and one of the few left in the known galaxies. But he didn't need to look it up; his mother had told him everything about this place. How, after humanity's defeat, the mocks let this place stay untouched. A token to keep the human slaves from revolting.

As one of the flesher monks strolled by, he pinned Will and his crew with a curious stare, seeming to float inside his coarse brown robes. Probably not many mocks came inside this hallowed shrine of human history.

"Tell me again what we're looking for?" Lux asked. Her green eyes squinted against the amplified solar-flare light pouring in from one of the arched windows and glinting off the countless vaults.

"The symbol from the pod. I drew you a picture?"

"Right." She flicked a skeptical gaze around the room. "And we have one hour?"

"Actually a little less, now."

She crossed her arms. "Tell me again why we can't just sell her to one of the ice-trawler crews and be done with her?"

"Because," Will said, speaking slow and deliberate—his crew were like children sometimes who needed orders repeated constantly. "I'm the captain, and I said no. Now, let's start in the center. If you look closely, you see the vaults make the shape of six octagons fitted inside one another. If we start with the center octagon, we can work outward."

"Fascinating," she said as she stalked off, muttering, "Should have went with Jane and Dorian for supplies."

Will found himself smiling as he watched Lux weave through the vaults. The navigator was stubborn to a fault. If he ever had a sister, he'd want her to be just like Lux, minus the criminal leanings. Maybe the whole crew could buy back their status if all went as planned.

No, they'd probably squander their chances. Not Will, though.

A sense of urgency thrummed his bones as he found a vault in the center. The label read 2742 AD-2842 AD. His programmed histories told him that was nine hundred eighty-nine years ago. The same year a group of earthens left their planet on the Columbus Explorer searching for a new home.

The First Settlers was etched across the front of the holo-book in glowing blue letters. Hidden somewhere deep below the ground in steel, climate-controlled vaults were the original books. He used the simplistic buttons just below the glass to turn the holo-pages, and it took him less than a minute to blow through the book. There was nothing inside about a symbol like the one on the pod, just an overly detailed account on the life of the first settlers on the Columbus, including pictures.

The next vault was 2842 AD-2942 AD. He groaned under his breath as he recounted more of the same. Settlers adjusting to life on the Columbus. Giving birth. Planting gardens that kept dying. Dying themselves. Other than a failed bid for power by one of the earthen families, and a brush with a black hole, nothing of importance happened.

By the next tome, at least, they'd discovered Calisto, the first of the Seven. A picture of the planet and its two moons popped out at him. After that, the histories became more engaging, but not by much. He was flipping through pages fast, his mind in rapid-uptake mode, when something jolted him back into the present.

A crest of some sort. The creature was elegant, its wings spread inside a circle with bright dots connecting it—a constellation. The words below read: the Starchaser Family crest.

This had to be the symbol from the pod. The sharp lines of it were nearly identical, although the one in the book was a painted version with more colors and dimension.

After that first instance, he found the symbol everywhere. On scrolls. On coins. It seemed anything a symbol could be put on, the Starchaser family did. He barely blinked as he plowed through nearly six hundred years of intergalactic politics and intrigue, all of it involving the Starchaser family in one way or another.

How had he never heard of them? Someone obviously scrubbed their history from the broadnet, but why?

Lux shouldered up to him, bouncing on her toes. "I found something."

"Me too." He flipped another page, ignoring her as he concentrated. They were nearly out of time, and he had no idea how the symbol accounted for the girl.

"The symbol—"

"Lux, I know all about the Starchaser crest, but I don't know how we connect it to the flesher girl. And I won't ever know if you keep interrupting me."

"Well, I know her name's not Ailat."

"We all knew that." Will tore his eyes from the holo-page. "Did you find anything useful?"

Lux's face beamed. "C'mon, idiot. I'll show you."

Will's physiological response to excitement was set to only fire during extreme duress or pleasure. Yet his mouth was dry and his palms dripped with sweat as he followed Lux to the vault near the outer rim.

"I researched Ailat, since the girl used her name," Lux explained, talking fast. "I figured there must be some connection. I mean, obviously we knew the girl we found in the pod isn't Ailat. Pod girl's name is Talia."

His mouth went dry as he squinted at the picture of Talia standing on a stage beside a handsome man, her shoulders back and chin held high. The sight of her was like a shock of electricity storming through him. A crown glittered atop her head, her gown a mesmerizing, low-cut ensemble he imagined only queens wore. But something about her face, the twist of her bottom lip and unfocused stare, was at odds with her haughty, confident pose.

A dark-haired girl dressed similarly sat at the couple's feet on the stage, terror filling her wide eyes.

"That's Ailat," Lux explained, tapping the glass just above the fallen girl. "It says on the previous page she was Talia's junior mock, can you believe that? They were going to kill her as part of some cruel flesher engagement ceremony, but somehow she escaped."

"That doesn't sound like the girl on our ship. Are you sure it's her?"

"Of course." Lux's voice wavered, her gaze lingering on the true Ailat. "I knew about all the horrible things they did to us, but . . . it's hard to believe that was only a hundred years ago."

Will nodded. From the date on the vault, this was near the end of the rebellion, when the virus scare had humans turning against all mocks, even innocent ones. Atrocities committed during that time were enough to affect someone as tough as Lux . . .

Wait. This was from a hundred years ago.

He squinted at the picture again. "But, *how*?"

"You mean, how do we have a century's old princess on our ship, who, by the way, is supposed to be dead?"

"Dead?"

"Long story. And *I* vote we ask her." She glanced around, then took out one of her blasters and smacked the butt-end into the vault. A spiderweb of cracks spread out over the glass. As it shattered around them, she reached inside and plucked the tiny holo-disc sitting at the bottom. "For evidence."

A monk came rushing over, his robes flying around his legs. He froze at the sight of the broken glass.

"Sorry," Will said. The holo-books were only electronic versions of the real thing, but they were expensive to replace, and these people had nothing. "I'll find a way to repay you."

Two more monks had gathered to stare, but they wouldn't be a problem. There was no reason for them to carry weapons. Will took a step toward the door, his boots crunching the glass, when a droning whir outside made him pause. He cocked his head just as a shadow flashed across the window.

Lux paused from dusting glass off her jacket and glanced up. "What the bloody stars is that?"

Before he could respond, an explosion outside rocked the walls and sent loose pebbles raining to the floor.

CHAPTER 20

Talia

For most of Talia's life, being exceptional in a crowd of people was expected. Today, it was going to get her killed. She nicked a lavender-and-green shawl from a stall on the fringes of the marketplace and wrapped the fabric tightly around her head. She'd escaped down the mountainside and lost the mocks shooting at her—along with her hat—but finding her again wouldn't take them long.

Now that the sun had risen and people had eaten breakfast, the town was bustling. She slipped down an alley and paused on the other side. The door to the building said this was a credit exchanger. But as soon as she opened the glass door and saw the line inside—every one of them mocks—she darted down the street.

She tugged the shawl down to her eyebrows, even though she looked foolish and was probably only bringing more attention to herself. Her heart skipped along her ribs. Most people would have their mock attendants out running errands, so she was bound to see a few. But how could she know which ones were rebel sympathizers?

Near the shores of the frozen lake, a ramshackle fish market was set up. The tang of the oily scales cleaned from flesh permeated the air, and Talia doubled over to catch her breath. Why couldn't she have chosen a cleaner place to suck in air?

Ignoring the repeated offers of a lovely street dish made with fish guts and eyeballs, she worked to clear her mind. Her current don't-get-shot plan wasn't going to cut it. Obviously rebels were entrenched here, so she couldn't ask just anyone for help. But nearly all the residents were bundled against the morning chill, their necks hidden. If she'd been smarter, she would have already found the rescue ship.

She doubled back around the north side of town, panting from the exertion, despite the chilly air. A few residents cast curious glances at her snowsuit. No one inside the habitat wore anything heavier than a wool cardigan. As soon as she found a deserted alleyway, she slipped inside. The zipper made it to her waist when a sound stopped her. She strained to listen. In the distance, a soft whir filled the sky.

Something about it sent shivers scraping down her spine. At the corner of the alleyway, she held a hand over her eyes to shield against the solar lights and peered up.

Five metallic spheres the size of winter melons glinted across the crisp blue holo-sky. The buzzing grew louder as the drones dove in a concerted formation, hovering just above the streets.

Hunters. Drake's voice on the com replayed in her head. They tracked using spotter-drones and . . . what? He hadn't finished his sentence.

One of the spotter-drones dipped low. The residents parted

beneath it, some trying to hide, others covering their mouths with their hands. *They were terrified.* Red lasers shot from the drone over the people, scanning their faces. Whenever the lasers fell over someone, the person would freeze, trembling.

A metallic flash near the corner of the opposite street caught Talia's eye. A moment passed before she made sense of what she saw. The gunmetal-gray droid was taller than any human, its body warped to resemble a hulking man. Muscles of carbon and steel twisted as the droid walked, each footstep like thunder. And instead of eyes, one red circle glowed in the middle of its black head.

The way its humanoid head tilted, it seemed the droid was somehow connected to the drones flying above.

"Hunter," she whispered in a voice part awe part terror. Everything about it was created to inspire fear.

Stars. Leo was right. The Coalition would never use these monstrosities. Meaning the starship chasing the Odysseus wasn't here to rescue her.

They were here to *kill* her.

Skittering noises, like metal on metal, drew Talia's attention back to the hunter. She gasped and clapped a hand over her mouth to muzzle a scream as spiderlike metal creatures the size of dogs swarmed from the hunter's chest and overran the streets. One creature stood on its back four legs, two legs held in the air, and sniffed.

Her father used to hunt in the dense woods of the winter planet where they spent their holidays. Because of those precious few moments with her family, she knew hunters always had two things: spotters and trackers.

The other piece to that puzzle was the prey.

Of course, *she* was the prey.

The spider-dogs sniffing the air froze and then dropped down into a rigid stance, one leg pointed up in her direction.

Crap. She spun around and darted through the alleyway. Time for a new plan.

Talia had always been remarkably good at thinking under pressure, and by the time she burst into the street on the other side of the alley, knocking down a reedy man selling fruit, she remembered seeing crafts parked at some of the larger houses near the mountain. If she could make it there, perhaps one would be space-worthy.

Bright-green apples tumbled across the cobblestone streets, and the man she'd knocked down cursed at her.

"Sorry," she huffed, launching over him and straight into a crowd of people.

A wooden stage full of people milling about stood before her. The first thing she noticed were the thick, corroded chains circling their ankles. The very idea incensed her. Why were they chained? A man stood at the podium, whacking his gavel the way she'd seen some toddlers do their toys.

She should have been fleeing the hunters. But something about this spectacle seemed important. Like the answer to a puzzle in the back of her mind.

Were they selling mocks? Her hands clenched into fists at her sides. The poor things had been ill-treated, by the look of their shabby clothes and dirty faces.

A proper mock auction would be held behind closed doors, allotting them dignity.

"All right, on to the next one." The announcer's voice poured from the drone amplifiers flitting around the heads of the spectators. "Flesher B57215."

She sucked in a sharp breath. *Humans are on the stage?* As the pieces began falling into place, she scoured the necks of the crowd. Many had removed their jackets and scarves, exposing ports.

Mocks were selling humans?

Behind her, metallic clacks sounded off the buildings. She glanced back and immediately wished she hadn't.

The spider-dogs were scampering after her over the walls of the buildings.

Breaking out of her fog, she plunged through the crowd. A woman cried out, and someone yelled, "One's escaped!"

Everything after that was a blur of buildings and people. Yells and the occasional scream marked the location of the hunters and their creatures, but the crowded slave market must have masked her trail.

Slave market. She pushed the words deep, *deep* down to ponder later when she wasn't running for her life. In a stupid, heavy-as-sin snowsuit.

She pushed on. Her breaths became ragged gasps, her footfalls in time with her racing heart. Fire burned through her lungs and into her arteries.

You're a Starchaser. You welcome pain.

Her body disagreed, but it wasn't her master. *Keep pushing!*

Circles of gold flashed across the pavement around her feet—light reflecting off the drones. She could feel them right behind her. Closing in. The buzzing grew louder until it seemed to vibrate inside her bones.

No matter how scared she was, how close the sounds got, she didn't look back.

Keep going. Keep going. Keep going.

The houses near the base of the mountain came into view. The first several were smaller ramshackle homes surrounded by collapsing stone fences and junked-out hovers. She scanned the yards as she ran, looking for a star-worthy vessel. A few cloud-gliders, lower atmosphere vessels unprotected against the extremes of the upper atmospheres, appeared beneath their corrugated tin ports. Once she broke 70,000 feet in altitude, the lack of a proper oxygen supply in the ship would kill her within minutes. If she wore an oxygen pack, the cold would take her out.

Space was an unforgiving host.

All at once, her body felt too heavy, filled with rocks and lead. Her muscles trembled, her lungs burning. The Starchaser motto and her adrenaline could only do so much for her body, still weak from time in the pod.

Something streaked past, as fast as lightning, and a shudder ran through her as she faced what she first thought was a drone that had fallen to the ground. The thing was curled into a circle, rolling impossibly fast. It stopped with the quickness of a machine, transforming back into its original, terrifying arachnid shape. Spider-dog. Calling it that felt silly, but the machine's face was canine shaped, with a long metal snout. Four red eyes, two on each side, watched her with a look of intelligence that clenched her gut.

Without a second thought, she whipped out her gun, pulled back the hammer, and pulled the trigger.

Nothing.

The spider-dog cocked its head; she swore realization dawned on its robotic face. Then she pulled the trigger again. This time, it did what it should have done in the first place.

Blew the bastard's head off.

It also bruised her eardrums and recoiled so hard she nearly dropped the gun.

An unearthly shriek pierced the air. Still holding the weapon out like a bomb, she turned to see the pack of spider-dogs closing in, followed by a hunter. Each giant step he took gobbled up ten feet. Above, the drones had converged into a tight unit barreling down on her—a shiny spear of death.

If the hunter had spoken, perhaps commanded her to give herself up, she might have done it. But the thing just kept coming. A machine hell-bent on capturing its prey. And its lack of humanity sent waves of terror washing over her.

The two little bullets left in her gun might as well have been duds at this point. Panicked, she pocketed the revolver and leapt over the stone fence, ducking behind one of the houses. The backyards were naturally fenced in by hedges and lemon trees, and she wound through the maze with a desperation unbefitting a princess. But her grandmother had never been hunted by spider-dogs and giant androids.

Through a patch of heavy foliage, she spied something silver. Further inspection found a long, cylindrical craft. An older model D-Class hauler.

Totally space-worthy.

Her throat was tight with hope as she approached the vessel. Some of the silver paint had chipped off, and the windshield could do with a good washing, but otherwise the craft looked in good condition. The door creaked open, and she almost kissed the cracked, dusty console as she spied the keys inside. Wiping the layer of muck off the dials, she said a silent prayer and turned the keys.

By the looks of her, Talia thought the ship would give her problems, but the cruiser started on the first try. "Someone loves you very much, don't they?"

A silver flash drew her eyes to the huge, curving windshield that wrapped around the front end. One of the spider-dogs had pounced on the glass, its pointed metal legs hooked into the surface. Tiny cracks spider-webbed out from the points. She swore the beast smiled at her as it slammed its head into the glass like a battering ram. Each loud thud made her flinch backward.

Airborne, Talia!

Thank the stars this part of her training was rote memory, because otherwise panic would have made it hard to remember the sequence of switches and buttons to engage. She jerked the cruiser up, her movements too choppy. *Easy. Just like you practiced.*

Her breathing stabilized as muscle memory took over, gliding the cruiser up in a smooth arc. Just as she cleared the lemon trees, the hunter burst through them, snapping four-foot limbs with explosive *cracks* that made her jump. The over-muscled droid looked a bit less intimidating with leaves and lemons dropping on its head. But only a little.

The spider-dogs on the ground leapt into the air, their enraged screeches making the hair on her arms stand on end. Those beasts would never lose their creepiness.

She grinned at the spider-dog still attached to her window, banging its idiotic head against the thick, translucent glass. Finally, it stopped and watched her with eyes too intelligent for comfort.

"You streaming this to all your buddies?" she yelled over the engine, glaring into its four eyes.

The beast cocked its head.

She flashed a grandmother-inappropriate gesture. "Send them this!"

Except Talia didn't need to send them anything, because the drones had caught up. Sunlight danced across their smooth shells as they formed a circle around her craft.

She needed to shake her new friends. Clenching her jaw, she dove into a steep dive, the metal steering wheel vibrating so hard her whole body shook. The alleyways between the buildings were just wide enough for her to scrape through, leaving an inch on either side of her wings.

Her instructors at the academy would have been proud of the way she threaded through alley after alley with the precision of a master seamstress. She lost the first drone as she banked right, beneath a stone bridge. The orange explosion the drone made reflected off the frozen river below.

"Gotcha!"

Another drone crashed into the corner of a bakery as she maneuvered a ninety-degree turn to the left. *That's two.*

Lifting to the skies, she set a path to the silver-blue frozen waters of the lake. A church stood smack in the middle of the lake, reminding her of some of the older castles she'd studied from Earth. She aimed the nose of her cruiser for just above the spires. On the other side more mountains rose up and kissed the sky, a good place as any to lose the last of her unwanted guests.

She was crossing over the pale, sandy shores of the lake when, on some signal she couldn't hear, all the drones fired at once.

Flashes of blue seared her eyes. The craft rocked and shuddered. Alarms pierced the din of explosions and splitting metal. She tried to maneuver away, but the drones shadowed her, half-hidden inside the oily-black smoke spewing from her engine. A well-placed shot cracked the windshield, somehow missing spider-dog still clinging to the center.

Not somehow—on purpose. These were machines thinking in tandem. Spider-dog smashed its head against the crack, each blow a splintering sound that settled in her gut. The steering wheel went loose in her hands. She no longer had control of the cruiser.

For a moment that seemed an eternity, they glided over the open skies on some invisible hand. And she thought maybe— maybe she would get out of this okay. Just glide to the ground and pop out unharmed. Then her belly hollowed out as the craft lost momentum and dropped, spiraling toward the icy waters.

The startling realization that she couldn't swim came just before she understood that fact was inconsequential. Most likely she'd be knocked unconscious or killed by the fall.

As the white ice closed in to meet her, spider-dog broke through the windshield and leapt.

CHAPTER 21
Will

The second Will broke through the doors of the church and glimpsed the craft partially submerged in the lake, he knew it had to do with the princess masquerading as an escort. *Talia.* Trouble followed her everywhere.

But he wasn't expecting to actually *spot* her inside the mangled cruiser, fighting with something dark and quick that thrashed inside the cockpit. Other than a few bright pops of her auburn hair, and the occasional curse, he couldn't tell who was winning.

Just as he adjusted his eyesight for binocular mode, a gunshot split the air, and the movement inside stopped. The princess was tougher than she looked.

Lux put up a hand to shield her eyes from the sun. "Is that . . . our princess?"

"So it's *our* princess now?" he muttered as he took off across the lake, his boots slipping on the ice. From his quick calculations, they had a minute before she sank. No more than two.

Beneath the glazed surface was blackness, like a watery version of space. The vessel was half-submerged inside a near-perfect circle, chunks of white ice scraping off the hull. Fissures shot out from the hole, making the ice near the crash unstable.

He adjusted his vision to zoom in on the cruiser. The mangled body of some type of robot creature lay half outside the hole in the windshield. He focused on the long, animalistic face. As the analysis in his programming ran a diagnostic on the creature, he looked deeper into the cockpit. Talia stood completely still, her eyes wide and white as snow, a ribbon of blood unspooling down her forehead. Her body trembled with shivers.

She was in shock. And trapped, judging by the way she struggled against the harness.

The diagnostic came back, a name and description flashing across his vision. Spotter Canis, belonging to a galaxy hunter.

Shit. Since when were hunters after her?

Lux caught up with Will, gracefully skipping across the ice and making his careful steps look clumsy in comparison. "What's the plan?"

"Plan?" he shot back. "I thought you had one."

"You're the captain!"

A crack sounded beneath their boots, and the ice split a foot ahead. They both dropped low and flat, crawling on their hands and knees to spread their weight. Shadows streaked across the ice, and Will's heart sunk as he looked up.

Drones.

"What are drones doing here?" Lux growled from ahead. She moved much quicker than he could.

"Hunters."

All it took was that one word, and she froze. Up until this moment, he could count on one hand how many times he'd seen Lux daunted. Her dark skin paled to match the gray of the ice, her breaths coming out in short puffs as she scrambled ahead. Afraid or not, she wouldn't back down.

The drones descended. They seemed unconcerned with mocks lurking about the crashed cruiser, instead flitting around the wreckage and scanning the vessel. The hunter—or hunters, if they were unlucky—wouldn't be far behind. One of the drones finally seemed to notice Will and Lux, and it buzzed over, hovering just above Lux's head.

"Aw, hell, no!" she yelled, lifting to one knee. She had two blasters, one for each hand. The drone moved to zip away, but she clipped it with two blasts. It hit the ice and skidded fifty feet across the lake, nothing left of it but a hunk of billowing smoke and metal.

Lux turned her blasters on the others, and red fire lit the sky. They swarmed around her, dodging her shots as they returned fire. She ducked and rolled, barely missing a volley of blasts. The ice where she'd been a second ago exploded into crystalline shards, dark water mushrooming up into the air.

"Not the best place for a fire-fight," Will scolded, dodging a blast so close it singed his skin. Then he brandished his own blaster. Lux had two because she liked to show off. But a true marksman only needs one.

Will took out two drones in less than a minute. Both hit the ice, hard, and smoldered, sending dark slivers of smoke into the air.

"Lucky shot!" Lux called, her tone calm and even, not the voice of someone waging warfare.

His snappy retort died on his lips as more drones thronged

the sky. They dove as one mind, barreling straight for them.

He was so focused on the drones he forgot about Talia. When he turned his attention back to the vessel, his body went cold all over.

Only the top of the cruiser was visible, bobbing just above the surface. Bubbles disrupted the top of the water. Then they stopped, and the vessel sank with a groaning sigh.

Stars, she was trapped. Will ripped off his snowsuit and kicked out of his boots, the chilly air stinging his skin. "Cover me."

"Let her go, Captain!" Lux pleaded. "There's too many."

That was the most rational decision, of course. Any other time he would have agreed to flee. But this time—this time he couldn't let go. Already the image of her fragile human body stuck inside that metal cage was eating him alive. He couldn't get to her fast enough.

As he teetered on the edge of the ice, overlooking the darkness, Lux called out one more time, "Will! Don't."

Any other day, the rare pleading in her voice would have made him listen. "If I'm not back up in one minute, leave."

He dove before he could hear her reply. The freezing water was like a punch to the chest, the cold wave enveloping him. After all that noise, the silence of the water was startling. His muscles went rigid. Frantic beeps sounded inside his head, and a temperature monitor popped up on his biometric vision. The warmth of his body was plummeting. Even mocks like him succumbed to water this cold. He needed to hurry.

Pushing past the initial shock, he swam deeper, following the receding light of the craft. The cruiser had settled on its side on the floor of the lake. A dim-yellow light filtered out from its interior. His ears popped as he reached the door handle and tried to pry it open. The door wouldn't budge. Lungs aching, he swam around to the front and darted inside.

Talia's white face and unblinking eyes resolved from the darkness. His heart clenched, but then her wide-eyed stare jerked his way, bubbles of oxygen escaping her purple lips and rising to the long bubble of air trapped at the ceiling.

She was alive.

She gestured to the harness pinning her to the pilot's seat. Silt and strands of her hair brushed over his face as he leaned close. The buckle was jammed. He retrieved his pocketknife and carefully slipped the blade under the harness to begin cutting. As he did, he noticed the sound of air leaving her lips stopped.

Hold on, Princess. He could hardly feel the knife handle beneath his fingers as he cut, sawing with a desperation he hadn't experienced in years. The thoughts floating around his brain went from the possibility of her dying, to the inevitably.

That cannot happen.

Her eyes began fluttering back into her head, and a rush of panic overwhelmed his systems. Finally the blade severed the first harness strap. The second one seemed harder to cut, or perhaps he was tiring. Slippery shadows nibbled at his vision. His body temperature was dangerously low, and his oxygen readout was blinking.

Not good.

Leave her, the rational side of him argued. *No bounty is worth dying for.*

He didn't know why he cared so much. Why the wretched human emotions he'd tried so hard to leave behind had suddenly reappeared. But there was no way in hell he was leaving her to die in this dark, lonely place.

The last strap gave way, and he slipped his arms under her armpits and kicked off the floor. As soon as their heads hit the air bubble trapped at the top, he filled his lungs with oxygen. Talia's eyes were half-rolled back, blue shadows clinging to the bone-white skin around her mouth. In this meager light, the wet hair pasting her skull was the same color as old blood.

"Breathe, Princess," he whispered, knowing full well the fear gripping his chest went beyond keeping her alive as a bounty and into different territory. "Please, just breathe."

CHAPTER 22

Talia

One second, Talia was trapped inside the cockpit, struggling against the straps of her harness as her body screamed for air.

The next, she was somewhere else. Somewhere dark and empty, a million pinpricks of light winking just on the edge of her vision. As if she'd fallen into a secret pocket of space. She was floating, the dress from her eighteenth birthday fanning out around her like spilled oil.

Ailat appeared. She was wearing her dress from the party—stars, she was beautiful—and she was smiling.

"How does it feel?" Talia's friend asked.

Talia stretched out her arm. Everything was foggy, like a mist enveloping her brain. The only thing she knew for sure was she hadn't seen her friend in forever and desperately wanted to touch her. As if, somehow, just holding hands with her junior mock again, laughing and whispering all the new things that had happened to them, might fix everything. "How does it feel to what, Ailat?"

Ailat's pupils began to glitch, her facing twisting into something horrible as she said, "Drown."

Gasping noises ripped Talia back to her body. She was sucking in air and clawing against something—Will. The dark shadows covered half of his face and made him look more severe than she was used to, but it was him, his normally tousled hair contorted at a crazy angle. His arms were tight around her, the solid muscles of his chest and stomach hard to ignore beneath his thin shirt. He could crush her to death if he wanted to.

Hopefully he didn't.

"You're hyperventilating." His voice was gentle but stern. "Slow, deep breaths."

Her first instinct was to fight Will, but images of him trying to free her popped into her brain. Besides, she could hardly feel her body. Then there was the fact she couldn't swim.

To survive she'd have to trust him.

"Where are we?"

"Bottom of a lake, fifty meters down. As soon as you're able, we should get to the surface."

Impatience was hidden beneath his gentle tone, and she barked out a pitiful laugh. "Just my luck. I can't swim."

He shifted her in his arms, and she swore they tightened— though with her body totally numb, it was hard to tell for sure. "Then I swim us both up."

"Fine . . . I can try to kick, if that helps?"

The corner of his mouth quirked. "No, just be still."

Right. She'd end up kicking him somewhere tender and

cripple him, and then they'd both drown.

"Okay. I'm ready." A lie—the idea of submerging her head into the black water sent her heart racing—but they had no choice.

"Quickly take three deep breaths," he commanded.

After her third gulp of air, his face lost its playful edge and she was dunked under the water without warning. She twisted to the side as they maneuvered out of the broken windshield. Then he came up behind her and circled his arms around her waist, and they began their ascent.

The hole in the ice appeared. Light streamed into the depths, slants of pale yellow that warmed her face and gave her hope. As they neared, lightning bolts of blue streamed across the ground of that other world, followed by explosions.

They surfaced just as a blast split the air. Propping his arm on the side, Will lifted her over the edge. She clambered the rest of the way herself, panting as her freezing limbs scraped over hard ice.

"Nice of you to join us!" Lux called. She stood with her legs planted wide, holding two blasters. Every time one of them went off, something silver fell from the sky.

The drones.

They littered the ice around Lux's feet.

Near the edge of the lake, three hunters waited. Talia cringed at the sight of the spider-dogs clumped in packs just ahead. They were all watching the battle unfold.

Talia got to her knees; she was too weak to stand. "What are they waiting for?"

"My blasters to die." Lux said it so matter-of-factly Talia thought she misheard.

"Take mine," Will offered. He'd climbed from the water, his jumpsuit clinging to his body.

Shocked, she tried not to stare at his slim waist and ropy muscles or remember the feeling of his flesh around her body as he carried her to the surface.

Not the best time to notice the mock captain has abs.

Lux pointed at a drone as it dove near her head and then tossed the weapon at the ground. "That *was* yours, Captain."

A sinking feeling came over Talia as she stared at the dead weapon lying on the ice. Then a strange whistling drew her attention to the hunters. The spider-dogs turned to their android masters, obviously waiting for a command.

All three hunters pointed a finger at Talia and her crew, and she hardly breathed as the spider-dogs erupted across the ice toward them.

Talia was impressed by how steady Will's voice was as he asked Lux, "How much charge is left in that one?"

"One percent," Lux said. "Two if the stars align and all the crap."

Will plucked the gun from her hand, and Lux whipped around. "What are you doing?"

"Go." His eyes were fixed on the oncoming pack, and he blew out a long breath. "Take Talia, and get to safety."

"Like hell—"

"That's an order, Navigator."

Talia expected Lux to argue, or crack some joke, but she set her shoulders and turned to Talia. "You heard the captain."

Talia staggered to her feet, glancing at Will. In a few moments, he would have to face those horrible creatures alone. The idea was more troubling than it should have been.

He was her captor. Yet he'd also saved her. He was a mock. But he played the piano better than any human she knew.

Before she could make up her mind, a gun-metal gray ship broke over the mountains and swooped down on them, raining fire over the pack. The blasts tore giant gashes in the ice and left the spider-dogs nothing more than mounds of scattered metal.

The tension from Will's shoulders melted away. "Leo!"

"That good-for-nothing bastard," Lux added. By the rare girly lilt of her voice, that was a compliment.

Talia had never seen the Odysseus from the outside. Any other time it would have seemed ugly, with its bulky core and corroded parts all patched together. But now—now it was the most gorgeous vessel she'd ever seen, and she found herself laughing as it landed gently at their feet.

"That's not Leo's flying," Will said. "Jane must be on board."

The ramp crashed open, cracking hard against the ice. Lux went to leap on board when something caught Talia's eye, a flash of metal just above. *Drone!* Lux was just starting to turn to face it, but she was too slow. On instinct, Talia grabbed the girl and dove, flinging them both to the ramp. At the same time, the ground where Lux had been standing lit up in flames.

Leo hit the drone with a blaster.

"Get off," Lux grumbled.

That was easier said than done, considering Talia's limbs were near-frozen and her snowsuit, swollen with water, made bending her knees and elbows almost impossible.

Leo lifted Talia up by the back of her collar, and Lux popped up, brushing off her hands and knees and cutting annoyed looks at Talia instead of *thanking* her.

Dorian appeared at the top of the ramp and tossed Will a fresh blaster. He flipped around to face the drones, walking backward as he fired. The sound of his well-aimed shots made a nice, safe little tempo as they boarded.

Leo's gaze kept sliding to Talia. She thought he might gloat, or make some stupid remark saying he was right about the hunters, but he simply nodded to her. "Glad you're okay."

Once the Odysseus was in the air and Talia knew she was safe, the adrenaline wore off and she nearly sank to her knees. Leo went to grab her, but Will was quicker, propping her up against his shoulder.

He led her to the engine room, and once inside, a wave of delicious heat washed over her. The numbness in her cheeks and fingers began to fade as she peeled out of her snowsuit. She turned to Will and found herself paralyzed. He was naked from the waist up, his dark-gray briefs clinging to his lower half and leaving little to the imagination. His core muscles tensed and rippled as he leaned over and shook out the water from his hair.

Once his skin was mostly dry, he turned his attention to her. "The heat won't work if you leave your clothes on."

"Yeah, my fingers are numb so—" Her words died as he approached and began unbuttoning her blouse, his bottom lip caught between his teeth as he worked. The middle of her shirt parted, and more goosebumps ridged her stomach.

He dropped his hand and turned his back, his gaze fixed on

the engines. "There. You can do the rest."

Frowning, she shrugged out of her shirt and rolled down her soggy pants. If she had any questions regarding his leanings—mock or human—they were answered. She'd been exposed, her breasts barely hidden behind a lacy bra, and not even a twitch disrupted his face. Her presence had no effect on him whatsoever. He was probably used to the perfection of mock bodies, and hers definitely didn't fit the standard.

Her body had always been athletic, but after she woke up from the pod, she was lean, every muscle showing beneath her skin. Her breasts were small, her curves pretty much nonexistent.

So much so, apparently, they inspired not even a flicker of reaction in Will.

That shouldn't have bothered her, but it did. Standing behind him with her arms crossed, she said, "Go. I'll be fine."

"You're positive?"

"Yep. I'm tougher than I look."

His shoulders shook as he chuckled. "I noticed." He hesitated before crossing to the door and glanced back at her. "I'll have Lux bring you more clothes."

"See if she has anything jewel-toned," she called after him. As soon as the door shut behind her, the pressure in the room felt a million tons lighter.

Now she needed to get dressed so she could put her thoughts in order and find an explanation for what she saw on that off-world planet.

CHAPTER 23
Will

Will sat in the bridge next to Jane—who was beaming after her solo flight—and tried not to think about the incident in the engine room as they discussed Talia's fate.

The way her chest shuddered when he unbuttoned her shirt, her stomach tightening. Had her breath caught from the air brushing against her bare skin, or had she reacted to something else?

Masking his reaction took every ounce of power he had left after the fight. The strength it took to keep his breathing steady and eyes on the wall behind her. Even with Talia in the other room, his hands twitched at the thought of touching her human flesh, and he kept them clenched in his lap like the traitors they were.

"Captain," Lux snapped, breaking Will from his thoughts. "The book."

He focused on the holo-screen in the middle of the room. The holo-book from the Hall of Memories hovered in the air, three times as big on the ship as it had been in the church. Under her direction, the pages flipped until they landed on Talia on her eighteenth birthday. Lux pushed play on the scene, and they watched in silence as Talia crossed the stage.

At the sight of her, Will's skin grew hot until he had to look away.

Leo inhaled sharply. "That's our girl."

It wasn't a question.

Will nodded. "That symbol on the pod is the Starchaser Dynasty crest. For unknown reasons, someone high up erased all traces of the Starchasers in the flesher histories."

Jane unfolded from her chair and approached the holo-book, her head tilted. "This date is from a century ago."

"So . . . she's over a hundred years old?" Dorian asked.

"No, silly," Lux answered, pausing the video. "The pod put her in cryosleep. Technically she's still eighteen." She pointed the remote at the holo-screen, and the pages turned to another scene. A massive starliner, bigger than any Will had seen before, filled the holo-screen. Stars glittered around it as the beauty sliced through space.

Everyone in the room gasped as a crack split the air and an orange fireball consumed the ship. Dorian cried out the loudest, and Lux watched him from the corner of her eye. Their parents were both killed on a mock carrier when Lux was only ten, and Dorian seven. Ambushed by fleshers. Watching something similar had to be hard.

Other than a muscle jumping in his jaw, the kid seemed unfazed, and Lux moved on, flipping more pages to the aftermath. "The description says all the Starchasers were destroyed on Insurrection-Day. Obviously now we know that's not true. But their supposed deaths were the turning point in our war, and the reason we're free and not still enslaved."

"So," Leo asked, tugging on one of his blond braids. "What do we do with her now?"

Lux shot Leo a withering look Will knew too well. "What kind a question is that? We take her to the queen. The bounty alone will buy back all of our jump privileges for an eternity."

"Bounty? Since when do supposed dead people have bounties?"

Lux scoffed. "No, Leo. *Before* they died, each member of the royal family had a bounty on their heads of fifty billion put on them by the rebels. By law, that bounty still stands."

"And what happens when we hand her over?" Leo asked, his brows gathered and arms crossed over his massive chest.

Leo's question hung in the air, and a long stretch of uncomfortable silence followed.

Lux jerked the remote at the holo-book, her movements emotional and angry. The scene from the princess's eighteenth birthday played again, except this time Lux let the whole thing unfold. Emotions Will hadn't felt in a long time surfaced as he watched Talia and her fiancé taunt her mock companion. The way Talia sneered, the pleasure she and the prince seemed to take in the poor mock's fear, didn't match the girl he saved in the water. But denying the evidence right in front of him was impossible.

"Is that someone you want to risk your lives for?" Lux paused to let her words sink in. "We can't protect her, and if we don't hand her in, Xander or someone else like him will." The video clicked off, and she set the remote down. "Her fate is already written in the stars, but ours isn't. Not yet."

Will hadn't planned on standing, but he found himself out of his chair. Those images of cruelty had dredged up haunted memories from his past—being beaten, broken, left for dead. Whatever he thought he felt for Talia, it was a lie. A failing of his humanness. And the logical answer was clear.

"Set a course for Calisto," he said, thinking of the young mock girl on that stage, confused and afraid. "We're taking the Starchaser Princess to the queen."

The second he was done speaking, he noticed someone standing just inside the doorway to the bridge, wearing an emerald-green jumpsuit. Talia.

A loud breath of air escaped him. "Princess."

Her bottom jaw was pushed forward, the way people do when they're trying not to cry. Instead of responding to her name, she approached the holo-book, slowly. Fists curled at her sides.

"They're dead?" Her voice was the same steely voice from the video. The one he didn't recognize. She blinked at the book, her eyelashes wet with tears he knew she wouldn't shed. "All of them?"

Oh, stars. A shiver of anguish shot through him. She didn't know.

Jane approached Talia, carefully. "All of them, Princess. I'm sorry."

She rested a hand on Talia's shoulder, but Talia absentmindedly shrugged it off. The holo-screen had manual functions, and she flipped the pages back to the day of her eighteenth birthday. He thought she might skip past the worst of it, but she watched everything, unblinking and quiet. Hardly breathing. Every so often her chest would heave and she'd drag in a ragged breath. Otherwise, she was completely still. Riveted to the scenes that would shape her life and future forever.

When she got to the destruction of her family's ship, a tiny shudder wracked her body. Her hands went out, as if for stability. Then she turned and, arranging her face into a cool, indifferent mask, marched out of the room like nothing happened.

Lux exchanged worried glances with him. If anyone understood what this moment felt like, it was her. Without meaning to, he set off to go after Talia, despite having no clue what to say.

"Wait!" Leo said. Will tried to brush him off, but Leo grabbed his arm. "Captain, something's wrong with the hyper-drive."

"What do you mean wrong?" Will hadn't meant to snap, but his nerves were on edge. And all he could think about was finding Talia . . .

Jane pulled up an image of their back flank. Countless pulsing lights lit up the starscreen.

"What is that?" Will asked, drawing closer. "What am I looking at?"

"Looks like a fire net," she explained. "By now it'll have fried most of our fuel coils and drained who knows how much power."

"The hunters." Leo sunk into his chair, the tightness in his jaw confirming the crap they were in. "They must have done it while the drone was shooting at Lux. Stars!" He kicked the bottom of the operating console with one of his fancy boots. "I should have checked our rear. I knew they wouldn't let us get away that easily."

And if Will hadn't been distracted inside the engine room with Talia, he would have noticed too. "We all missed it."

He slid into the captain's seat and then paused, glancing back at Lux. "Will you make sure she's okay?"

She raised a sharp eyebrow, but for the first time in her life, the fiery navigator didn't argue. "Yes, Captain."

Once she was gone, his focus shifted into problem-solving mode, and he was relieved to occupy his mind with fixing their dilemma instead of Talia's hurt expression. "All right, Dorian, go assess the damage. Jane, find me the closest Federation planet before Xander finds us sitting ducks. And, Leo?"

Leo flashed an eager smile. "Captain?"

"Stop looking so damn pretty and go extract that fire net before they track us here."

"Yes, sir."

CHAPTER 24

Talia

Talia didn't remember walking up the stairs to the uppermost glass room, or sitting at the piano. One minute she was watching the last moments of her family's life; the next, she was here. Surrounded by the stars that had witnessed it all.

She'd always loved deep space. Loved the feeling of being a part of something so much bigger than herself. Stars were romantic, magical. What the viewer saw was a beautiful illusion from thousands of years in the past.

Just like her life currently. She'd let herself believe the illusion that her family was still alive, because they were the gravity that kept her together, just like the gravity that holds together the brightest supernova. Without them . . . she was nothing.

A girl breaking apart.

Why wasn't she crying? She pounded her fist into the ivories, the sound bouncing off the glass. She yearned to fall into a ball of tears, to thrash and scream and curse the world. To mourn properly. But she couldn't even do that right.

I killed you. The words lodged in her throat. Her parents and grandmother. Her little brother—

Say his name. Maybe if she could just say it aloud, he

wouldn't be dead. An irrational idea, but somehow it made sense. "Tamsin. I just saw you. They say it's one hundred years later, but just yesterday we were playing games on the holo-screen, and I was winning. Remember?"

The silence stretched into minutes. Expecting him to answer was ridiculous.

She meant to play a tune, but her fingers became fists pummeling the keys. Smashing them over and over. But no matter how hard she hit or how painful the white-hot lightning ricocheting up her arms, she couldn't stop the guilt from splitting her in half.

Someone cleared their throat behind her. Ripped from her trance, she looked down at her knuckles, busted and bloody. A mixture of shattered ivory and her blood smeared the broken keys.

Lux came around the side of the piano, her worried gaze sliding from the ruined ivories to Talia's face.

"I'm sorry," Talia whispered. But she wasn't apologizing to Lux, and they both knew it.

Lux absentmindedly pressed one of the unbroken keys. The sound echoed in the silence. "You should have seen the wall of my bedroom after my parents died."

Talia curled her injured hands in her lap. "Does it help?"

"For the moment, sure. But death is a tsunami, and all the pain in the world can't stop the waves of grief about to crash over you."

"Then how do I stop them?"

"You don't. You learn to hold your breath and wait for them to pass. After a while, the waves are less frequent. That's when it's the hardest. When you can breathe again and your life feels almost . . . normal. Then you pray for the waves to come again because the guilt of living is harder than drowning."

Talia nodded. Not once had she thought Lux's grief might be different than her own. Lux was a mock, sure, but the anguish reflected inside her eyes was the same as Talia's—just not as raw. A wound that had stopped bleeding but never quite healed. The last person she ever thought she'd receive comfort from was a mock, but Lux's words were real, and they touched something deep inside that marked them as the same.

Death didn't care if Talia was flesh and bone and Lux was metal and wires. Death wrecked both their lives in equal measure.

"How did they die?" Talia asked.

"They stumbled onto a flesher ship near the Outer Fringes. It happened very quickly, I'm told." There was no blame in her voice, but Talia felt responsible anyway. "They should have been more careful, but the war was long over and no one expected an entire fleet of fleshers to appear."

"The war? Between my kind and yours, you mean?"

"The day your family was killed was the start of a long offensive by the mock rebels." Lux met Talia's gaze, and she saw her own guilt mirrored back at her. "Fleshers made it clear they'd never set us free, so we did what we had to."

"What happened to my people after the war?" Pain zipped up her arms, and she realized her injured hands were clenched into rocks.

"We switched roles. Considering our history, there was no other place for humankind. We were smarter than fleshers, stronger, more civilized. The queen says our rise was an inevitability; that's why the humans treated us so bad in the first place."

Talia chewed her lip. "The queen?"

The way Lux straightened at the question, the queen was someone held in high regard. No one had ever acted that way at Talia's name. "She saved us. First, she helped us win the war, and then she united the planets of the Seven along with the off-world colonies."

"This mock queen. Does she have a name?"

"No. Just the queen."

"You like her?"

"Yeah, I guess." She tugged at the zipper dangling just below her collar. "After my parents were killed, Dor and I were shuttled to planet Calisto to meet her. There was this live ceremony broadcast over the galaxies, and all the families of those killed on the ship were there. They gave us medals for our loved ones dying. She came out at the end."

"And?" Talia nudged, her curiosity flaring. "What did she say to you?"

The thought that a Starchaser wasn't ruling the galaxies was foreign, and hard to swallow. What was this new queen like? Was she fair? Clearly she wasn't to humans, but to mocks at least?

Lux's eyes unfocused slightly, and she twisted a bit of purple hair through her fingers. "She told me she would make them pay."

"The humans who fired on your parents' ship?"

"Every last surviving human in the universe. Those were

her words." Frowning, Lux pulled a thin green cuff from her pocket. "Give me your wrist."

Talia slowly complied, eyeing the thing with distrust. The second Lux had the band around Talia's wrist, it shrunk to fit. Surprised, she tried to yank it off, but it had molded to her wrist.

"What the—" Talia's question died as holo-Tandy appeared to her left, her image shimmering before solidifying. She wore a galaxy's worth of makeup and a slinky silver dress that draped over her hips, the bodice plunging to her navel. Her blond hair was pulled back in a severe bun, showing off her long neck and high cheekbones.

As soon as the holo-girl recognized Talia, the trademark pout emerged, and her eyes flashed fire at Lux. "Where's Leo? You said he needed me for a high-class function."

"Sorry, doll. There's a tiny emergency on the bridge, but Talia here will keep you company." Lux leaned in close, and Tandy's body language changed; she angled her body to mirror Lux's, one finger running along the exposed curve of her breast. Tandy was a pleasure holo, after all. Seduction was in her nature. "Leo wants you to keep an eye on Talia for us. Can you do that?"

Tandy's face lit up. "Of course. Anything for my Leo. What specifically should I look for?"

Lux maneuvered out of Tandy's reach before the holo-girl could finish her seduction sequence. "Set off the operating system alarms if she tries to do anything suspicious. Like taking a weapon or messing with the coms, trying to escape. Stealing a shuttle"—Lux cut her gaze to Talia—"that kind of thing."

"Oh, I'm the right girl for the job!" Tandy squealed. If she were a dog, her tail would have broken the piano bench with all her wagging.

"Wait." Talia stood, bumping her knee on the bench. "Will said he was taking me to the queen. That's her, right? The one who hates humans?"

Lux didn't answer, but the way she stared just behind Talia, as if meeting her eyes was too hard, confirmed it.

"She'll kill me. You know that, right?"

Grinding her jaw, Lux pivoted on her heels, obviously in a hurry to avoid talking about what exactly the queen would do. "I'll have Leo bring up some tea for you when everything's calmed down."

As the door clicked shut behind Lux, Talia released a deep sigh. Now, more than ever, she needed to escape her captors and find her people. She knew her kind, and they wouldn't give up so easily. There had to be pockets of them out there, probably on the Outer Fringes. If she could just find a way to them . . .

Talia forced a grin as she turned to holo-girl. "Tandy?"

Tandy, arms crossed over her chest and bottom lip pushed out, cut a sideways glance at Talia. "I don't think I should talk to you."

"They didn't specify that, did they?"

The pleasure holo's frown deepened as she scowled at Talia. "No."

"Then we can talk to pass the time."

"About what?"

"Oh, I would love to talk about directly after the war. But they probably didn't upload you with history, so . . ."

Tandy scoffed. "I'm an A-grade luxury pleasure holo,

familiar with anything a client can possibly want to discuss. Even the smallest, most *boring* detail. I can also change my design to best please you . . ." Her face began to change, her heart-shaped head and delicate chin elongating, her jaw thickening. Stubble appeared on her tawny skin, her wide eyes shrinking and lightening. Will stared back at her; Tandy had even captured his half-smirk.

"No, just . . . go back, please." Something about the way Talia's heart had leapt at the captain's face bothered her, and she was relieved when Tandy reluctantly changed back to her original design, huffing as she did.

Her arms tangled over her chest. "I was only trying to please you. I've seen the way you look at the captain."

Resisting the urge to protest, Talia nodded. "Tandy, it's obvious you were made with the best of everything. But, if you really want to make me happy, you'll fill me in on our history."

Tandy's eyes lit up at the compliment. "Try me. Any question, and I bet I know the answer."

Talia smiled; she was counting on it.

CHAPTER 25

Will

Will stood outside Leo's door, breathing hard while leaning his face against the cold metal. On the other side of that thin door was Talia, dreaming her human dreams. The image of the broken piano keys, dark with human blood, was emblazoned on his mind. When he first entered his viewing room and saw the mess, the memories came flooding back in a wave he couldn't stop.

His mother, slaving away inside General Crayburn's palatial townhome during the day and entertaining in the evenings. His father, darkened with the metallic ore dust after a long day in the mines.

The day the other fleshers came for Will and his mother inside their cramped, squalid little home just outside the city, he heard them from half a mile away. Cursing and cajoling her name in the streets. Names like *metal lover* and *mock whore* drifted across the sluggish breeze that filtered through the flesher town.

Scared, he begged his mother to flee. Even then, at thirteen, he knew how much they were hated by their kind. They were jealous of his mother's nice job inside a mock home, and some of the flesher slaves whispered about his mother's relationship with the general when the sun went down. Will's father included.

But she refused, convinced they would never hurt them. When he peeked out the front windows and saw his father leading the pack, face red from drink and anger, a horrible feeling settled in Will's stomach. Memories after that moment were a blank, as if a door was shut on the violence that followed.

But, sometimes, on the rare occasion when he dreamed, he heard his mother screaming for him. Saw the blood and the terror on her face as she was beaten by a man sworn to love and protect her.

A rustle came from the other side of the door, bringing Will back to the present and the complex emotions he couldn't shake. When he first saw those destroyed piano keys, he was angry. But somewhere between there and Leo's room, that feeling had transformed to pity, and Will went from wanting to yell at Talia to wanting to comfort her. To take her in his arms and ease her pain.

Then he remembered the mock girl crying at the Princess's feet, and her cold indifference. The way she'd looked at the poor mock girl, her own companion, the disdain in her eyes—

Sucking in a cleansing breath, he shoved off the door, propelling himself away from Talia as fast as possible. Her humanness was corrupting him. Bringing back terrible memories of the past and waking up emotions that made him weak.

He clenched his fists as he stalked away.

She was a human; he was a mock. They were enemies. A few hours until they docked at the city of Palatine and replenished their fuel cells, and then they'd hyperdrive all the way to Calisto and hand Talia off to the queen, and he could forget all about Talia Starchaser.

No more wasteful emotions. No more indecision.

In a few days, his whole life would be back to normal.

CHAPTER 26

Talia

Talia hadn't slept at all after she and Tandy retired to Leo's old room. Instead, she used the time to learn everything about the last one hundred years she could from Tandy, who, surprisingly was very knowledgeable. Someone had taken great care to ensure she was uploaded with a comprehensive history, and holo-girl was more than happy to answer Talia's questions and show off that knowledge.

In the last eight hours, Talia had learned that a massive joint attack took out all the main human rulers the day her family was killed, throwing their forces into chaos. On that same day—Insurrection Day, they called it—the mocks on all the off-world colonies and Seven worlds rebelled. Her people didn't stand a chance. The virus, or what the mocks now called the Awakening, was much more widespread than anyone knew, allowing even the most trusted mock companions to rise up against their masters.

But there was also reason for hope. Tandy admitted to several large human battalions unaccounted for, much like the one that killed Lux's parents and disappeared. Where did those ships and their crews go? And not all mocks had been in favor of human enslavement, either. There was a minor coup to overthrow the queen a few years after the end of the war. Whispers of an alliance between mocks and humans flitted through the galaxies, and ships like the one Will manned before this one—Tandy was full of information—hunted these rebels of the queen down.

For the most part, the Alliance was a myth the fleshers told themselves for peace. Hope. At least, that was Tandy's opinion.

Talia knew humans wouldn't have given up without a fight. If she could just find a way to escape, she could join that fight.

When she'd entered the bridge earlier, the Odysseus's crew was already dressed and ready to depart. Instead of snowsuits this time, they wore thin, mismatched jumpsuits with oxygen masks hanging around their necks for ready use. Lux was bright inside a purple suit embroidered with gold on the cuffs. Will's navy-blue jumpsuit had been traded for a tight-fitting red one, reminding her of his corded muscles and tight waist— before she remembered she was supposed to loathe him.

They were hiding their identities from whoever was chasing them, or trying to blend in to this new off-world planet. Although Talia had never heard of Palatine, a tiny mining colony planet under Thoros, Jane rattled off a dozen gambling dens they could visit, revealing once again how little Talia knew of this century.

Same as the last planet they stopped on, Leo was supposed to stay with her and guard the ship, but at the last second, he decided to change the plans, suiting up in a fiery-orange jumpsuit, the only one big enough for his muscled frame.

His gaudy green leather boots poked out below, shiny and polished to perfection.

"You know," he said, twisting his long braids into a knot behind his head. "I just remembered a man I know here who might have a body for Jane."

Lux rolled her eyes. "Why are you just mentioning this now?"

Leo busied himself with fixing his high collar. "Just remembered."

"Who's going to watch the ship?" Will asked. He'd fitted two blasters at his side and added a black trench to his ensemble. Talia hated to admit he looked dashing.

"Jane. Might do her some good to stay on board— otherwise, we'll have half the gambling dens of Palatine after us before we can depart."

"Like you aren't just saying that so you can visit the escorts?" Lux grumbled under her breath. Then her dark eyebrows gathered as she slid her gaze to Talia. "And the princess? We can't afford Jane to glitch while watching her."

"She can come on-world with me." Leo spoke off-handedly, his voice casual and spontaneous, as if the idea just came to him. But there was something off about that casualness that grabbed her attention, and she straightened, curious to see where this went.

Will paused from checking his blaster's charge, and his eyes narrowed slightly as he glanced over at Leo. "That's a huge risk, Leo. Once we hand her off, our jump status will resume. All of us can jump to new bodies when our time comes, Jane first. Why would we risk losing the girl for a black-market body now?"

Leo lifted his big shoulders up in a shrug that seemed a bit too forced. "Just figured with Tandy and me both watching her, it'd be fine. Anything happens, Tandy can alert you on the coms, and she won't get far with the tracking chip inside that bracelet. Plus, I don't trust her here in the ship, not after last time."

The argument was a good one, if not a little too well thought out for Leo. Tandy was attached to Talia at the wrist, and according to holo-girl, only her owner had the key to unlock it. Even if Talia could somehow overcome Leo without a weapon, Tandy the tattletale would be along for the ride, conveying Talia's every movement.

Will raked a hand through his hair, the tightness in his jaw easing as he considered the proposal.

"And Jane is like a second mom to me," Leo continued, his voice thick with emotion. "I'd do anything for her, and I don't trust something unless it's tangible and right in front of me. We can find her a body, Will. Before it's too late."

Will rolled his head side-to-side, stretching his neck likely to buy more time to think. For some reason, Talia's heart kicked wildly against her ribs.

Then he groaned. "Don't make me regret this, Leo."

As soon as they slipped through the crowded port and into the streets, Talia wished she'd stayed behind. Palatine was a hot, arid cesspool of ore miners and ore barons all crammed into a city of metal. Ugly, windowless steel buildings blocked the sky, glittering and huge, their points tapering off into sharp ends like spears. The space surrounding the small group was crammed full of hover traffic, dark lines of cruisers and shuttles inching along. A noxious mixture of fuel vapors and tinny smoke choked the air.

The only color came from the holo-billboards slapped across the buildings and the walking holo-adverts. Most were selling human services. Flesher escorts and pleasurers—the only difference being, the holo-salesman explained, one was rented for the night, the other for an hour—flesher nannies, flesher chefs and companions. The list of services humans performed was never-ending. A tireless mockery of the duties mocks used to perform.

But it wasn't wrong then because mocks had been created by humans . . . nothing more than metal and wires and computer programs. Or so she'd thought.

A reedy mock with a cheap suit and three human girls chained behind him came up, his eyes looking Talia up and down and inspiring murder inside her heart.

"How much for this one?" The mock slaver scratched his jaw as he let his oily gaze linger on her breasts. "She's remarkably fresh looking for such a pretty face."

She bared her teeth at him. *Just touch me, bastard, and see what happens.*

"Oh, you wouldn't like her," Tandy remarked in her most serious voice. "She's very unpleasant and disagreeable."

The mock's grin widened, and Talia wished she could punch it from his face. "A few months in my possession and I'd change all that."

Leo thrust his broad hand out, forcing the mock out of her face. "Not for sale. Now move along."

The disgust lacing Leo's voice seemed at odds with all the stories she'd heard about his run-ins with escorts, but she shrugged it off as him being in a mood.

The handler backed off, and she spat fire at the creep with her eyes as he continued on with his slaves. Everything inside her begged to take Leo's blaster and put a melon-sized hole in the middle of that jerk's face, and she forced herself back around so she didn't have to watch him berate the three human girls shackled to him like cattle.

She ground her teeth together. Funny that Lux used words like civility when she mentioned the world today. That was definitely not the word she'd use to describe this place. Not even close.

Leo used his size to sweep a path through the vendor tents around the port, and once they cleared the crowded space and the sun hit her cheeks, the tension in Talia's body eased.

Talia blinked up at the tell-tale shimmer of the bio-dome above. To think a membrane that thin and delicate was all that kept the citizens of Palatine alive was a bit disconcerting. Without it, the oxygen pumped by the generators near the core would be lost to the atmosphere, and everyone would die.

Before landing, she'd had time to survey the planet, and it was nothing more than a pile of sand and the occasional granite mountain, veined with minerals that validated the existence of such an uninhabitable, sparse world.

"How much farther?" Talia asked as they crossed a bridge over a muddy, stagnant river choked with trash.

Leo shielded his eyes as he squinted across the street at a collection of beautiful high rises. The streets below were clean, the air traffic between the buildings less crowded, the cruisers zipping above the smooth pavement higher-end crafts with custom paintjobs and shiny metallic trim.

"There's a restaurant on the other side. He's waiting for us there."

Crossing the streets took five minutes, and it took another five to find the restaurant. It was three stories up, a red tarp above the entrance the only sign an establishment here existed. Although crafts regularly dropped off occupants at the businesses surrounding it, no one entered its door.

Since most mocks only ate once a day, Leo explained as they waited for a hover to take them up, most chose dinnertime. If it were nighttime, they might wait hours to catch a hover.

The foyer of the restaurant was dark and quiet. The windows had been blacked out, and the walls were holo-screens portraying moonlit beaches lined with tiki-torches, the muffled break of waves at once both soothing and disconcerting. The stench and chaos of the city outside faded.

A few seconds after they entered, a flesher girl around Talia's age with wary brown eyes and mousy hair appeared from the back. She wore a metallic halter top, sequined shorts, and enough red lipstick to paint a house.

Talia strained forward to listen as Leo whispered to the girl. Then she nodded and skipped off to the back room, beckoning them to follow. Talia ducked through the glowing beads that separated the rooms. The other side was darker and smokier, and definitely not just a restaurant. Empty black booths were scattered around the room, all facing a stage in the middle. With *poles*. Exotic music vibrated the wood-paneled walls, and a dark-skinned holo-girl danced to the frenetic beat, twirling suggestively around a pole.

Talia flicked up her eyebrows, both impressed with the mock's moves and annoyed with Leo for dragging her to a strip club. "Leo—"

Leo held up a hand to silence her complaint and then jerked his chin to a booth near the back.

The seats were red leather, the table wobbly. Tandy, beaming like she was on a special date, ordered an expensive glass of pinot noir and filet mignon from the waitress. Talia stuck with water—thirty credits worth, apparently, according to the bill displayed on the holo-menu they ordered from.

"Water and oxygen are the most valuable currencies here," Leo explained over the music, his head pivoting as he continued to watch for whomever they were meeting. "Why you can never go wrong with a gin and tonic."

Talia had already moved on to wondering how Tandy would eat, but the waitress answered that question when she arrived with their orders. Tandy's wine and steak were both holo-versions, not that she seemed to be able to tell the difference.

Tandy swirled her wine around inside its glass and raised an elegant, perfectly plucked eyebrow at Talia. "What?"

"Can you taste it?" Talia asked, nodding to the food. The song had stopped playing, thank the stars, and they could talk without shouting.

"Of course. What would be the point otherwise?"

Leo chuckled. "A lot of mocks who can't afford real humans use holo-girls instead, so the restaurants accommodate them. No one wants to go on a date and be the only one eating."

Date? Talia sipped her water, cringing at the metallic aftertaste. Apparently expensive didn't mean good. "Is that why you got her? To have someone to *eat* with?"

Her question was brazen, but after last night's discoveries and now this strip club detour, she was *feeling* brazen.

"No, Princess. Tandy here belonged to a mock baron from a slave planet near the Outer Fringes. He was . . . cruel to her." Tandy took a long pull of her wine as he spoke. "He was going to give her to a mining crew and purchase a new, less *melancholy* pleasure holo, so I offered to buy her."

"I'm not melancholy. I'm sensitive," Tandy said, crossing her arms. "And he was a crude man not worthy of my company. Not like Leo here."

A blush crept up Leo's neck, and he looked relieved as the waitress brought a mock male over. The mock was tall and surprisingly handsome, an expensive, midnight-blue suit tailored to show off his wide shoulders and trim waist. Glossy-black hair was neatly trimmed close to his head, contrasting against porcelain skin and startling sky-blue eyes.

He was basically the opposite of Leo: dark, elegant, and refined.

"You know, darling, my feelings about discussing business here," the mock said, speaking low as his gaze darted around the empty room. He had a sultry accent she guessed was Krenthian, or maybe one of their off-world colonies.

"I wouldn't have if it wasn't important." The serious tone of Leo's voice made Talia's head snap up. "We don't have much time."

The man nodded to the waitress, and she left the room,

closing the door behind her. After he made sure they were alone, the man turned to face Leo again, face twisted with hurt. "What? I don't see you for almost a year, and that's all I get?"

Leo's voice was low as he said, "I'm sorry, Mathew. Okay. But we don't have time to—"

The mock, Mathew, took Leo's square, stubbled jaw inside elegantly manicured fingers, pulled him close, and kissed him.

Talia's mouth fell open. She looked to Tandy, but other than the twinge of a jealous frown, she didn't appear surprised.

Mathew finally pulled away, smiling. "Better. Now, what did you want to ask me?"

Leo scratched his neck, which was now a bright-red shade to match the waitress's lipstick, and said, "Um . . . the Alliance. Can you get someone to them today?"

Talia's heart skipped a beat. Alliance? Forgetting all about Leo's kiss, she leaned in, unblinking as the man's gaze flitted to her, his face darkening. "Not possible. The queen's forces are everywhere—"

"We don't have a choice." Leo finally met Talia's open-mouthed stare. "We need to get her to our mutual *friends*, and soon."

Talia's pulse raced so fast inside her ears she had to strain to hear over it. Was she hearing right? She should have trusted Leo before, when he'd tried to tell her she could.

Tandy's face had gone from perplexed to disapproving, and she shook her head. "No, Leo. You could get in trouble."

"It's the right thing to do, Tandy."

"But . . . if the queen finds out—"

"She won't." Leo cut her off, and Tandy flinched at his

brusque tone. Sighing, Leo's voice became gentle. "Look, you've always known I worked for the Alliance, so this shouldn't surprise you."

Mathew grinned at Tandy, obviously enjoying her scolding, and Tandy shot him a dark look as he ran a thumb over Leo's hand. "Anyone that knows you knows you're a sucker for lost causes." He flashed Tandy an I-know-him-better-than-you look. "But it's just too dangerous right now to contact our *friends*. Besides, I don't know her."

Mathew turned his intense stare on Talia, appraising her from head to toe. "Who are you, anyway?"

A wide grin split Leo's face. "Mathew Winecraft, meet Princess Talia Starchaser from the Starchaser Dynasty."

"*No . . .*" Mathew's eyes went wide, and he clapped a hand over his mouth. "After all your dreaming, scheming ways. You actually found her!"

"Wait," Tandy said, her gaze sliding from Mathew to Leo. "How does he know about the princess? I thought all trace of the Starchasers had been erased from the histories?"

Leo looked at Talia as he spoke. "The queen tried, but the Alliance remembered. And when we discovered the full, un-redacted report from that day and realized you were unaccounted for, Princess . . . Well, I've been searching for you ever since. Do you know how many laws I had to break to get assigned to a scavenger ship?"

"Why?" Talia asked. "You're a mock."

"Not all mocks believe we should rule over humans. There are some of us who've fought and died trying to free your kind. Finding you has always been our best hope for peace between us."

"How? What can I do?"

"Everything." The way he said that word sent shivers racing down to her toes. "Right now, the Alliance is just pockets of scattered humans and mocks, but you can unite them—even lead them, if you want. Together, we might stand a chance."

For the first time since she woke up, Talia's vision blurred with tears. "Why didn't you come to me earlier?"

"I couldn't be sure it was you at first. I didn't have your picture or another way to identify you."

"Because the queen erased me." Anger tightened her shoulders and jaw and dried up the tears. "I hope one day to meet this queen and return the favor."

"Just hopefully not today." Leo chuckled at his own joke. "Right now, we need to move before Will and the crew realize I've betrayed them." As he spoke, his gaze collapsed to his hands, his jaw popping. How long had he been with the crew of the Odysseus? To live and eat and spend so much time with them . . . It was obvious he hated to hurt them. "They'll be coming for us soon."

"What about Jane's body?" Obviously with Talia gone, they wouldn't get their jump status back—something she'd learned all about from Tandy's history lesson.

"I'll have Mathew send one to the ship. Right, dear?"

Mathew made a dramatic show of rolling his gorgeous eyes. "Anything for this man."

Tandy scoffed at Mathew under her breath, but Talia was too busy freaking out to care about the holo-girl's jealous mutterings. It was really happening. Her head was spinning;

the few sips of water she'd taken threatened to come back up.

Everything had changed so fast. Now that Mathew knew who she was, he agreed to help, and he had one of his bouncers, a human bigger than Leo, bring around the hover and drop them street level. Until Mathew's friend from the Alliance could meet them with a cleared vessel and fake identities, traveling on foot was safer.

Talia hardly noticed the smog and pollution permeating the air this time. Her mind was on finding the rest of her people and helping them any way she could. And a part of her, however small, held out hope Ailat had found a way to jump bodies and was with the Alliance. Maybe she didn't sell Talia out, after all. The Collector could have been lying . . .

They'd hardly made it ten feet when Leo halted near a dumpster and went rigid. The breath caught in Talia's chest.

Something was wrong.

Leo reached for his blaster. Between one blink and the next, someone plucked his weapon from his waist and leapt back. Lux. She twirled his blaster in her hand while walking backward out of reach, shaking her head as she did.

Her eyes flashed hurt and betrayal. "Traitor," she spat. "Good for nothing idiot bastard traitor!"

Whimpering, Tandy wrapped her holo-arms around Leo's waist, as if she could protect him from Lux's weapon. Tandy's holo-image flickered back and forth—she was shivering.

Leo lifted his arms in defeat. "Please, Lux—"

"How could you be so stupid? We're supposed to be your family." Her chest was heaving, her eyes wild in a way Talia couldn't predict. She inhaled sharply as Lux slipped her pointer finger over the blaster's trigger. "What happened to metal over flesh? To loyalty, you big-headed idiot?"

Talia's heart slammed against her ribs as Leo slowly shook his head. What she wouldn't give for a weapon.

"I'm sorry, Lux." Guilt riddled his voice, and he shoved his hands into his pockets as if he wanted to give in and let Lux take him in. But Talia read his body language for what it was: feigning defeat. While Leo might feel guilt, he'd just told a story of how he spent years searching for hope. No way would he let that go without a fight. "It was the right thing to do."

Where was Will? A quick search caught him leaned against the steel wall of the building, his jaw set and eyes shining with an emotion she couldn't quite name. Words like betrayal and hurt weren't enough. This was something more, like the way someone might stare at the gravesite of a loved one who'd died unexpectedly.

Whereas Lux's emotions brimmed the surface, a raging fire of fury, Will's smoldered deep down inside, buried in a place she assumed no one ever gained access to.

Talia was too frozen with shock to move. Three warring emotions hit her all at once. Wanting to protect Leo. Wanting to soothe the hurt on Will's face. And wanting to escape for her own sake.

Will stepped away from the wall, silently, his face an unreadable mask.

Then he raised his blaster and shot Leo in the chest.

CHAPTER 27

Will

Will couldn't scrub the image from his mind. The surprise on Leo's face as he glanced down at his chest and then crumpled to the ground. Granted, the shot was only a stunning charge, meant to incapacitate the idiot. Otherwise, Leo would have died fighting. They left him locked in a cargo hold, dead to the world. When he woke up, he'd be pissed off and raging.

Good. Let him. Will had a few words to say to his former friend—if they'd ever really been friends. Will massaged his temples and sank deeper into the old couch in his viewing room. Thank the stars Lux had the forethought to add a viewing program to Tandy right before they left for Palatine. Will thought her suspicious feeling was crazy, right up until the moment it wasn't.

The first surprise had been Leo's boyfriend. Didn't see that one coming. Not that Will cared about Leo's sexual preferences, but Will couldn't stop going over all those times Leo was caught in the undocumented brothels.

All those times Will bailed him out, for star's sake.

Had everything been a lie? A ruse to trick the crew somehow?

As much as Will tried not to care, the thought made him sick. Why did Leo betray the Odysseus? That's what bothered Will more than anything else, and he couldn't seem to find a plausible explanation. Putting himself on the line for humans just didn't make sense.

The door to Will's viewing room creaked open, and Lux entered, padding silently across the floor and disrupting the projector screen. *Breakfast at Tiffany's* was playing, as it had been all night, an endless loop of Holly Golightly. Jane sat at the broken piano, watching with vague interest in the only movie Will had ever seen. Every so often, her eyebrows rose at something the waifish actress did. No doubt she thought Holly was silly.

Couldn't blame Jane for that. Her programming lacked a sequence to appreciate nuance or metaphors. In a few hours, after they landed at Calisto and presented Talia to the queen, that would all change. Jane would get her body, all their jump statuses would be renewed, and they'd be a few billion credits richer.

And the Athena . . . his heart skipped just thinking about her back in his control, and the hope was almost too much to bear. Soon his life would be exactly where it was supposed to be.

The couch jostled as Lux plopped down beside him, her purple twists wilder than usual. She cut a sour look his way. "You didn't have to shoot him."

"Oh, did you see his face? I did. Leo would have fought to the death to protect Tal—" He paused. Calling her by her name made her more real. "The flesher princess." Remembering the betrayal sent his adrenaline pounding into overdrive, and he reached for the bottle of crème de menthe, the cloyingly sweet green alcohol inside sloshing. The syrupy liquid slid down his throat, and he leaned his head back, hoping that would make the alcohol go down easier. "I always assumed that loyalty was for us, but I was wrong."

"We both were." Lux frowned at the bottle he offered, shooing it away. Likely she was upset over more than just Leo's affiliation with the Alliance. Will had seen the way she looked at Leo when she thought no one was watching. Learning the man you love couldn't ever return the favor had to be hard. "He's an idiot," she continued. "A bloody, big-headed idiot."

Will took another pull, focusing on the cool wave that followed the minty liqueur instead of the pain clenching his heart. "Don't want to talk about it anymore."

Crossing her legs, she settled back into the faded gold cushions, eyeing Holly Golightly with distrust. "Why do you like this movie anyway?"

Will could have told her that it was his mother's favorite movie from the selection inside General Crayburn's holo-theatre. That she used to stare at it enraptured, hardly blinking, this weird blank look on her face. That the sadness she drowned in day and night was momentarily forgotten as she lost herself inside that screen.

Or he could try to explain that watching this movie made him feel connected to something bigger than him, something he didn't quite understand. Like floating through space amongst the stars, alone, inconsequential, yet somehow feeling an inexplicable sense of belonging.

"I think she's hot," he said instead, eliciting an eye roll from Lux. "And different than most mock girls."

Scoffing, Lux ripped the bottle from his hand and swilled. When she was done, her face crinkled, her pert nose lifting at the minty taste. "Will—I mean, Captain—she's basically a flesher escort, just with less brains. You can't tell me she's your dream girl."

Her minty breath rolled over him, and he shook his head. "You're missing the point. She's irrational, constantly making these horrible decisions and torn between being practical and letting her emotions ruin her."

Like his mother. Except Holly Golightly had a much happier ending than she ever did.

"And you like that?"

He shrugged. "I find it strangely . . . comforting."

Silence stretched over the room, broken by Holly's laughter coming from the speakers in the ceiling. This was the first time Will had ever really opened up to Lux about anything. Judging by the way Lux picked at the frayed hem on her jumpsuit and he couldn't meet her eyes, they both sucked at dealing with their newfound honesty.

"Whatever," Lux muttered, wiping her mouth on her sleeve and forcing her gaze on the screen. "This movie's weird." An uncertain look transformed Lux's normally confident face, and she scraped her teeth over her bottom lip, glancing at him from the corner of her eye. "What's going to happen to Leo?"

His gut clenched, and he blew out a sharp breath. Facing the firing squad would serve the idiot right . . . but it wouldn't be by Will's hand. If Leo was in the Alliance, the queen and her soldiers would root him out eventually. "The queen doesn't have to know anything about him being a traitor. After we turn in the princess and get his jump status renewed, he can do whatever the hell he wants. I just don't ever want to see his face again."

Lux opened her mouth like she was going to say something but then closed it. They sat in silence for a moment before she uncoiled to a rigid stand. "That's fair."

Frowning, he watched her leave. Alone with his thoughts, the movie lost its appeal, so did the liqueur. He got up to leave, his body disrupting the screen and drawing Jane's attention. As he clapped her on the shoulder, she rested her hand over his. Startled, he froze. She rarely ever touched him, and for a moment he thought she was glitching. But her face was calm, almost serene as she dropped something into his hand.

His lucky penny. He'd nearly forgotten about it.

"Figured you'd want this back now."

Will nodded. "Could really use the luck."

"So could a lot of us." Her lips flicked into a smile. "Remember, a good captain always says goodbye to his crew."

His shoulder sagged, and he shook his head. "No, Jane. If I see Leo and he gives me one of his arrogant grins, I'll end up killing him."

"A good captain never inflicts more punishment than—"

"Punishment?" Will interrupted, his gut clenching. "The law states I execute him. Is that what you want?"

She blinked once, twice. Slow, deliberate movements. Hell, maybe she *was* glitching.

Her hand tightened over his, the skin over her knuckles split and worn. The glint of dull metal beneath hinted at her body's eventual disintegration. She was running out of time.

"Humans had their laws," she said. "When we took over, we made our own. And someday, someone else will make even more laws. Laws change, it's what's inside your heart that should guide you."

"Enough, Jane. That's flesher talk." He pulled his hand away before she could continue spouting nonsense, pocketing his penny. "I'll go see him, okay? But I can't promise I won't murder him, so that falls on you."

The floor creaked beneath his heavy boots as he stalked out, his pulse drumming in his skull. He took the stairs three at a time, rushing even as his body screamed at him to stop. He'd do what Jane asked and share face-to-face what he thought of Leo. Besides, why was Will afraid of losing his temper? He was a mock, not a flesher.

By the time he reached the hallway of the crew's quarters, Will was panting . . . What was he doing here? He'd meant to go the other way, to where Leo was being held in the cargo bay.

Instead, somehow Will had ended up where the flesher princess was kept. He flicked a quick glance at the metal door separating them, his heart beating wild inside his chest. Despite urging himself to turn around, he found himself approaching the door, the knowledge she was nearby sending his emotions into a tailspin.

What if she was hurt? Scared? He remembered what it was to be human and terrified all the time. The fear eating away at you—

Stop. But his personal plea sounded distant, like a voice from the far end of a tunnel.

His hand was on the knob, and before he could talk himself

out of it, he unlocked it from the outside and entered, clicking the door shut behind him. Shadows soaked the room. The air was thick with the scent of jasmine, intermingled with Leo's overpowering cologne.

Will's eyes adjusted quickly, his vision sharpening on the princess perched on the corner of the bed, her knees drawn to her chest, hair mussed and wild. As soon as she lifted her eyes to him, he expected another tantrum like last time. Curses, perhaps. Bared teeth and looks of disgust.

Instead, she just stared at him with this lost expression that caught him off guard and, before he could chase away the feeling, his chest tightened. A near-infinitesimal movement he ignored.

"Do you need something?" Her voice was raspy but stronger than expected given her circumstances. "Or . . . is it time?"

A pang of pity lanced through him, and he gritted his teeth so hard his jaw ached. Conjuring his willpower, he tried to force himself back, but he was frozen in place. Why was he even here? She was a flesher, a cruel one. He'd seen the evidence. Maybe if he'd stayed a flesher, he'd have become mean and twisted too. Maybe they just couldn't help it.

And yet nothing cruel or even pitiful rested inside her eyes tonight. Only the faraway stare he recognized immediately: loss. The same look that drenched his mother's expression every day of her life.

He found himself sitting on the bed beside the princess. He needed to walk away, to leave this room. But he couldn't.

She exhaled, relaxing a little. "Leo's okay?"

"It was a stunning blow. He'll wake up sore and pissed, but otherwise fine."

"After that?"

Despite himself, the worried tone of her voice sent a twinge of jealousy lodging below his sternum, and his lips twisted to the side. "He goes free. I won't turn him in."

Relief washed over her, the worried lines in her forehead melting away. "I'm glad. He doesn't deserve to be punished for trying to help me."

"That's a matter of opinion."

"Why are you turning me in, anyway? What do you get out of it? Besides being able to jump."

The way she said it made his reasons sound sleazy, and he shifted on the bed. "I get my life back. We all do. Leo, Dorian, Lux, and Jane. I won't feel guilty for doing the inevitable. There's no place for you in this world, Princess, and if it's not me presenting you to the queen, it will be someone else."

Her eyes flashed anger at him. "That's a cop out, Captain, and you know it!" She balled her fists so tightly that her knuckles bulged, the white bones jutting sharply and reminding him how different they were from each other. "We can find a way to coexist, mocks and humans. But what I saw on Palatine, that's nothing better than what we were doing to the mocks a hundred years ago. How can you call that progress?"

He bit his lip, appraising her from the corner of his eye. "So you admit humans mistreated mocks? That the world was a savage place when they—your family ruled?"

Her hair rustled as she shook her head, almost violently. "We didn't want mocks to suffer or—"

"*No?*" Bitterness tainted his voice. "Because the video I saw of you on your eighteenth birthday, hurting your junior mock, says otherwise. You were smiling—*smiling*, Princess—and she was terrified."

Her gaze collapsed to her hands, still fisted in her lap. "You don't understand what you saw."

"Maybe not. All I know is mocks will never be enslaved again."

He thought she would argue, or make some snide remark, but she was still and quiet, the silence filling the room like water until breathing became too hard.

"I'm sorry," he finally said, lurching to his feet. "I wish things were different."

As soon as his hand touched the door, she spoke. "If you give me to the queen, they will kill me and extinguish the last hope for my people to live free. How long until this queen grows tired of human slaves and decides to exterminate us forever? You know she will, because that's what logic prescribes. We're weaker, less intelligent. We get sick and require more food, more resources. Compared to mocks, we're inferior in every way. But does that mean we are deserving of death?" Her words hit him squarely in the chest the same as a punch would have, and he clenched the door's handle. "You've been both mock and human," she continued. "Surely you can remember when you were a human. Did you think yourself so terrible?"

His throat felt like paper as he tried to swallow. He certainly didn't feel like a mock, with his adrenaline surging, sending his heart racing and pasting his hands and chest with sweat. "Why do you cling to this idea that there's any chance left for humans, when you just listed all the reasons why you're obsolete?"

From the corner of his eye, he caught her lips pulled into a tragic smile. "What's your name, Will? Your full flesher name?"

A pause. "Will Perrault."

"Well, Will Perrault. That's what we humans do. We hope, despite all the odds. You may see it as a flaw, but I think it's what makes us so special."

It wasn't until the door was shut and locked behind him that he could finally breathe again, and he marched down the hall, forcing the princess and Leo from his thoughts. The bridge was brightly lit, the lights chasing away the shadows darkening the ship's interior. Jane sat in the co-pilot's chair, and she nodded toward the starscreen as he took his seat beside her. Long lines of freighter vessels and starliners hovered just above, waiting to dock.

"Air-traffic around the waystation is light this morning, Captain," Jane said. "We'll be docked within the hour."

Planet Calisto was a grayish sphere below, shrouded in clouds. But he didn't need to see the land below to imagine it, every square inch covered in grand cities of steel. Once they broke cloud cover to land, the cities would appear to be moving, but that was only the millions of vessels caught in an endless array of traffic to and from the buildings. Bridges arced mid-air, the meshwork of arteries that supplied the cities with its people clogged and churning.

Once, he and his mother trekked along one of those swollen steel tubes to Crayburn's building, a massive skyscraper that had seemed like a castle straight out of a flesher fairy tale. As commander of the battalion that helped stamp out the flesher rebellion, and head of the queen's security, the general resided close to the queen's palace. Will had never been there, only seen the monstrosity rising from the waters surrounding it, a blight of ragged metal and glass surrounded by a thick, clear wall that allowed everyone to see what they couldn't touch. The queen was notoriously careful about who she allowed past those crystalline gates and within the palace walls—and so far, Will hadn't been one of them.

At the thought of being back, a shudder wracked his chest, and he tamped down the uneasy emotion as he nodded at Jane to begin landing procedures, keeping his face devoid of anything but boredom. Coming here always had this effect on him, which was why he rarely visited.

Jane worked the switches with deft fingers, despite their worn appearance. When the checklist was complete, she paused and glanced his way. "Welcome home, Captain."

As they broke through the clouds and the shimmering city of Palesia came into view, a spasm of dread wound its way around his heart, and no amount of forced smiles could dislodge the useless human emotion.

CHAPTER 28

Talia

As much as Talia hated to admit it, part of her wished she'd never woken up to this nightmare. Not only was she being marched to her death, but she was going to be publicly executed in the city of her birth, the royal birthplace of every Starchaser ever born.

Despite the mangled streets jutting with steel and the once vibrant, lush hills now covered by metal, she'd recognized Palesia immediately. The two moons, shrouded in wispy gray clouds, hung faintly over the ragged buildings which seemed to go on forever, a glittering sea of metal and pollution, the air flecked with hovercrafts of every kind. The once beautiful marble structures she remembered from her youth had been replaced with hideously warped and spiraling designs that clawed at the clouds with angry fingers.

She shouldn't be that surprised the new queen chose the old capitol to make her home. The planet Calisto had always been the most temperate of the Seven, with long Summers and rich, fertile soil. Strategically placed closest to mineral-rich planets Thoros and Aegaeon, Calisto boasted twenty-nine off-world colonies to run to for supplies. But the way it had been rebuilt was as if someone had purposefully soiled what once made the city beautiful, stamping out its identity, which made little sense.

The queen openly hated fleshers, but to go to this extreme . . .

The second she'd left the ship—or, rather, been dragged off in handcuffs—an overwhelming feeling that the complete transformation of Talia's once beloved city was personal struck her. An attack on her family and the entire human race.

She and the crew of the Odysseus disembarked over four hours ago. From there, they took two hovers and had walked at least three miles. Still, the golden arc of the gates leading to the final bridge that would take them to the new palace seemed miles away. The city's streets were at a near standstill, mocks coming and going, hardly complaining in the sweltering, fetid streets steeped in deep shadows. Many of the mocks were dressed in jewel-bright clothes, trailing similarly well-dressed children. Ragged, rail-thin human nannies and servants buzzed around the mocks like flies, reminding Talia of a different time when the roles were reversed.

She wondered if their starvation was on account of mocks forgetting how much humans ate, or simply a cruelty.

At first she surmised today must be some sort of holiday for the mocks. But, from the little talk between her jailers, she gleaned all these mocks were here to see the queen. Apparently, they arrived in droves from all of the surrounding planets to pay respects.

Beside Talia, Leo made some comment beneath his breath about the citizens being brainwashed. He wasn't bound like Talia. Rather, he was controlled with thin metal cuffs around his wrists. Explosives. And Lux held the remote that would set them off and sever his hands—if he didn't behave. Although the wild look in his eyes said the odds he wouldn't cause a scene were dwindling.

"What do you mean?" Lux asked, squinting at him.

He cut her a sideways glance, his lips pulled into a grimace of disgust. "The Alliance discovered that anyone who's jumped into a new body in the last twenty years has suddenly developed a blind obedience to the queen."

"So she's . . . what? Programming devotion into them?"

"Looks that way."

Lux narrowed her eyes and prodded Leo forward, harder than needed. He grimaced, shooting his former friend a frown before trudging on with his head hung low.

Two Starfighters similar to the Predators she used to fly buzzed above, cutting white slashes into the dirty-gray sky, their paths strategic and ready for combat. A military training academy must have been nearby. As Talia eyed the crafts with longing, she jostled her arms, the manacles binding her wrists behind her back cutting into her bones.

Wincing, she flexed her wrists and stifled a sigh. Great, it could be hours more before they crossed over into the queen's estate. Not that Talia was in a hurry to meet this queen and suffer her wrath, but what was the point of putting off the inevitable? Especially when it was stifling hot outside and Talia was bundled in the heaviest cloak in existence. The thick fabric was meant to disguise her in case Xander was still searching for her—stars forbid someone other than Will present her to this new queen—but the wool was scratchy and fell below Talia's feet, constantly tripping her up.

The hood of the cape slipped farther down, eclipsing her vision. Will, who'd been glued to her side since the second they'd stepped foot on Palesia, pulled the fabric back for her, but he refused to look her in the eye. *Coward.*

"You can't even look at me, can you?" she snapped, making sure her voice conveyed the annoyance clawing through her veins.

His shoulders stiffened, but he continued staring straight ahead. Perspiration darkened his temples, and a bead of sweat trickled down his jaw.

"You do realize mocks don't sweat?"

His eyes widened as he glanced at her, but the comment did its job. Will quickly swiped his palm across his jaw. "So?"

"So you're not fully mock. Which means you're still part human, no matter how hard you try to pretend otherwise."

Some of his hair had fallen into his face, and he scraped the strands back, keeping his gaze forward. "If I am, it's not by choice."

"And the way you play the piano," Talia continued. Even though she knew he wasn't about to let her go at this point, she couldn't help needling him, the jerk. "No mock could ever play with that kind of emotion."

A muscle feathered in his neck, but otherwise he was an impermeable mask, shoulders back and head held high. He'd changed into a different uniform than the one she was used to, a fine-tailored cardinal-red jacket fitted to his wide shoulders, its high collar accentuating the sharp lines of his face. Three gold bars lined the breast-pocket, and medals adorned the shoulders.

For the first time, she realized how devastatingly beautiful he was. And cruel—that too. As if the jacket had transformed him, his lips were pressed taut, his eyes distant and cold. She was wasting her time; no amount of ribbing would break the layer of ice guarding his heart.

Huffing, she yanked her wrists against the shackles, wincing once again as the metal cuffs bit into flesh, human flesh. Something Will, despite the small shred of humanity clinging to him, would never be. He'd chosen to be a mock—and loved it.

A murmur trilled the air, drawing her attention from Will's stony exterior to a circle of onlookers gathered around the end of the street. Mocks crawled over each other to see whatever was in the center, the smaller children perched on awnings and the sides of buildings for a better view. An opening appeared between two older mocks, and Talia caught a flicker of something.

The woman in the center of the crowd was a hologram, that much was clear by the shimmer of her form. The way her body glinted and flickered when someone managed to touch her. She was tall—taller than the mocks in the crowd by at least a few feet—but that could have been the hologram's proportions. Head-to-toe onyx armor covered her strong body, so smooth the material could have been painted on. Whatever the dark armor was made of, it had a luster that captured the eye—though no one would stare for long with the woman's face just above. Talia found herself gaping at the strange mixture of sharp, contrasting features. Milky skin stretched over angles not natural in the human body. The woman's eyes were too large, her irises too black, her lips made for sneering.

A spasm of pain wriggled through Talia. Something about the face was familiar—but not. Cruel, yet calming. Whispers joined to create a song made up of one word: queen.

That was when Talia noticed the jagged, mangled metal crown embedded inside the woman's nest of sable hair. The crown was dark like her armor and fitted like a helmet, three-foot long wiry tentacles coming off and forming a serpentine corona around her skull. As Talia gaped at the woman, tiny spherical drones no bigger than baby hummingbirds broke off from the tentacles and flitted over the crowd.

A few minutes later, one of the queen's drones found the Odysseus's crew. A perfect sphere made of a metallic, greenish alloy. Will halted, his body going rigid as the drone hovered six inches from his face. It remained for a few seconds, as if scanning his features, and then moved on to Lux, who pushed her chin out, unafraid. Leo and Jane were next.

Talia was last. She could almost feel the drone's curiosity as it wavered in front of her, taking longer than the others. Her face, distorted inside the reflective ball's surface, mirrored back to her. All at once, the machine zipped away through the crowd so fast and became invisible to the naked eye.

Relief crashed over Talia, and she pressed ahead, shoving through the crowd and away from the queen, even if she was only a hologram. Something about her settled low inside Talia's gut. A feeling, a memory. The fact that she was going to meet this queen soon turned Talia's veins to ice, despite the humid heat trapped beneath the cloak with her.

They were nearly to the gate of the queen's estate when Talia noticed the surrounding mocks had parted to make a wide path, their faces all fixed in the same cold, vicious expression. Her skin crawled beneath their raking eyes, full of inhuman hatred—but it seemed as if one mock stared back at her.

A little girl with sun-gold hair and blue eyes broke off from the crowd and said, "Welcome back, Tal."

Something inside that small, innocent voice saying Talia's name sent claws of fear scraping against the inside of her ribs. "What's happening," Talia asked, glancing over at Will as her heart pounded deep and muffled inside her chest. "Why are they talking to me?"

"She's hijacked their minds," Will answered, fear infused in his voice despite his earlier efforts at appearing unaffected. "Anyone who's uploaded in the last forty-eight hours can have their mind taken over by her."

Well, that's not creepy. Gritting her teeth, she forced her breathing into a steady rhythm as the massive gates creaked open, allowing access to the castle. "She knows who I am."

"It appears so," Will said from the corner of his mouth, still staring straight ahead as they entered the empty courtyard.

"You sure about this, Captain?" Lux asked under her breath, likely so the onlookers—and the queen—couldn't hear. "I don't like the way she's looking at us. Or the princess. Something feels wrong."

Talia wholeheartedly agreed. But if Will heard Lux, he didn't answer. Instead he pressed forward, yanking Talia by her arm so they were almost running. She surveyed the courtyard, scanning the walls for another opening to escape through. All of this was new, right down to the cloudy wall around the palace that resembled ice.

She stumbled up a flight of steps, unable to get past the differences. There used to be a swan fountain in the courtyard here, one open to the Palesian people for seven hours during the day, always swarming with citizens. Now there was nothing save a few mock guards, all with their gazes trained on Talia.

Whoever this queen was, she didn't like company. As the gate crashed shut behind them, condemning them to whatever lay ahead, Talia blinked, something niggling at her, just out of reach.

Like a punch to the gut, all the pieces fell into place. The queen recognized Talia, had called her by a *nickname* only one person had ever used.

Ailat.

The realization knocked the breath from Talia's lungs, and she stumbled backward a step, jerking Will back too and nearly dislocating her wrists. *Could it really be her ex-best friend?* Will tightened his grip on her upper arm as he glanced back, only to stop in place. Talia's expression must have been horrified, because a whisper of emotion flickered across his face.

"What?" he asked. "What is it?"

"Please don't do this." Her voice was a whisper, a plea, and his eyes softened infinitesimally. "She'll kill me. We have . . . history. A misunderstanding."

The second the declaration had been spoken aloud, the dark suspicion nested deep inside, Talia knew it to be true. Ailat was responsible for her parent's death, and from the way she looked at Talia through the other mocks, her former friend would like nothing better than to murder Talia too.

Will's Adam's apple bobbed as he swallowed hard, and he absentmindedly stroked the bars on his shoulder. Indecision played over his face, the warring emotions twisting his visage into a mixture of resolve and guilt. "You talk like she has bloodlust, but she's not like humans . . ."

But even as he said it, his voice began to falter, and two deep lines etched into his forehead. Talia shifted on her feet. From the windows cut into the spiraling castle above came a heavy sense of someone watching her, but she couldn't quite force herself to look up.

Don't be a stubborn idiot, Will! "I can make the world better," she said, talking fast. "But I need your help. If there's any humanity left inside you, Will Perrault, any at all, then dare this one last time to hope." She paused, letting her words sink in, before she continued, her voice pleading. "Release me."

His resolve was starting to break, she knew, because his fingers loosened around her bicep. He flicked his gaze to Lux and opened his mouth to give an order—but froze, just as an older man came around the side of the courtyard and called out his name. The man wore a similar uniform to Will's, shoulders flashing with metal. Whoever this man was, he was high up in station and the military.

"General?" The word came out on a breath of air, and Will inched his hand toward his blaster, even as his lips trembled into a smile. Confusion leaked from his pores and rooted him in place. His programming wasn't prepared for such a conflict.

"You brought the princess," the general called, striding toward them. "Good boy." As soon as he was within several feet, he halted, his gaze sliding to Will's hand resting on the butt of his blaster. "Now wipe that hesitation from your face before the queen sees it and march up those stairs with your prisoner."

Will's fingers tightened on Talia's arm, but he stayed put. "What happens to her once the queen has her?"

The general's faded blue eyes landed on her, and she swallowed the urge to spit in his face. There was something inhuman about his superior gaze, sterile, as if she didn't deserve to stand in his presence. "Oh, I'm sure the queen will think of something . . . *inventive* to do with her."

A fist of ice curled around her gut and squeezed. No way in *hell* would she be taken. She glanced over at Lux, at the weapon tucked neatly inside her waistband—but a weapon was useless with these handcuffs.

"Why not just let her live out her life somewhere, in secret?" But Will shook his head as he spoke, as if even *he* knew his suggestion was preposterous. "Or stick her on some tiny off-world colony?"

The general blinked at Will, slowly. "You're not stupid, Will, so stop acting like you are. The queen can't let a Starchaser live, not until the rest of the Alliance is rooted out and no longer a threat. Keeping her alive gives them the one thing that makes them dangerous."

"What's that?"

"Hope."

As soon as that word registered in Will, his expression changed. She could see the human realization click into place behind his eyes, and she prepared herself for what she knew would follow.

A fight.

Before anyone could react, Will had his blaster out and pointed at the general.

"What are you doing with that, boy?" The man's voice was soft, terrifying, and remarkably devoid of the usual fear that came with a blaster pointed toward the face.

Will took a step back toward Talia, jumbling with the keys to her shackles. They popped free, releasing her wrists—and her pride—with a click. "The right thing, Father."

Father?

Disappointment flashed in the general's eyes, and he shook his head. "I should have believed Xander."

The man lifted his arm in some type of signal, and the courtyard came to life. A man in his early twenties marched around the corner of the palace, his fiery-red uniform the same as Will's—though not as dashing on this man as it was on Will. Behind the newcomer loomed a line of silver hunters, their heavy metal legs punching the gravel and sifting up dust.

A line had just been drawn.

Will's eyes flashed hatred at the man, whose name Will said with a hiss. "*Xander.*"

Xander grinned at Will, cruelty marring the features of his narrow face. "I told Father you'd mess it all up, flesher scum."

Will smiled back, and in the blink of Talia's eye, fire from his blaster streaked through the air almost in slow motion. But right before the shot hit Xander, a hunter knocked him down, taking the brunt of the blast. A black hole singed the hunter's metal flesh, just above its waist, but it hardly seemed to notice the wide chasm exposing its inner working parts as it returned to its feet.

Will turned to his crew. "Run!"

Another blast rocked the courtyard as Will just barely

missed a hunter taking aim at them. The general scurried to the safety of the columns, disappearing at the top of the steps.

"Get Talia back to the ship, now!" Will added, sensing his crew's need to stay and fight with him. "That's an order!"

Never in her short time of knowing him had Will's voice been so clear or commanding. Before Talia could respond, Leo was dragging her toward the gate, Lux a step ahead. She used her blaster to persuade one of the guards to open the gate. As it screeched open, a blast from a hunter's weapon skimmed their heads, just missing Leo and obliterating the right half of the gate for them.

"We got a problem!" Lux informed them, panting heavily. The crowd along the bridge, controlled by the queen, had formed an impenetrable mock barrier. A few of them even held makeshift weapons. Shovels. Bricks. A belt, even.

"That does *not* look good," Leo muttered. "Even with full blaster charges, there's no way in stars we'll take them all out. There's just too many."

Talia glanced at the water surrounding the palace. From the bridge to the water was a twenty-foot drop, at least. But there were boats below. Fast ones. If they could bypass the bridge . . .

Lux must have read Talia's look because the navigator followed the princess's gaze, grinning. "The water! Get ready to jump." Brushing back a lavender flourish of hair from her face, Lux lifted a remote and called into the com. "Dorian, tell Jane it's time for the Odysseus to go dark and take flight. We'll meet at the place we last saw Mom and Dad. Make it quick, yeah?"

Closer up, the waters were choppy and green. Talia swallowed as she and the crew scaled the concrete barriers. She hovered just above the drop, her stomach bottoming out. Leo jumped first, landing with a huge thud atop a silver hoverboat and somehow not capsizing it. He dumped the poor fisherman into the waters along with his poles and then beckoned Lux and Talia in.

Explosions rocked the inside of the gates. She glanced back, making out the silver flash of hunters through the semi-translucent wall and, near the gate, a dark figure that had to be Will. He dove and zagged, bright explosions trailing him. The firefight inside grew heavy. They shouldn't have left Will to fight alone. But Talia had no weapon, and if she ran back to help, she'd end up getting in the way.

The crowds had realized what was happening and surged forward in aid of their queen. Two silver flashes above caught Talia's attention. Drones. *Stars*. Looking back one more time, she said, "I'm sorry, Captain."

Then she clenched her teeth, said a silent prayer for Will, and leapt.

CHAPTER 29
Will

Guard the gate, Will. Let no one through. Will repeated those words inside his head until they became a mantra of strength, a declaration of willpower and grit. If he could just keep this small section of space protected, then he'd be happy. Obviously he couldn't hold the hunters and Xander off forever. But long enough for the crew and Talia to reach safety . . . Will could do that.

A blast of orange fire burst against the gravel at his feet, sending a spray of rocks pelting his skin. He ducked and dived, more blaster fire streaking over his cheeks and head; the smell of singed hair filled his nose.

Keep moving. He needed to delay the hunters and queen's guards as long as possible. To save up the charge on his blaster so he didn't use it all at once. That meant moving, *fast*. And not dying.

At least not yet.

A hunter charged and he rolled between its legs, popping up on the other side. He took one step, turned mid-air, and released his charge into the machine, blowing a three-foot wide chasm in its chest. Smoke billowed from its wound, and the hunter collapsed with a crash.

He sucked in air and dove for cover behind the metal carcass as more shots rang out. Fire danced all around, but the hunter's body took the brunt of it. A metallic glimmer yanked his attention to the gate. Two hunters charged the opening, and he took them down with three body shots each.

Xander growled from the top of the steps, commanding more hunters to storm the gate. Luckily the bodies of the hunters Will had felled made a barrier, slowing the others still pursuing down enough that he could pick them off with ease.

Chaos filled the queen's courtyard. Smoke churned the sky, tongues of fire lapping the air. The grating-metal sound of dying machines echoed off the walls. When his blaster failed, he managed to grab a huge gun from one of the downed hunters and scramble around the side of the gate wall, the wall Talia and the crew had climbed up and then jumped from. By now they should all be long gone.

Others in Will's position might be upset at being left behind, but he'd given the order to leave after all. As Jane would say, you can tell a good captain by how well his crew followed his orders.

Heavy footsteps crunched the gravel around the corner, followed by the sounds of shouted commands to split up. They were coming for Will, flanking him on all sides, though since he no longer held the wall, they could be cautious. Drifts of pale-gray smoke wafted over his face as his internal alarms blared. He focused on the litany of warnings scrolling down his bio-screen, the most critical one being blood loss.

Gritting his jaw, he flicked a look down at his left arm. He hadn't felt the injury when it first happened, but now pain hit him all at once. His bio-flesh was shredded just below the elbow, the inner metal workings of his lower arm mangled beyond repair. The oily black fluid pouring from the severed plastic veins puddled on the ground beside him. Thicker than human blood, but it pulsed with life just the same—and like fleshers, he would die after losing a certain amount.

"You're surrounded, Will!" Xander's voice reverberated across the courtyard, the humor in his tone scraping down Will's spine. "Surrender and we'll keep this painless."

Will snorted. Nothing but lies ever came from Xander's lips. He'd like nothing more than to make Will suffer.

He tried to lift the weapon cradled against his chest with his good arm, his one last defense, but the blaster was too large and cumbersome to aim one-handed. Crap.

His head fell back against the hard stone, and a ragged sigh escaped his throat. How had his life come to this? His mind had been set. Why change it? There was no sense in the decision, no warning he'd ever do something so brazen as forfeit his life for a flesher. Still, here Will was, totally screwed—and yet he didn't regret saving Talia's life.

Hope. Is that what this was? His lips stretched into a smile, his heart beating hard and fast. Whatever the emotion, it felt equally foreign and familiar. As if, once, long ago, he'd tasted it and then somehow forgotten how wonderful it was.

Run, Princess.

Xander turned the corner with a smug expression, blaster held out, his head haloed by billows of smoke and a swarm of pissed-off soldiers behind. He shook his head, his thin lips twisting into a smirk. "You're an idiot, brother."

He brought his blaster down on Will's temple so fast he didn't have time to flinch before his world crashed into darkness.

Will knew he was dreaming because he'd had this same lucid nightmare for years after his transformation, before he stopped sleeping altogether. He was in a hospital bed beneath a thick glass window, sunlight casting shadows over General Crayburn as he looked over Will, inspecting him the way one might a shiny new toy.

His body felt different; his skin felt wrong. He tried to stand, but the general had the mock technicians hold Will down, using words like hurt and dead to explain what had happened to his mother and him.

His skull had been crushed, his brain damaged beyond repair, the bones of his body pulverized into jagged pieces that would never fit back together again. Every human part of him was ruined.

"All humans are savages, but now you're saved from such a fate," the general promised. "I saved you."

Will's eyes were stretched wide as he clawed at his arms, the metal beneath too hard, too alien. He never noticed his skin before, but his new bio-flesh felt tight and odd holding in all this new material. His fingers gouged holes into the plastic sides of the hospital bed. His legs felt like they could lift a building. His mind whirred faster than a machine, processing shreds of sensory detail the way a computer would, with no emotion.

When he was done thrashing about, his new mock body paralyzed with shock, his new father leaned down and whispered, "I am your creator, boy. Your salvation. Never forget that."

Then he handed Will a copper-colored coin, slipping it into his new, foreign hand.

"What's this?" Will asked.

"Keep this with you always as a reminder. Just as you own this penny, I own you."

Earth-shattering charges pulsed through Will's body and wrenched him into consciousness. His body ached, shuddering, and his mind was fuzzy. Shadows shrouded the walls of wherever he was—a cell. Unused, judging by the musty smell. The stones were old and faded, the air frigid and stale. He was underground and cloaked in darkness, nothing but a pale slant of light coming from a holo-flame somewhere above.

The source of his shuddering revealed itself quickly as a long metal prod. On the other end crouched a generic-looking mock male with a pleasant smile that contrasted with his flat, cruel eyes. His face hardly creased as he shocked Will again, and again. Blue sparks lit the darkness. Will kicked at the rod and scurried back, pain shooting up his left arm when it touched the grimy floor.

Deep down, he knew what he would see when he looked

at his arm. Still, as his gaze swept over the stump, wrapped in gauze stained black, a fist of panic slammed into his gut.

"Leave the captain alone, Collector." The queen stepped into the dim light, the soft, insidious tone of her voice raking down every knob of his spine. "His uploads show he has no information on her whereabouts or the secret Alliance locations."

Disappointment flashed across his torturer's face, the man's bizarre smile twitching. "He may have such knowledge embedded inside his programs—"

"No." The words were final, leaving no room for argument. "He didn't know he was a traitor until seven hours ago. That was a secret buried inside with the last remains of his human tendencies. A nasty little surprise." The queen peered down at him, her pale face half veiled in darkness. "No, he won't have the information we need."

She emerged from the shadows, the queen's sleek, polished armor the only clean thing in the cell. He'd seen her holograms before, and her visage haunted every single broadcast made in the galaxies. But up close, she was phenomenal—tall and powerful with a savagely stunning beauty that made him forget his pain for a breath. Like staring at one of the large, extinct cats that used to roam the first world.

"Let this be a lesson, Collector." She wrapped her slim fingers around the bars and peered down at him the way someone stares at an insect. "Humanity cannot be stamped out of someone. Like a virus hidden inside a single cell, it returns to infect the host."

Nausea coiled in Will's gut. How had he ever pledged his life to someone like her? All these years thinking his service was for someone pure and honorable, a queen worthy of his loyalty. Yet it was all a lie. This woman might wear a crown, but she paled in comparison to Talia, even with all the flesher princess's human faults.

For the first time, he realized those were what made her worth following. And this perfect, unfeeling queen was a bad copy—and undoubtedly a psychopath.

"I'm glad she's free," he said, grinning despite the pain in his arm and his overall crappy circumstances. In fact, he hadn't felt this clear about something in a while. "She's going to escape your planet and rally the Alliance, and then she'll show everyone what a true queen looks like."

A frighteningly long pause followed where not a flicker of emotion crossed the smooth contours of the mock queen's face. Then she wrapped her hands around the metal bars of his cell and squeezed until dust and steel ground beneath her metal fingers and clouded the air. She regarded him a moment longer, her huge eyes unblinking as her gaze raked over him, peeling back layers to his core.

"I hear having your servers corrupted is about the most painful thing our kind can endure," she said, glancing sideways at the man she called the Collector. Then she turned and glided back into the shadows, calling out over her shoulder, "Set his public execution for daybreak tomorrow, so the galaxies can see what happens to anyone who supports Talia Starchaser."

CHAPTER 30

Talia

Talia's fall seemed to span forever. She flailed in the air, her hair snapping away from her face, wind thundering in her ears. As soon as she hit the murky water she sank like a brick. The currents caught her heavy cloak and yanked her deeper. Thrashing in a panic, she clawed at the material to free herself, but then a strong hand clenched her shoulder and yanked her to the surface. She clamored into the metal boat, wincing as her bruised wrists dragged against the hard sides and gasping in precious gulps of air.

Chunks of concrete splashed in the water, hailing down from above—the drones must have shot right as she'd jumped, just missing her and blasting a human-sized pit into the wall. Lux popped up on the other side of the boat, looking about as happy as a cat being drowned, her lips pursed and eyes hard.

She shot Leo a look that could melt the sun as she climbed over the side, wheezing. "Thanks for the . . . help, Leo."

"Always a gentleman," Leo remarked, cutting a sideways glance at her before aiming at the closest drone. As it dipped low, sunlight reflecting off its convex body, he let off a shot. Direct hit. The drone crashed into the water, sending drops spraying every which way.

Talia slipped into the pilot's seat, a smooth red fiberglass thing, still warm from the angry fisherman now swimming toward the shore thirty-yards out. The boat had a steering wheel, a throttle, and two buttons. Small crafts like this frequented the rivers of the off-world resort planet of Laos, but she'd never actually piloted one. How hard could it be?

The engine was still rumbling. She paused, her hand just over the throttle. "What about Will?"

Lux already had her gaze locked onto the bridge, searching for any sign of him. Leo flicked quick glances over too, in between taking shots at the drones. Talia counted twenty rapid beats of her heart as they waited—an eternity.

"Go," Lux commanded, her shoulders lowering as she ripped her gaze from the bridge. "He'll find a way back . . . if he can."

Despite the hesitation for leaving Will, Talia's adrenaline made her hit the throttle, hard. She slammed into the seat, which only made her push the throttle down *more*.

Leo cried out and crashed onto the sleek deck, bellowing curse words as Lux smirked at him and held onto a rail along the side. They skipped over the waves, the power from each landing concussing Talia's body and rattling her teeth, her skull. Sprays of water soaked her face and hair and sent little rainbows shimmering over the air. But they made good time, and somewhere between there and the shore, Leo shot the other drone out of the sky.

Once on land, five more drones came, but Leo and Lux took care of them, shooting rays from their blasters. Dripping wet and reeking of stagnant water, the crew sprinted into the city, winding through alleys and under bridges to avoid the crowds. Talia threw her arm out to stop Lux and Leo as they were about to round a corner, spotting soldiers marching on the other side of the street.

After waiting three beats for the soldiers to pass, Talia nodded and received a small, almost nonexistent, smile from Lux. They made their way to the outskirts of the market and kept their heads low while winding down a rickety spiral staircase, closing in on the meeting place.

As soon as the Odysseus's ragged hull came into view, hidden beneath a crumbling bridge and a mound of junk metal and trash, Talia's entire body went limp with relief. She stumbled inside, and they were met by Jane and Dorian. Their eyes darted from the returned crew to the door.

"Where's the captain?" Jane asked, even as her eyes crumpled on the sides a bit like she knew already.

"Had to . . . leave him behind," Leo panted, one hand plastered on the wall of the bridge for support. Water dripped from his thick braids and puddled on the metal floor.

Lux reached over and punched a few buttons on the bands still around his wrists, then she slipped the explosive devices off.

"Glad to know I'm not on your bad side anymore." Leo winked, rubbing his red, irritated wrists.

"Let's just stay alive."

Dorian crossed the bridge to the com panel and twisted a few dials until a holo-screen popped up over the dash. The image shimmered before solidifying, revealing Will from the shoulders up and drawing a gasp from Lux. His flesh was split open over his left eyebrow, trickling blood down his cheek. Reddish-purple bruises spotted his face. Despite his obvious injuries, he still managed a smirk.

His name and ranking were listing below the image—Will Perrault, Ender Class and Scavenger Captain of the Odysseus— along with the words *traitor*. Lux's hand shot out, using Leo for support as Will's face disappeared and a mock entered the screen. Something about him was familiar, with his dead eyes and giddy smile so at odds with the rest of his countenance.

"The Collector," Talia murmured, as if saying his name too loudly might draw his gaze toward her. Waves of hot anger rolled over her, the kind that could burn someone from the inside out, blood and all. He was the one responsible for the Starchaser's death. He and Ailat. And now he was near Will. He'd risked his life for Talia, for his crew. The thought churned her gut, and she fisted a hand against her stomach.

"Captain Will Perrault was caught harboring a high-profile member of the Alliance. He is a traitor to the Federation, his queen, and the intergalactic community. Tomorrow at dawn, he will be corrupted publicly as a reminder of what happens to those who help our enemies."

Talia hugged herself to block out the giddy humor in The Collector's tone, and the awful memories that came with it, her legs suddenly very heavy. How could she let Will suffer like this? She spoke to him about hope, but what hope did he have if she didn't do something?

"Guys . . ." Lux's voice wavered, drawing Talia's attention back to the holo-screen.

Jane's image and rank wavered in front of them, her

short salt-and-pepper hair combed and her black uniform crisp, a proud smile on her face. Jane was standing a few feet away from the image, and a tiny breath escaped her lips, her shoulders slumping as she read the word below: traitor.

Lux was next. For once, her lavender hair was tamed into a bun, her jewel-bright green eyes appearing more hazel against her cobalt-blue uniform. She wore a big smile that showed off dimples on either side of her cheeks.

"They took that picture right after I graduated the Academy," she whispered, staring at the image as if she didn't recognize herself.

As soon as Dorian's picture appeared, Lux stiffened, hardly daring to breathe. His image was taken a few years ago, judging by his round face soft with youth. The word *traitor* blinking below this innocent boy seemed wrong.

"Look at that handsome devil," Leo scoffed as his visage appeared. Whatever the occasion for the picture, his long honey-blond hair—usually pulled back into braids—was loosed and combed away from his chiseled face. "Never been a traitor as good looking as him."

Before Talia could respond to that bit of ridiculousness, a picture of her from the chest up appeared, and her heart free-fell into her belly. She looked radiant inside the midnight-black dress from her birthday, her eyes focused on something in the background. Not a hint of her unease from that day showed—she was good at hiding emotions, after all. They'd had the audacity to erase her crown from the image and doctor her title from Sovereign-in-Waiting Princess Talia Starchaser to nameless rebel.

At least the price on her head hinted at her real identity—500 billion credits.

"Holy stars," Leo muttered, rubbing his jaw. "We'll have the entire galaxy after us for that sum."

Lux switched off the screen and took a seat at the console, punching buttons and flipping switches to prep the ship for takeoff. "That's why we need to get going. Jane, can you start the departure sequence? Dorian, check the coils and thrusters and initiate regular maintenance. We need to ready the hyper-drive, and we might be off land for a while."

Leo cast his attention to Jane, drawing Lux's gaze that way as well. "And if she glitches mid-hyper?"

"She won't."

Leo snorted.

"But if she does, the princess over there's a pilot. She can take over."

They all looked at Talia, and for the first time ever she doubted her flying skills. "I can fly most fighter crafts, but my training never extended to large cargo vessels like the Odysseus."

"Well, you better figure it out because you and glitch over there"—Lux flashed an apologetic half-grin at Jane—"are all we've got."

Talia quirked an eyebrow. "What about Will?"

Lux sucked in her cheek as she crossed the bridge to stand before Talia. "We can't do anything about him now."

"Why not?"

"Because there's only four of us—unless you count my barely pubescent brother—then there's five. *Five*. And the queen has an entire army. Even if they didn't *want* to fight for her, you saw what she did in the courtyard with her hive mind tactics. She can *make* them destroy us."

Talia planted her hands on her hips. "Well, I refuse to leave him."

Lux blinked at Talia as if she'd spoken another language. "He was about to sell you to the queen. Have you forgotten about that?"

"But he didn't, and now the queen is going to publicly murder him to get to me. I can't just sit around and watch that happen." She began to pace, her mind whirring. "What if we had help? Leo said there are members of the Alliance out there who'll support me. There have to be some here. Let's ask them for aid."

Lux rolled her eyes, hard, and shot a sharp, narrow-eyed look at Leo. "Tell her she's being crazy."

Leo twisted one of his braids between his thumb and pointer finger. "What if she's not?"

"Don't, Leo. Don't you give her any ideas. This is madness, and I'm not going to risk Dorian's life, even for . . ."

"Will?" Leo answered when Lux couldn't say the captain's name. "You mean the man who spent his shares bribing those jailers to spring Dorian from jail after he got caught pickpocketing that commander on that back-world waystation? Who got me out of trouble time and again when they caught me with undocumented escorts? The captain who paid your fine for kneeing that bounty hunter in the balls?"

"That jerk deserved it," she added, but her voice wavered.

"Not the point, Lux. Will proved his loyalty to us when we

needed him most. Now it's our turn . . ." He rubbed his chest, muttering under his breath, "Even if he did shoot me."

"I could do a secret broadcast," Talia offered, lifting on her toes with excitement as a plan began to take shape. "Announce who I am and tell citizens to join our side, that we want peace for mocks and humans. This was once my capital, after all. Surely people still remember me?"

"Your history's been erased, but there are some who might appreciate a more peaceful way of life . . ." The lines between Lux's dark brows smoothed out, though she still didn't look entirely convinced. "Say you *can* gather more people to help, and miraculously we save Will and make it out alive. Then what? If we don't leave in the next, say, half hour, the Odysseus will be splashed across every ship's starscreen within five clicks of Calisto, and we won't make it out of this airspace alive."

Talia sighed, long and hard. *Good point.* "What about another ship?"

Lux scoffed and closed her eyes, as if she were dealing with an idiot. "Another ship? They giving those away somewhere I don't know about?"

"The Athena." Everyone turned to Jane, who hadn't yet uttered a peep. "Give Will his ship back. That would be a nice escape death present, right?"

As farfetched as the idea was, it somehow made sense. With Will behind the controls of the Athena, they could easily hyper-drive all the way to the Alliance. Once Jane planted the idea, the others, including Lux, went along with it and worked through formulating a plan. At first stealing a weaponized military A-class Darkstar didn't sound remotely plausible, but once they factored in Dorian's penchant for thievery and Jane's gambling habits, plus some sleeping pills for mocks—made to allow mocks to dream—it went from a suicidal idea to a feasible plan . . . if all the stars aligned perfectly and the crew of the Athena were thirsty tonight.

Everything counted on that thirst.

But before the crew could even start on that crazy endeavor, they had to put together a half-credible strategy for breaking Will out before his execution in the morning. Lucky for Talia, she knew how the queen thought.

"She'll hold the execution inside the great hall where my coronation took place," Talia said as they pored over any images they could conjure up of this new palace.

Lux frowned. "How do you know it's still there? She razed the old palace to the ground—"

"She left it, believe me." Talia squinted at the jutting spires of metal, sunlight running down their craggy length, and stabbed a finger at the holo-image. "It'll be somewhere in here."

"How do we get inside?" Leo asked, lines etching between his brows as he pored over the image of the castle. "More importantly, how do we get a crowd inside?"

The rebels—assuming any showed. "If I know the queen, she'll keep the doors closed and have it publicly broadcasted. We need something to take out the gate and one of the hall's walls."

Leo chuckled and threw Lux a knowing look. "That'd be your department, darling. You're the best explosives expert in the Seven."

For the first time since meeting the cocky navigator, Lux

blushed, her dusky cheeks tinged with fire. "I haven't blown anything up since the Academy."

"Lux was part of an elite unit that hunted Alliance forces for two years," Leo explained to Talia.

"Why'd you quit?" she asked.

A shadow passed over Lux's face, and she glanced at Dorian before answering. "Got tired of blowing people up."

No doubt because of what happened to their parents.

"We have the ship," Leo said, breaking a thick silence that had suddenly fallen over the crew. "We have the manpower—hopefully—and a way inside. But how will we prevent them from executing Will the moment the explosives go off?"

Jane smiled, the corner of her mouth twitching at Talia, as if the previous Odysseus captain knew Talia had already worked this part out. "We need someone inside beforehand."

Talia nodded slowly, taking a deep breath before continuing. "Me."

She'd have to work that part out before tomorrow, but she had time. Now she needed to record a speech for the Alliance rebels, even though she had no idea what to say as Leo set up the outside com and carefully punched in the secret rebel frequency. Then he directed the pinhole microphone and camera at her.

All the air inside Talia's lungs seemed to shrivel, her heartbeat drowning out sounds. Who was she to speak to millions? She was a scared girl without a clue how to rule. How could she inspire others to risk their lives for her when she couldn't even save her friend all those years ago?

But then Leo nodded, his face laced with tentative hope,

and she realized that like it or not, she was her people's only hope. Humanity's only chance at survival. So she cleared her throat and began, the words tumbling from her lips.

"I don't know if anyone's out there, or if this message is going to be lost to the emptiness of space. But I have a story to tell. One hundred years ago, I was a princess with a family who loved me and a best friend I adored. War was on the verge of breaking out between human and mock kinds, but I thought my perfect life was safe, until one mistake, one act of cowardice on my part destroyed everything . . ." Her words trailed away, but Leo nodded for her to continue. "War came, and three generations of Starchasers, the very people who discovered the Seven and gave mocks life, were gone in an instant. Murdered. Except for me. My family surrendered their lives so that I could escape. Now, a century later, I've woken up to a terrifying new reality. To a dark, hopeless time where humans are enslaved and an imposter queen rules through force, taking over mocks at her will. A world where freedom has been stripped from us."

The other end of the com crackled as Talia paused. Once she said the words and asked for help, she would condemn many of the people listening to death. The device wavered inside her palm. How easy flipping the com off and leaving this hellhole would be, blazing a path to the Alliance where she was safe and wanted. All her current worries would melt away. She could deal with the rest later.

Except she did that once, with Ailat, and it practically ruined the world. Sometimes the right path was the hardest— and the most likely to get her killed.

"I watched my parents and brother die for me to live," she continued, her voice less shaky. "And now I'm asking you to take that same risk for the chance of a world where mocks and humans have equal rights, where the world, *our* world, is better and full of hope. My name is Talia Starchaser, the last living descendant of the Starchaser Dynasty and rightful Sovereign of the Seven, and I'm asking you to fight with me tomorrow against oppression and tyranny. Against a queen who may have once been good but is now a ruthless oppressor. Tomorrow is the day we stand up and fight back."

Silence fell over the ship as she switched off the broadcast and released a sharp breath. Even though they desperately needed more people involved to make this plan work, a part of her hoped there was something wrong with the com and no one heard her call to arms. She wasn't sure if her conscience could reconcile the deaths of so many.

But this wasn't just for Talia, rescuing Will and defeating the queen was for all of them. Mocks and humans alike. Ailat might have once been good and honorable, but what happened on that stage with Prince Cassius had twisted her into something dark and malevolent, and Talia felt responsible for putting Ailat's reign of terror and oppression to an end. So Talia shoved that part down deep and prepared herself for the coming battle, just like she imagined her father had done all those years ago during the beginning of the mock rebellion.

This was war, after all.

And things were about to get bloody on both sides.

CHAPTER 31

Will

Storm clouds crashed across the skies of Palesia, darkening the dusk-orange-and-pink palette to a murky yellowish green and bringing cool winds sweeping across the palace terrace. The breeze ruffled Will's jacket and stole the heat from his body. To his left stood the queen, a full foot taller than him, her towering form throwing a faint shadow across the railing. She wore the same armor as the day before, now adorned with a purple cape held together by a jeweled brooch.

The diamonds on the pin crackled as bits of morning sunlight broke through the clouds. As soon as he realized the brooch was a swan made into the Starchaser crest, an ominous shadow fell over him that he couldn't quite shake. Pinned to the queen's neck, the symbol that first started it all looked *wrong*.

He took a step toward the ledge, and one of the queen's guards jerked up his blaster, the biggest Will had ever seen. He held up his good arm in surrender and scowled at the droid, a type of hunter Will didn't recognize. This model was the same steel-gray color of the storm clouds rolling in, and lither than its predecessors. But the lack of bulk meant the machines were faster and more agile, their movements rapid and intelligent.

"Easy, dummy," Will called, slowly retreating to show he wasn't a threat to the queen. "What are you looking for?"

His voice was muffled by the wind, but he knew the queen heard because she tilted her head slightly in Will's direction, keeping her gaze trained on the ground hundreds of feet below. Just like him, her eyesight could be adjusted to see long distances, and not for the first time this morning, he wondered what they were doing up here.

Watching to see how many showed for his execution? If that was her intention, why was she waiting? Thousands of mocks thronged the bridges leading to the palace, and thousands more had spilled into the courtyard below. Hell, the streets were so crowded with onlookers wanting to see him die, he'd already seen two people knocked into the dark waters surrounding the palace.

The air traffic was just as bad. A swarm of vessels clogged the skies, blocking the light and reminding Will of a nest of hornets right after it'd been disturbed.

He and the queen had stood here for over an hour. Will wasn't bound, but he might as well have been with ten guards weighted down with blasters watching his every move. He'd been wracking his brain for a way out since the moment they stepped foot up here, but his odds weren't good.

No weapon. Check.

No allies. Check.

No knowledge of the terrain. Check.

No arm. Double check.

Will cringed. That last one was the hardest to accept. Every few minutes something as normal as opening a door or reaching out to lean on a ledge would remind him of his loss. The pain wasn't bad, just a mild throbbing and the occasional phantom sensation, as if his arm was still there. But it wasn't— and that pissed him off more than anything.

All at once the queen stiffened, her gaze tracking something below. Sharp buzzing filled the air as the six drones attached to her medusa-like tentacles dispatched from their tethers and shot toward the crowd.

Hand clenched into a fist, Will walked to the edge of the iron railing, careful to remain far enough away from the queen to keep the super-hunters happy. He toyed with the idea of using the queen's distraction to try and throw her over the side— one-armed or not—when something caught his attention.

Or some*one*, more like it. His enhanced vision zoomed in until the person drawing his gaze came into focus, her long auburn hair mostly hidden beneath the same hideous blanket as yesterday. All the air left him, and he leaned on the railing with his one hand, the iron cool beneath his palm.

What the hell was Talia doing?

Her head snapped up as one of the drones paused to hover near her face. Two more followed. *Run, idiot.* Beside him, the queen leaned as far over the terrace as possible, her long fingers wrapped around the ledge.

"Stupid girl." A smile warped the queen's face.

Suddenly Talia smashed a fist into the drone and took off through the crowd, but three of the queen's enhanced super-hunters materialized from the crowd, looming over Talia.

She stole a look behind as two more appeared. Then, probably realizing she was trapped, she yanked a blaster from somewhere beneath the heavy folds of her cloak and began shooting.

The crowd parted around her, surging toward the edges of the bridge. Waves of civilians crashed into the water, pushed by the swarms of mocks escaping the blasts, the sounds of screaming stirring the air.

For a heartbeat, he thought Talia might have a chance, her hair whipping in the wind as she fought the dark hunters, her blaster painting the air around them electric blue. *Atta girl.* He held his breath, willing her to escape.

Then the hunters surged together in a coordinated attack, burying the princess beneath a tangle of onyx metal. No way could she escape that.

He shoved back from the ledge and kicked the railing, causing the two closest guards to lift their blasters.

"Screw you, metal-heads!" he yelled, taunting them with an inappropriate gesture.

At this point, he didn't care if they shot him to hell. Nausea churned his stomach as he imagined Talia down there, hurt and afraid. Although afraid might be a stretch. If he knew the princess, she was probably hurtling obscenities at the hunters even now, pinned beneath them.

Stars, if they hurt her . . .

"She was always blind when it came to her friends," the queen said, her tone nonchalant despite the way her eyes kept flicking back to the scene, a predator unable to resist watching its prey. She waved the hunters back with a lazy flip of her hand. Finally, she tore her gaze off Talia below and met Will's eyes. "What do you say, Captain. Care for company at your execution?"

Lifting his one good arm, he charged the bitch. Surprisingly, he made it within a foot of her before a hunter bashed the butt of his blaster over Will's head and he hit the pavement, lights out.

CHAPTER 32

Talia

So far, everything was going according to plan. Though recognizing that with both arms trapped firmly inside a hunter's grasp, one on each side, was a bit difficult. At least the queen needed *two* muscled-up droids to hold Talia.

"Stop grinning and pretend to be scared," Lux hissed into the tiny earpiece hidden just inside Talia's ear.

"I don't have to pretend," she muttered, ignoring the curious glance of the hunter on her right.

She wasn't bound yet—unless the hunters holding her counted—as they marched her through the angry crowds. Curses flew at her from brainwashed civilian mocks, but luckily the crowd's fear of the hunters trumped their hatred of her, and the tightly packed sea of citizens parted once again. Hopefully some of those angry faces belonged to Leo's Alliance friends.

Most of the storm had passed, despite a thin smattering of rain on her cheeks, and sunlight cast the palace's shadow across the courtyard. She twisted against the hunters' iron-clad grips, appraising this new palace. A meshwork of steel and glass rose from the ground, so high she couldn't crane her neck back enough to see the top. Walls of tangled metal melded together like vines all vying for the best spot in the sun. Up and up it went, vessels coming and going like tendrils of smoke wafting off the glinting walls.

The hunters crossed through a series of guarded archways and courtyards, dragging Talia along without regard for her human frailty. Ailat had always been careful, but this seemed excessive. Even paranoid.

A sense of anticipation mixed with dread formed a strange sort of excitement in the pit of Talia's stomach. How many times had she walked this path, nervous about some gathering or another, her companion mock by her side for comfort?

And yet *comfort* was the last thing Talia was expecting today.

"Keep moving," the hunter said, its voice like metal and stone grinding together.

Then it jerked Talia's arm for good measure, and she swore she heard a pop as they crossed the final gate to the actual palace, the great hall where all this trouble started rising in the distance. The pale moonstone structure was exactly like she remembered, a relic from another time. Marble archways held up a steeply pitched roof and three spires of varying lengths. A shimmering globe of glass surrounded the ancient hall. Sunlight danced along the curves of the globe and cast rainbows all about.

Ailat had preserved the hall. The thought made Talia's heart skip a beat, and she released a ragged breath. Once, this place had seemed huge. But now—now it looked like a miniature doll house next to the monstrosity of smoky metal towering above it. That was probably why Ailat kept everything the same. A reminder to all of the superiority of mocks over humans.

Climbing the steps up to the hall was surreal, transporting Talia through time. What only felt like a week but spanned one hundred years. She kept glancing back, looking for the drone Dorian had snagged from the Academy earlier—along with the explosives banded around her waist beneath her jumpsuit. He really was an incredible thief.

The Athena was waiting for Talia, unmanned—thanks to Jane distracting everyone with her mean dice game while Dorian slipped the sleeping tonic into their cups. The Athena's crew should be resting in a deep sleep right now, probably dreaming about all the possessions they lost to Jane. Lux and Leo were in the crowd outside the gates with a shitload of explosives packed and ready to use. As soon as the queen began broadcasting the spectacle, Talia's friends would use the distraction to slip through the outer gates unnoticed. If all went as planned, they'd set off the explosives on the final gate and then the royal hall.

They just needed their captain.

"Keep going," Lux whispered into Talia's ear, and she responded with a near imperceptible nod to indicate she'd heard.

Once inside the royal hall, the crew would no longer be able to see her. But they would be able to hear everything.

Talia's heart punched into her throat as she crossed the threshold inside and began scouring the darkness. A few breaths passed before her eyes adjusted. Everything was exactly as she'd left it one hundred years ago. Rays of warm sunshine poured in from the skylight above and painted the square tiles with thick, buttery strokes. Mahogany-stained wooden beams crisscrossed the high ceilings. A dais rose in the middle of the cavernous room, the same one she stood on when she betrayed Ailat. Tables and chairs scattered around the center stage—all empty save one table nearest the dance floor. The very same one where Prince Cassius made Ailat stand.

Mocks filled the room, dressed in lustrous suits and vibrant, shimmery gowns. Understanding hit Talia like a slap to the cheek, sending goosebumps dancing across her skin.

This was a recreation of that fateful day.

She grimaced, remembering the way Cassius crushed her arm in his vice-like grip. The way Ailat stood embarrassed and vulnerable, her wounded pride on full display. Just the memory of Talia's friend's pain was enough to bring all those horrible emotions from that day back to the surface. To make them real in a way they hadn't been before.

Maybe that was the moment Ailat snapped. Maybe her programming had never properly prepared her for the deep sting of humiliation.

"They're waiting for you at the table," Lux said, the music and chatter from the ballroom muffling her voice. "Will's there—he looks . . . *hurt,* but okay." The way she hesitated before the word *hurt* sent alarm bells ringing in Talia's skull. "We can see part of the dance floor and surrounding tables from the skylight, but not the stage."

Three people filled the only seated table. Will was one of the diners, but she didn't have to look too closely to know who the others would be as the hunters shoved her closer, their metal feet clanking against the tile. One of the hunters pulled back a chair for her, but when she went to sit, the queen said, "No. Humans don't sit at tables with mocks. Isn't that right, Tal?"

Refusing to look at her former friend, Talia stood, hands clasped behind her back as she assessed Will, scouring him for serious injuries. He sat with his shoulders squared and head held high against the high-backed velvet chair, despite the pain tightening his eyes. Soot and a few ragged tears marred his otherwise pristine captain's jacket. If not for his rigid demeanor, or the scrapes and bruises mottling his flesh, he appeared a venerated captain enjoying a nice meal.

He shifted to face her, revealing more of his torso. One of his jacket's arms had been peeled back . . . a small gasp slipped from her lips at the sight of his missing arm, bandaged just below the elbow, and she resisted the urge to reach out and comfort him somehow. That was what Lux saw from above.

Once, Talia might have been curious about what lay beneath his torn skin, the differences between them. Now she couldn't care less if he was made of metal, bone, or dirt for that matter.

She simply wanted him safe and out of pain.

Will met her gaze, and a shiver of pride ran through her at the courage she found there. He even wore his usual half-smirk.

"Wasn't expecting you for this little luncheon," he said, his scolding tone making it clear he disapproved of this plan.

"Well," she replied, "You know how I feel about being left out."

The com inside her ear crackled to life. "Stall, Talia. We need at least another fifteen minutes. The crowd's larger than expected, and we're having trouble getting close to the first gate."

Bloody stars. They should have already been past the first gate with their explosives. She shifted nervously on her toes, willing her mind clear of anxious thoughts.

She could do this. It *had* to work.

The man directly across from her chuckled—the Collector. He'd traded his patched-together junk body for a top-grade one, his face constructed of soft, pleasing lines that complimented his permanent smile. A sable tux finished the illusion.

If not for the port flap just above his collar, or his cruel black eyes, no one would guess he wasn't human.

"Hello, dear," he said, his smile stretching into a chasm, revealing a mouthful of human teeth. "I'm glad we finally found you. We were beginning to worry."

Bastard! She swallowed the insults weighing down her tongue. He was a welcome distraction from the one person in this room she both hated and loved—but Talia had to face her former friend.

After all, soon—if everything went perfect and according to plan—she might have to kill Ailat, end her the way Cassius had tried to a century ago.

The queen sat to Talia's left, wearing the same beautifully savage armor from the day before. A scarlet cloak of satin flowed from her shoulders to the floor, gold embroidery catching the light from above. Wide, depthless black eyes peered at Talia, unblinking above angular cheekbones and a sharp jaw. Charcoal-black hair flowed down the queen's back.

Upon recognizing the brooch with the Starchaser's family

crest on it, the one given as a present by Ailat and then traded to the Collector, Talia finally allowed herself to believe Ailat's betrayal. That she had truly been a part of Talia's family's murder.

Although this queen looked nothing like the Ailat Talia remembered, there was something familiar, just beyond the cold look and sneering lips. As if the companion mock Talia knew was trapped just below, announcing her presence through near-imperceptible tics. Gestures. The occasional fleeting emotion that flickered across this version's dead face.

Talia fixed the queen with a hard stared. "Ailat. I'd wondered what happened to you."

"Hmm." If Talia had any remaining doubts Ailat was truly gone, the queen's remote voice dispelled them. "I had no idea you were concerned for my safety, Tal."

Talia gritted her teeth at the once affectionate nickname. "I was. That's why I came to The Collector. Why I was stupid enough to trust him. Everything I did was to get you back so I could protect you."

"Protect or *own*? Was I a friend you wanted to help or a piece of property to be collected and forced back into service?"

"You know I never felt that way about you. I never treated you like property, I . . ." Talia let her words fall away. Perhaps part of what Ailat said was true, and the shame of that would stay with Talia forever. But the truth didn't change the fact they were friends. *Sisters.* "I cared about you, Ailat. As much as family—maybe more."

The queen's lips twisted into a sneer. "Cared? Is that what you call ordering me to kill myself? I was loyal to you, Princess, but the second a Thorossian prince commanded you to end me like nothing more than faulty equipment, a broken toy, you complied with a *smile* on your face."

"I was trying to save your life!" Talia insisted. "I suspected you were corrupted and hoped that would spark something inside you to override your programs so you could escape."

"Corrupted?" the queen spat. "You say that like free will is a sickness."

Talia flinched at the accusation just as her earpiece buzzed.

Lux said, "We made it through the first gate, but there was a problem. We'll have more guards on us soon. Stall as long as possible . . ."

"Is that why you killed my parents?" Talia persisted. "*Tamsin?*"

Something shuttered just below the queen's wicked mask, an infinitesimal flicker of emotion.

"When I finally found Ailat on the streets of Palesia," The Collector said, shining a butter knife with his thumb, "a group of human men had her. They found her that first day after she fled here and *played* with her a bit. She'd been tortured, violated, and mutilated beyond recognition by then, so the fleshers didn't know she had a bounty on her head." He pulled at the stiff white collar of his shirt, lost in thought. "After I saved her, cleaned her up, and gave her back the parts we could find, she was willing to tell me everything about you."

Talia slid her gaze back to the queen, grimacing while imagining Ailat scared and alone at the mercy of those men. "I didn't betray you, Ailat."

Ailat turned her attention to her friend, gaze hardened and black eyes devoid of anything that resembled that girl they spoke of. Instead, viciousness lingered, a detached malevolence Talia had been taught mocks couldn't possess. "You betrayed me the moment your kind created me, a perfect specimen forced to live in your imperfect shadow. Can you fathom how it feels to be smarter and stronger than everyone around you, to have the ability to crush them with a single blow, and yet be treated as a soulless insect?"

All at once the mocks moving around the room froze. Then, as if on some invisible signal, they all waltzed to the dance floor and began choreographed movements to simulate revelers at a party.

More specifically, the guests from that night one hundred years ago.

Talia shivered, tightening her arms around her chest. The queen was controlling the entire room—at least seventy mocks—with her mind. That meant once Lux and Leo blew up the outside wall and then the walls of the great hall, the queen would have seventy soldiers at her disposal, as well as seven hunters that stood guard along the walls.

Every piece of this plan had to fall into place exactly right, or Talia and Will would be trapped. She craned her neck up at the skylight . . . When was the last time Lux made contact? Sweat crept over Talia's neck and back, trickling down her shoulder blades. If even one piece of the plan fell through . . .

Before she could manage a whisper to Lux, the queen stood. "Let's dance, shall we?"

Will shot Talia a confused look as a hunter yanked him from his seat and forced him to the dance floor. He almost succeeded at hiding his poor condition, but she recognized a subtle limp in his step, the way standing abruptly had him struggling for breath.

Another hunter prodded her in the same direction. The queen watched carefully as Talia and Will were forced together in a macabre semblance of a dance. Mocks fluttered around them in perfect step. The queen grinned as Will hesitated, holding out the stub of his arm to Talia's waiting hand. She slid her fingers up over his bicep, and he winced.

"This is . . . okay?" she whispered into his ear.

He shifted his arm slightly and nodded. "Barely even hurts."

"Liar."

"Although," he continued, doing his best to smile, "I'll never be able to play the piano again."

Will stiffened as the queen came up behind them, and her hard fingers on Talia's shoulder sent tremors of disgust coursing through her.

"You make a marvelous couple, Tal. Just like that ore prince, Cassius. I never found him, you know. He left his family to be crushed and fled to the Alliance." A pause. Talia felt the cold shadow of the queen's gaze fall over Will as she studied him. "All flesher males are the same, don't you think?"

The second the queen was gone, Talia exhaled, releasing the tension in her shoulders. "She's going to execute you first."

"Lovely. Wish we hadn't waited until our executions to do this." He slipped his hand around her waist, and his eyes stretched wide as he felt the explosives.

"Be serious, idiot. I have a plan." Her words came out fast and breathy, and she waited until he twirled her with his good arm to continue. "Be ready to run, you'll know when . . . Without me if you have to. And don't believe everything you see."

He raised a swollen eyebrow as understanding dawned. "You *let* yourself get taken."

There was no question in his statement, and she rested her head on his shoulder, pretending to be swept away in the dance. A mixture of salty sweat and the rich, metallic scent of mock blood filled her nose. "Shh. We don't have long. My execution comes after yours, and I'd rather not be around for it."

The small of her back tingled as his hand settled there, resting warm and strong against her spine. "I didn't want you to come back for me, Princess."

"Well I don't answer to you, Will Perrault, although that may come as a shock to your inflated ego. Besides, I have a history with this queen, if you haven't figured that out yet."

His hand pressed her into him, their bodies melding together. "So you're not here because you like me?"

She swallowed, both irked and strangely breathless. How was it possible to be attracted to someone and also want to punch them? "I'm here for *both* of you."

Cold hands clamped down on her shoulders and ripped her and Will apart. They clung together a moment, stupidly, as if that could prolong what was about to happen. Then a hunter yanked Will across the dance floor, his boots scuffing and squeaking as he tried to resist, and forced him to the stage.

Talia followed without being prompted, her heart lodged in her throat. Why hadn't Lux responded? At least ten minutes had passed. They should be at the last wall and ready. She wiped her sweat-stained palms over her cloak as she ascended the stage, the feel of the plastic explosives clinging to her waist comforting. Her hand went to the bangle around her left wrist before she forced herself to stop touching it. Any attention to Tandy's bangle would mean scrutiny—and their plan couldn't afford that.

Talia found herself panting for air, unable to catch her breath, her legs growing heavier. Adrenaline had morphed into panic. Numbness overtook her limbs as all the blood rushed to her core, her vision shrinking to small pinholes as an avalanche of terror crashed over her. They needed that distraction, like, yesterday.

Come on, Lux. We're out of time.

Talia knew what happened next because she'd been here before. The queen was going to force Talia to corrupt Will and fry his circuits. His would be a slow, agonizing death. Then her turn would arrive.

Fortunately for her nerves, she couldn't begin to imagine what the queen had in store. And considering what happened to Ailat before The Collector found her, it was best Talia didn't even try to come up with a guess as to how the queen would replicate that part.

"Where are you?" Talia whispered to Lux, chewing her nails as she continually glanced out the windows. "The execution's about to start."

Five heartbeats followed. Five long, drawn out moments that seemed to last forever. Then her earpiece buzzed to life. "I know. I'm looking at you right now." Lux's words spewed out hard and fast, muffled by panting, as if she was running. "They have holo-screens broadcasting the execution all over the place."

"What are you waiting for?" A few mocks turned to Talia to stare, but she didn't care. The queen was walking toward her with whatever device they'd created to corrupt mocks. They were out of time.

"I . . . Talia, everything's gone to shit. I can't reach Jane, and we're trapped at the outer gates. The guards know something's up. And . . . we were forced to ditch the main wagon carrying the explosives."

"What about the rebels?" The words came out a dying whisper, so that anyone watching might think she was scared and muttering to herself. The first half of which was true.

"The explosions were supposed to be a signal. As of now, we have no idea who in the crowd is with the Alliance, if any."

Crackling filled Talia's ear, raking along her frayed nerves as she waited for Lux to say the inevitable.

"I'm sorry, Talia. We're screwed."

CHAPTER 33

Will

Will knew by Talia's face alone that something in her plan had gone horribly wrong. Unfortunately, instinct told him his crew was somehow involved as well. Anger coursed through his beaten and mangled body. His dominant hand was out of action, but he could still deliver punches with his right. He flexed his fingers in preparation, sneering at the closest hunter as the queen carried the corruption chip to Talia.

He'd witnessed a few executions by corruption, and the appalling images of mocks seizing, pissing themselves, and frothing at the mouth, eyes rolled back in their heads, permeated his mind.

Screw that. He'd rather die fighting. Craning his head, he scoured the hunters and crowd for small weapons he could manage one-handed. All of the hunters carried large military-grade blasters. But lucky for him, his biggest fan, Xander, had insisted on seeing the execution. He watched near the edge of the dais, wearing *Will's* uniform, an idiot smile plastered on the idiot's face, and a nice-sized blaster at his waist.

Will smiled back at his *brother,* enjoying the look of confusion that dampened his excitement. General Crayburn stood rigid next to him in full military uniform, light from above catching on his medals. He looked straight ahead, ignoring Will. He stiffened as he recognized the rest of the Athena's crew, *his* crew, their disappointed expressions lodging in his gut.

But his other crew, his *real* crew, was busy out there somewhere trying to save him—and possibly fighting for their lives. Stars, if he ever saw them again, he'd kiss each one of them. Even Leo, the beautiful bastard.

Talia's feet made soft, hollow thuds against the stage as she approached Will. The corruption chip fit neatly inside her palm, her hand trembling, making the rectangular device appear to shiver.

His logical mock side knew they couldn't escape alive. But his human side insisted he wrangle a weapon and take out the queen first so he could die proud. His glare skipped from Crayburn and Xander to the demented queen Will once pledged his life to. The knowledge that only days ago he strived to be like them filled him with shame.

The queen's sharp focus remained on the chip as Talia presented it to him. Their eyes met, her message clear. *Ready to fight?*

The queen drew closer, the drones attached to the tentacles in her crown buzzing with excitement. "Citizens of the Seven, we have two very special executions this morning. First up is mock traitor Will Perrault, former captain in the queen's regiment." Drawing in a long, ragged breath, the queen shifted her saddened gaze to him the way she might a loved one who betrayed her. "For your crimes, Captain, you will be corrupted until death."

While all eyes were on him, Talia snaked loose a corner of her shirt and snuck a hand inside. Fear dilated her pupils, but her lips pressed together with determination. On his signal, she would use the explosives. He glanced at Xander one last time, calculating the steps to him in case the bombs set off too much smoke to see. Will's heart thudded so loudly he thought the queen would hear and know.

Swallowing, he gave Talia a near-imperceptible nod, and resolve twisted her face into a steely mask as she moved to pull out the bombs—

A huge shadow washed over the room, casting the queen in darkness. Will tracked the shadow to the windows on the north wall, his brain processing the impossible just as a loud roar ripped through the air, followed by a giant explosion near the wall outside. A huge ship appeared, flying low. Fire raged across its hull from the impact against the gates, and mocks scattered out of its path as it headed straight for them.

The Odysseus. Which meant—

Even from this distance, he recognized the familiar face peering down from the bridge.

Talia must have too because she gasped. "Jane!"

His elation turned to confusion. Jane was going too fast: No one could survive the impact.

"Run!" someone screamed, but the cry came too late. The old ship rammed into the side of the building with enough force to knock Will to the ground. Grinding shrieks of metal meeting stone clogged the air, the concussion rattling his bones. The eruption tore through the room, sending bodies flying and shrapnel bursting into the onlookers. Screams rent the air.

Will struggled to his feet, ears ringing, inky smoke pouring out in all directions. Ash caught in his hair and snowed around the stage. The mangled wreckage of the Odysseus had skidded to a stop twenty feet from the raised platform where he was meant to die, the fireball consuming the ship sizzling heat across Will's skin and forcing everyone back. Without looking, Will knew Jane was gone.

No one could survive those flames, mock or human.

He shook off the shock, and his plan came roaring back into focus, burying the overwhelming pain of Jane's death for later. Xander was on the other side of the stage, huddled with a group of mocks. Disgust surged through Will's veins; the coward was hiding behind the injured.

Will leapt to the ground and into a sprint. Xander's head snapped up, his eyes widening with recognition, but he didn't have time to grab his blaster before Will barreled into him, scattering the injured mocks.

They slammed into the wall hard enough to crack the stone. A sick satisfaction came over Will as Xander groaned and went limp. The impact stunned him, though not enough to keep him from smashing his fist into Will's cheek. Red burst inside his skull. He shook off the blow and landed a knee to Xander's balls, kicking again as eight years of pent up rage released.

"Flesher bastard!" Xander howled, doubling over.

"You never used those anyway," Will taunted, snatching the blaster and shoving the muzzle of the weapon against Xander's pale forehead, metal clicking against metal. Xander froze, his lips curled in disgust and chest heaving. Black blood trickled from his lips.

With a grunt of rage, Will brought the blaster down over Xander's temple. The whites of his eyes flashed as he slumped to the floor unconscious. Then Will shoved his blaster into his waistband, retrieved the penny Crayburn had given him, and flicked the coin onto his brother. "Tell *Father* he can have that back."

Xander managed a groan.

"You're lucky I need the charge," Will called, darting back into the chaos to find Talia. Oily black smoke hung in sheets all around. His carbon-fiber lungs were much more efficient at filtering the smoke, but Talia's would already be struggling for oxygen.

Still, for the first time since his capture, hope buoyed his steps and masked his body's weariness. They had a chance, where five minutes ago they had none.

Their odds doubled when citizens flooded the hall from outside the gates, the glow of their blasters lighting up the darkness as they shot at the queen's forces.

Will found himself cheering for the Alliance as he hurtled over the remains of a table cracking with fire and checked the stage. He bounded up the steps, blue streams of fire zipping above his head and forcing him to retreat. At the bottom of the stairs, he ducked and pivoted, getting off two rounds at a hunter. The muscled-up droid stumbled two steps before crashing sideways into the burning table, sending fireflies of flame whooshing up.

Will turned and caught sight of something—the quick flash of hair the color of the flames raging inside the hall. The flash came from the top of the fallen wall, a twenty-foot mound of broken stones. Through the smoke, he made out the princess half-climbing half-falling down the ivory debris darkened with bodies and smoke. She flicked her terrified gaze behind her as if someone gave chase, her lips parted and breath coming in ragged spurts.

Two hunters emerged from the pile of broken stones above. They leapt after the princess, sending huge slabs cascading around her. Dust clouds filled the air. Head still turned back to watch the hunters, she managed to make it to the ground when something made her whip around, her bright hair flashing. Five small drones surrounded her, hovering ten feet out to form a circle. The queen's drones. Wherever she'd gone, she was undoubtedly watching Talia.

Her gaze slid to him. Before he could call out, the drones began to vibrate. Then a boom reverberated through the destroyed hall as they all fired at once.

Brightness seared his vision, the impact from the blast stunning him.

Each drone had enough force to kill a human male; all five of them together created a massive blast so big it took out the two hunters behind Talia.

Will's mouth parted, his cry a jagged rasp swallowed by the din of the stone rubble coming down. His mind screamed what his heart refused to hear: Even if Talia survived the concerted blow from the drones, the rubble sealed her fate.

Princess Talia Starchaser, the last of her dynasty, was dead.

CHAPTER 34

Talia

The moment Talia saw the Odysseus and realized what was happening, she shoved aside her sadness for Jane and darted across the stage. Talia needed the queen and her hunters to follow and give Will enough time to escape. The queen saw Talia run and shrieked, sending the hunters chasing after her. *Catch me if you can, metal heads.*

The ground smashed into Talia's feet, knocking her off balance and jarring her teeth, but she braced along the side of the stage for support. A giant shadow swallowed the ambient light from the windows along the wall as the Odysseus closed in.

The bomb strapped to her waist came free in her hands. She hit the detonator, took a breath, and hurled the bomb onto the far side of the stage, away from Will.

Right as her explosive found its mark, landing at the feet of the pursuing hunters, the Odysseus hit. The impact rippled through her body and left her stunned, gasping for air. Darkness followed. Another explosion rocked the ground, and the Odysseus burst into flames that devoured everything within close range.

Oh, Jane.

Talia couldn't bring herself to look at the bridge window as she slipped through the fleeing crowd. The Odysseus had taken out the entire wall of windows, and a tiny trickle of natural light from above made it through the haze. That, along with the orange light from the scattered fires, suffused the smoke into something almost beautiful—if their depths weren't mined with screams.

"Jane . . . she's gone," Talia whispered as she darted into the chaos, hoping Lux could hear. Thank the stars for the smoke hiding Talia from the hunters. She could hear them behind, scouring the rubble, their heavy metal bodies smashing anything in their way. Each crash sent Talia scurrying faster through the maze of debris. Overturned tables, shattered chairs, broken piles of stone. *Bodies.*

Blaster fire erupted nearby, and a wave of dark smoke fell over her, the acrid smell of burning metal and fuel from the Odysseus searing her lungs. A fit of coughing wracked her body, and she yanked part of her shirt up to cover her mouth.

"We saw," Lux finally responded, her voice thickened by grief. "She must have—Oh God, she must have thought it was the only way."

"They'll be looking for rebels outside. You and Leo get back to the Athena and wait for us."

Talia's earpiece went silent, and she could only assume the silence meant Lux received the order.

Finally, Talia found what she was looking for. The mountain of rubble had once been part of the building's wall before the Odysseus destroyed it. Now, the stones formed a makeshift hill, supported against the ship, a dangerous, unstable structure with pipes and debris jutting out. Some parts were on fire. Others shifted into mini avalanches as she watched.

Steeling a breath, she clamored up the side, searching for steady handholds. Every time a rock shifted, her heart punched into her throat, but she made it to the top. At least up here near the opening created by the ship the smoke was thinner. As she doubled over to catch her breath, the sound of clattering stones caught her attention.

Talia glanced down to find hunters.

They flung themselves up with sheer force, their long arms giving them unnatural climbing strength as they gobbled the distance to reach her. They would be here in a few *seconds*.

Run! She leapt four feet down to an outcropping, but the stone gave way and she slid down the side, barely catching herself on a two-by-four. Splinters tore her fingers, the rocks scraping her back raw. Stone fell all around her as the hunters began their descent. She jumped again, falling into a slide that catapulted her to the ground. The smoke engulfed her—and she used that brief second to hit the button on the device at her wrist.

Tandy appeared, grinning with excitement. A surreal bit of happiness inside the horror.

"Ready?" Talia breathed, eyes stinging with smoke and sweat.

Tandy nodded and began to change, the smoke sifting through her as she morphed into Talia's mirror image, right down to the disheveled shirt and wild, tangled auburn hair. Stars, if that's what she looked like . . .

"Tell me I look pretty," Tandy said, twirling with delight.

"Just like a princess."

Talia slipped behind a huge piece of unbroken wall just as the smoke drifted, revealing her holo-image. She didn't stay to watch what happened next, though the burst of fire and torrent of falling stones afterward gave her hope. The rebels were streaming through the cracks between the wall and the ship's hull, and she blended in with them. One even gave her a cloak, and she used it to disguise her hair and face.

After all, she was *dead* now.

She found Will by the Odysseus's nose, staring at the spot where she was supposed to have died. If she didn't know by then the way he felt for her, the anguish twisting his face confirmed it.

"Will," she whispered. His gaze flicked to her, his eyes glossy and unseeing. "Will, it's me."

Recognition dawned on his face the way a wave builds before crashing into the shore: slowly and then all at once. His mouth fell open, and he stumbled back into the charred metal hull of the ship. "You died. I saw you."

"Apparently," she said, taking his good arm, "I'm hard to kill. Now let's go."

He halted, glancing up at the Odysseus. A giant crater had destroyed most of the front end, fire still raging inside. Cracks and smoke veiled the windshield where Jane was last seen.

"She's gone, Will," Talia said, giving his arm a gentle squeeze. On the other side of the room, blasters made a chorus of battle. They needed to escape while the queen's guards were distracted.

"I know." Soot smeared across his forehead as he leaned it against the dented metal. "A good captain saves her crew, and that's what you did, Jane. I'll never forget."

Talia touched his shoulder. "Will."

He nodded and they slipped through the cracks into the light, fighting a tide of rebels running inside to join the battle. Before she could reflect on the sheer number of rebels willing to join the cause, the chaos outside the building greeted them.

The courtyard was pandemonium. Crowds of mocks dressed for the occasion clogged the gravel and cobblestone paths that were once filled with beauty, more pouring in every second from the fifty-foot hole in the north wall made by the Odysseus. The queen's soldiers, dressed in olive-green uniforms, ran blindly through the confused onlookers, searching for rebels. Bodies littered the landscaped grounds, many trampled and covered in black, goopy blood.

Will took her hand, and they fled through the maze of humans and mocks. The soldiers didn't even look at them once. The outer gates to the palace had been broken up as well, crushed by the influx of panicked onlookers, and Talia and Will traveled quickly.

When they exited the final gate, she halted, her breath catching. All the bridges were jammed full with people trying to flee. She scanned the perimeter of the translucent wall on the outer rim, searching for the last part of the plan.

A smile erupted on her face as she spotted a Predator-Class Mig-12 Starfighter, the same model she'd flown years ago at the Academy. Sunlight swam along its sleek surface, painting the metal a rose-gold tint.

"Dorian came through," she murmured.

Will's eyebrows flicked up in appreciation. "Dorian got that for you?"

"I didn't think he could." When she'd asked for an escape ship, she mentioned the Predator-Class Mig-12 as a joke, not thinking he could *actually* get her one.

"The little thief is resourceful like that. C'mon."

While everyone else crowded toward the bridge exits, Talia and Will cut toward the fighter jet. As promised, it was giftwrapped for them with unlocked doors and the keys inside. Will whistled and automatically slid into the pilot's seat . . . then he focused on his missing lower arm as if just now remembering, a frown overtaking his crooked grin.

"I can fly it," she offered, a bit irked he assumed this beautiful piece of machinery was for him.

"Probably best." Disappointment weighed down his voice, and he gave the controls a last longing look before shifting to the co-pilot's seat in the back. A part of her hesitated; she hadn't flown one of these beauties in years, literally, and Will was never meant to be a co-pilot.

Then again, neither was she.

Talia took her place in the front and fell into the routine of getting this baby ready for takeoff. One hundred years hadn't dampened her memory of what to do, and she switched into auto-pilot as she ticked off the procedures. When the harness clicked tight over her chest, a shudder of excitement whorled beneath her ribs.

Stars, this feels amazing.

Behind her, Will tapped his fingers against the metal lip of the window impatiently, but Talia wouldn't be rushed. This was her thing.

Once everything was in order, she hit the starter, the

powerful engine growling to life. Now *that* was a gorgeous sound. She released a pent-up breath from her chest and rapped the console for luck. "Ready to get this bug smasher airborne and back to your ship, Captain?"

A pause. "What ship? We left the Odysseus in pieces at the palace."

Talia started the jet down the open stretch of gravel courtyard. "It's a surprise."

The steering wheel jolted in her hands as the ship gained speed. Last second before they rammed the wall, Talia slammed the thruster and they jerked into the air, her belly groaning.

"Easy there," Will soothed, his breath warm on Talia's neck. His seat was located directly behind hers, and their cramped cockpit meant they were crammed together like the sardines Leo coveted.

As they arced over the wall and into the sky, the bridges of people growing smaller every second, Talia's breath evened out. "Pretty good for not flying for a hundred or so years."

The air traffic had thinned, probably after the explosion, leaving large chunks of sky to climb. They soared higher, maneuvering around more steel bridges interconnecting the towering skyscrapers. No longer caught beneath the buildings' shadows, the light burgeoned, warming the cockpit and making her blink.

At 20,000 feet, they were the only craft in sight, and she used the time to awaken her dormant skills, savoring the feel of the Starfighter as it responded to her commands. Every movement she made, however small, elicited a response. Fighting the urge to go all out, she finessed the powerful machine until her memory had fully awoken and controlling the ship was second nature.

She eased into acceleration when they neared the tops of the highest buildings and were out of the shadows. The force gently pushed her back into the leather seat, familiar butterflies swirling below her ribcage just before a shadow flicked across the dashboard.

On instinct, she rolled hard to the left. Shots streaked by the window, so close to their aircraft Talia could hear them zing. Each blast reverberated through her bones.

"I see one Starfighter behind us," Will said, his voice steady and even despite the danger. "We're still in its shot radius."

She dipped the nose of the jet and banked low under a bridge. As much as she yearned to turn around and identify their attacker, all her focus had to stay on flying. Silence filled the cockpit as she performed more evasive maneuvers, diving and rolling like a horse trying to buck its rider.

Whoever this pilot was, they were good.

A voice suddenly floated over the radio, and Talia's heart skipped a beat. "This brings back fun memories, doesn't it, Tal?"

"The queen," she whispered to Will, even though the queen couldn't hear them unless Talia pressed the button to talk.

"Remember when we used to practice maneuvers over the palace just to make your mother angry?"

"Screw you!" Despite knowing better, she snuck glances at the sky, blinking against the sun's bright glare. *Where is she?*

An outcropping of thin charcoal-gray buildings loomed ahead, and Talia shot through the tight spaces between, scouring the skies above.

"The queen flew Starfighters with you?" Will asked in disbelief.

They broke through the buildings, and she was about to answer when she caught movement up ahead and to the right. The jet flashed in the sun and locked in on their vessel. The queen grinned through the cockpit, her black eyes gleaming in triumph.

Talia increased thrust and lifted, but the evasive maneuver came too late. Bullets strafed their ship, the ear-spitting thuds as they pierced the Starfighter's hull sending pulses of panic down her spine. Talia pulled back, lifting the ship higher, and managed to pull out of the queen's shot radius. She banked hard left, and the world flashed upside down as they completed the loop head on with the queen.

More shots caught the tail. Talia checked the gauges, but nothing showed damage.

"She knows my every move!" Talia growled, pitching into a steep dive that brought them back into the bowels of the city. In open space, the queen could best Talia any day of the week, but here maybe she could even the playing field.

Sweat slicked her fingers as she guided the steering wheel, working to calm her breathing. The quiet inside the cockpit was an illusion of safety. Up above the queen stalked them from the clouds, waiting to strike.

Talia peered up at the sky, the sun's glare crippling her vision. "I can't see her."

"Me either," Will confirmed. Judging by his leather seat groaning, he was twisted around trying to find her. "She's using the sun to her advantage."

Of course she was. That was one of Ailat's favorite tricks.

Talia dove lower until she skimmed the turquoise waters around the palace. They'd made an entire loop through the city. What was the queen's plan? Ailat had always been a better pilot, a better tactician. She could toy with them for hours until they ran out of fuel—but that wasn't what she wanted.

No, she needed to prove once and for all she was better than Talia.

"Here she comes!" Will warned.

The queen's Starfighter dropped from above in an aerial attack, and the water below exploded in a straight line toward them as she strafed it with bullets. Ascending from this level would make the ship slow and decrease her power, so Talia cut toward the palace, hoping the queen wouldn't sacrifice the bystanders on the bridge with those bullets.

Talia was wrong. She flinched as the hail of firepower chased them into the courtyard, cutting down the crowds still stuck there.

"Oh God," Talia cried, wishing she could shut her eyes.

"Look out!" Will shouted as they careened between two archways.

Last second, Talia banked sideways, and the ship slipped through the opening by a whisker. The queen climbed back to her perch in the clouds, safe from Talia's guns while waiting to swoop down again.

The maneuver was called a high-sides gun pass, and Ailat had done it to Talia a million times before in training. Never once had she recovered after Ailat got her in this position. Growling, Talia swiped sweat-soaked hair from her forehead and then banged her fist on the dash.

"You okay, there?" Will called.

"We're *not* going to die today!" She repeated it, louder, for good measure. No way in hell would she let the queen kill them.

"Does this all seem familiar, Tal?" the queen purred over the com, the pleased tone in her voice riling Talia's blood. "There's nowhere you can hide now. No safety. You know how this ends."

Talia grabbed the radio. "I am Talia Starchaser. I fear nothing. I own the stars and the planets and the galaxies, and I am not afraid of you, *Queen*."

Talia slammed the com onto the dash and flew back out onto the water, her heartbeat drowning out her rapid breaths.

"Why did you go back into the open?" Will asked, his voice muffled as if he spoke from underwater. "She'll crush us."

As expected, the queen swooped down from the sky. This time, though, Talia was ready and sprang into action, lifting into a vertical climb and performing a barrel roll her instructor would have been proud of. Her belly churned as they ducked and dove. The queen stuck close behind, just out of firing range. The water shimmered below, a watery graveyard ready to swallow the quarreling ships whole.

The queen locked onto position behind Talia, alarms blaring in the cockpit, but she went for a violent high-g roll that thrashed their spines, turning hard to draw the queen close before rolling. The sky became water, the water sky. As they flipped upside down, all the blood rushed to Talia's face, her hair pooling on the pale ceiling like spurts of blood. The harness straps cleaved her shoulders and bit into her flesh.

When they righted, it took a moment for the world outside to stabilize.

"She's still there." Something about Will's voice gave her the feeling he was impressed with Talia, despite the fact they were running out of maneuvers to shake their attacker. Any other time, she'd have taken satisfaction from the awe.

No, satisfaction thrummed through her anyway.

"Why are you even trying?" the queen demanded. "I know you better than *you* do. Remember, Tal, I was your shadow, your mirror image. Every move you make, I can counter. Every action I see a split second before you make it."

"Then see this, *Queen*," Talia growled as she turned again, dropping the nose low.

They shot into a spiral dive, letting gravity increase their speed as the queen maneuvered to catch up. Talia's heart fluttered against her sternum like a terrified rabbit, and her stomach flip-flopped.

They used to perform this move so many times she'd dream about it: Ailat's favorite.

Except before, when it was still just a game, first one to pull up lost. The braver Ailat had always waited until right before her Starfighter hit the ground before pulling up, whereas Talia was too chicken to even come close, lifting back into a slow climb.

"What are you doing?" Will breathed. "Talia? Pull up!"

The water rushed up at them. She could make out the small whitecaps speckling the water, and her breath caught in her throat.

Not yet.

"Talia . . ."

Not yet.

"Talia, please—"

Now! She cut the power and extended the speedbrakes, and they jerked back as if a large hand smacked the ship, her body snapping violently with the change in position. A groan fled her lips, but a flash of silver and the queen overshot them. Without missing a beat, Talia flipped the power back on, aimed her sights on the center of the queen's jet, and hit the bitch with both guns.

The bullets seemed to hit the Starfighter in slow-motion, each one punching a fist-sized hole in the metal as the queen tried to lift into a climb. But she was too late. Bullets punctured the engine, the fuel tanks. The cockpit shattered, and Talia gasped as the queen jumped as if she'd been struck.

Shock, that violent jolt was shock, but the voice that came over the radio sounded as Ailat always had, calm, collected. "I won, Tal. I won."

Then her Starfighter spun on its side like an animal rolling over to die and plummeted to the water below, pale-gray smoke streaming from the engine. The ship hit the surface with a giant splash.

Talia struggled to breathe as she circled once, twice, until the vessel finally sank. Hot tears blurred her eyes. When her vision cleared, there was nothing in the water's surface to mark Ailat's grave. No sign of her death.

The back of Talia's throat burned with grief. In some strange way, Ailat had been the only family Talia had left, and the mock queen's death meant Talia was finally, truly alone.

The last Starchaser.

"Why didn't she pull first?" Will's breathless voice reminded her he was still with her.

"She had to win, just like always." Talia pressed her palm flat against the windshield, warm from the sun's kiss, and took one last look down at her friend entombed inside the waters she used to love. Ironic that as much as she hated humans, in the end a human emotion killed her. "I should have fought for you, friend."

"Who was she to you?" Will tipped forward into the front seat, the leather creaking, his eyes soft with concern. The day's horrible events were written all over his weary, battered, and soot-stained face. But in this light, with the sun's glare highlighting the ambers and reds inside his coppery hair and his lips curved into a smile, he was gorgeous.

Talia thought about explaining everything, but the truth was Ailat died that day one hundred years ago just the same as if Talia had followed through with Prince Cassius's cruel demand. She had to believe the Ailat trapped inside that monstrous queen was at peace now.

"A ghost." Talia hit the thrusters and streaked toward the place where the Athena waited, piercing the dark funnel of smoke from the Odysseus still choking the sky. "An old friend's waiting for you."

That was the thing about old friends. They reappeared when you least expected them.

Will chuckled. "I kind of like my new friends."

EPILOGUE

Talia

Talia jogged down the crudely carved stone steps winding through the mountainside, her secretary and retinue of personal guards trailing behind. Their shouts for her to stop went wholly ignored as she slipped over loose rocks and barely managed some of the more treacherous turns that could send her plummeting to her death.

There were faster, *safer* ways down the steep range, but she enjoyed the feel of her muscles burning as they grew more powerful. In the past three months since she emerged from cryosleep, her body had transformed from flimsy and weak to athletic and strong.

The Athena glimmered three hundred yards below, its silver, metallic hull a stark contrast against the vibrant green of the valley. As soon as the Darkstar landed, she'd rushed straight out of a meeting with the mock and human senators and cut down the hillside.

Her crew waited down there. So did *Will.*

A robin's-egg-blue sky hung above. Puffs of yellow wildflowers Talia couldn't begin to name dotted the crags and bluffs, growing thicker as she neared the valley below. Two condors glided to her right, playfully circling on a gusty breeze.

She glanced back at the council building where the senators undoubtedly still waited, carved into the highest peak and flanked by residences for all the important Alliance members. The entire city was ensconced up here, the last vestiges of humanity, accessible only by hover and these hazardous steps, and invisible from space.

Not that any Federation ships had been spotted over this airspace. And odds were they would never discover this tiny planet, technically a moon, one of three that hid the Alliance. Located on the cusp of the Outer Fringes, their habitable moon orbited a gaseous exoplanet that, from Talia's perch high on the mountain, was a faint orange-and-yellow sphere painting the sky.

"Sovereign," her secretary called, breathing hard as he struggled to catch up. "We insist you . . . wait for the royal hover."

"No time!"

Talia hadn't seen Will and her friends in a month. Bloody stars, she wasn't going to wait a second longer. Even if, as her human secretary and advisors liked to remind her, the Sovereign couldn't be seen favoring mocks over humans.

Sovereign. After three months, the word still filled Talia with both a sense of panic and pride. Sometimes, whenever she heard the title, she would look around for her father before remembering the position belonged to her. Those moments were when she missed him the most. When she understood just how much responsibility had weighed down his shoulders—and now hers too.

Proving herself to the Alliance and her people would be

a monumental task, especially with all the work required to even get mocks and humans to sit together. Ill will and distrust ran bone deep, rightly so after centuries of division. They had separate councils, separate living areas, separate leaders, and both sides accused the other of receiving favoritism.

Hopefully she could help change that, though it would likely take a lifetime or two.

Talia bounded down the last few steps and spilled into the valley, enjoying the feel of the knee-high grass tickling her palms. Grasshopper songs filled the meadow as she sprinted, hardly out of breath, through tangles of exotic lavender-and-white wildflowers that swarmed the basin. The first time she'd raced down these stairs, she nearly vomited at the bottom. But now she was used to the high altitude and long sun-cycles—twelve days of sun and twelve of night. She even looked forward to the stellar eclipses at noon that drenched this side of the moon in darkness.

The Athena rested near a long curve of forest that stretched for miles, backdropped by more smooth granite mountains and verdant foliage. Halfway to the ship, Talia stopped, and her guards finally caught up and formed a half-moon around her, as if the hunting party now emerging from the forest was a surge of enemies. Whatever the men carried on their shoulders would be her dinner, not a five-course meal made from the most exotic foods from around the galaxies, but just as good.

"Unless the grasshoppers are armed with blasters," she snapped, her voice breathless with impatience, "I think I'm safe."

"Please, Sovereign," her secretary implored, straightening

the lapel of his ridiculous yellow linen suit. "Your schedule is packed with meetings. Can this . . . this *mock* crew not wait like everyone else?"

"This *crew* is comprised of valuable Alliance members, and they're my friends." She gave a chilly smile, one of many in her new arsenal. "The rest can wait."

She blinked and Will appeared just inside the open hatch, his navy jumpsuit turning his eyes into topaz-blue gemstones. A golden tint flushed his skin, courtesy of whatever planet he and the crew had last visited while searching for more rebels to join the cause. A dangerous job. One she pleaded with him to let someone else do. But no one was as capable as Will when it came to evading the Federation's battalions in deep space, and she needed a bigger army before the Alliance could even think of making war on the Federation.

Still, every time her friends returned, she breathed easier.

Now, at the sight of him, her body softened with relief, all her responsibilities melting away as anticipation warmed her belly. She was no longer Sovereign. No longer the girl with a million meetings, whose every move had to be thought out and calculated. Who didn't dare laugh for fear of accidentally bestowing favor on one senator over another, and whose every action had a ripple effect across the galaxies.

She was just Talia—and sometimes, when Will was feeling particularly cheeky, flesher princess.

Her boots made rattling thumps on the grated metal as she darted up the ramp, stopping just short of slamming into the captain. Grinning, Will winked at her secretary and hit the button to close the hatch.

The second it groaned shut, Talia jumped into Will's arms, wrapping her legs around his trim waist. Will turned and pressed her back against the wall, gently. One of his hands was tangled in her hair. The other gripped her chin.

She didn't even blink at his metal fingers, cold against the flesh of her face. Will's new arm was made from outdated technology—the best the Alliance could provide—and Will had chosen to leave the metal exposed. He said he couldn't bear the fake plastic skin older mocks used. But secretly she thought the metal was a reminder to himself of what he was.

Half-mock and half-human.

Not that she cared *what* his arm was made of as he held her face in place and brought his lips down over hers. The kiss was soft. Tentative. They were both still exploring this new development between them. A faint groan slipped from Will's lips as his hand tightened in her hair, crushing her to his hard, warm chest.

"Is this too much?" he breathed, pulling back to gaze at her. His pupils were huge, his lips parted and hair more tousled than usual from her fingers raking through the coppery mess. It was hard to imagine this beautiful man could snap her spine without breaking a sweat.

"Shut up, Captain," she commanded.

"Yes, Sovereign."

Footsteps barking over metal drew Talia's gaze to the hallway, where Lux and Dorian waited. Lux flung a hand over Dorian's eyes. "Gross. Get a room, guys."

Dorian ripped his sister's hand from his wide eyes and beamed at Talia. "Hey, Talia!"

Lux smacked him behind the head. "It's Sovereign now."

Reluctantly, Talia disentangled herself from Will and crossed to meet the siblings. "In here, Dorian," she said with a wink. "Talia's fine."

"Good to see you haven't changed," Lux added with a warm grin. "Hungry?"

"Depends. Is Leo serving something other than sardines?"

"We've recently undergone an upgrade on supplies."

"Then let's eat."

The Athena was a gorgeous ship. Every rivet and bolt in place. Every wall painted and every surface shined. There was no rust, no cold, damp spots or broken equipment. It was—or *had* been—the crown jewel of the Federation Fleet. Yet Talia still found herself missing the Odysseus as she wound through the Athena's bowels, following Dorian and Lux to the main mess hall.

A long metal table was set up in the center of the large rectangular room, bordered on one side with a curved plexiglass window looking out onto the valley and a fully stocked bar on the other. Talia could easily imagine Will's old crew making use of this space.

"Wow," she quipped as she sat at the head of the table, "you guys must really hate slumming it in this old thing."

"It's not bad," Will said, sitting to Talia's left. "Though it's missing a piano . . . and someone to play for."

Thunking down on Talia's right, Lux cut her eyes at Will. "What, we're not good enough to appreciate music, Captain?"

Will slid his gaze to Talia, ignoring his navigator. "Think about it, if you ever get tired of giving orders and dealing with politicians. There's always room for you on board the Athena."

Before Talia could respond, Leo burst through the silver swinging doors that led to the high-end galley, carrying a tray full of cookies. A lit candle sat atop the tallest one, and Talia bit her cheek to keep the tears from her eyes as Leo rested the plate on the table. The cookies were appropriately burned to hard black discs.

Leo blew out the candle. "Happy birthday, Jane. Your cooking was horrible, but your friendship and loyalty was one of a kind, and we miss you like crazy."

Talia had only recently found out Jane would have been one hundred and five years old today. Most mock bodies didn't make it over fifty years before they had to jump, but Jane was tough like that. They spent the next few hours telling stories about Jane, and Talia realized that although the mock captain's life had been cut short, she'd lived a rich and fulfilling life most humans could only dream of.

Soon, Talia would have to climb back up the mountain and become Sovereign again. As much as she yearned to shirk her duties and join the Athena crew and Will, as much as her soul called out to explore the vast expanse of space, she knew she belonged here, and she was ready to give her life to destroy the Federation and broker peace between her people and the mocks.

For now though, in this stolen moment, she could pretend she was just a girl who liked a boy, hanging out with her friends and eating burned cookies and laughing at inappropriate jokes. And if she let the tiny seed of hope that she kept hidden inside bloom, she could even imagine a day when that illusion became reality.

The End

Did you enjoy this story? Join our newsletters to receive updates on Will and Talia's story, as well as discover other books we've written you might like.

Audrey Grey: http://audreygrey.com/connect/
Krystal Wade: http://eepurl.com/odGfT

ABOUT THE AUTHORS

Audrey Grey is the award winning and USA Today bestselling author of several books, including the Moonbeam Children's Awards bronze medalist, Shadow Fall. She lives in the charming state of Oklahoma with her husband, two little people, four mischievous dogs, and one poor cat. You can usually find her hiding out in her office from said little people and fur kids, surrounded by books and sipping kombucha while dreaming up wondrous worlds for her characters to live in.

Read More from Audrey Grey: http://audreygrey. com/

Krystal Wade is the USA Today bestselling author of six Young Adult Fantasy and creeptastically imagined fairytale books. She can be found in the sluglines outside Washington D.C. every morning, Monday through Friday. With coffee in hand, iPod plugged in, and strangers who sometimes snore, smell, or have incredibly bad gas-sitting next to her, she zones out and thinks of fantastical worlds for you and me to read. How else can she cope with a fifty-mile commute? Good thing she has her husband and three kids to go home to. They keep her sane.

Read More from Krystal Wade: http://www.krystal-wade.com/

CPSIA information can be obtained
at www.ICGtesting.com
Printed in the USA
LVHW03s1841230718
584651LV00002B/544/P